BLOOD AND JADE

©2021 KEN LIZZI

*To the Millers, in appreciation of
all the weekends at the cabin.*

CHAPTER 1

Karl watched the woman emerge, blinking and bewildered, from the terminal into the glaring Cancun morning sun. The press of taxi drivers, shuttle bus agents, and timeshare touts descended upon her, momentarily concealing her from Karl's view. He shouldered through the crush until he could see her again, feeling rewarded when he did, as she was easy on the eyes. A massive hard-sided suitcase trundled behind her on click-clacking wheels, and she bore a backpack that appeared oversized on her petite frame. She was looking about, incipient dismay written on regular, porcelain skin features. *Eurasian,* Karl had time to note before hipping aside a solicitous local in loose khakis and an orange guayabera embroidered with a travel company logo. All the rest clamoring about looked like variations on this fellow: transit and tourist workers in the business of ferrying visitors from the airport to hotels and resorts, wearing ID badges on lanyards and holding clipboards. They began to disperse the moment Karl reached out to touch the woman's arm, his action alerting them that she was not a customer."Dr. Chen?" he asked. He hoped it was her; otherwise he'd wasted the last few moments while the actual archaeologist he'd been tasked to collect from the airport waited impatiently somewhere else. "Karl Thorson, from the dig. Professor Allison sent me to pick you up."

Karl watched her shoulders sag in relief, suitcase dipping and backpack lowering. She fumbled out a pair of sunglasses from a loop on the backpack, opened the frames.

"Oh, thank God. The immigration line was a bitch and a half. I thought for sure I'd get the red light at customs, but at least –"

"Come on," Karl said, "we've got to move."

"What? Can't I at least buy a bottle of –?"

"Can't risk losing him. He might have moved already."

"Who? Risk losing who? What are you talking about?"

"I'll explain while we walk. Here, give me that." Karl took the handle of her suitcase and, not waiting to see if she followed, turned and pushed through the crowd of arriving tourists along the sidewalk outside Cancun International Airport, Terminal 3. At least two or three planeloads must have recently landed, judging from the throngs intermingling, jostling, and making herky-jerky passage along a sidewalk just beginning to soak up the tropical morning sun. Oncoming tourists parted before him, the breadth of his shoulders making his near six feet seem somehow even taller. Even some of those moving in the same direction slipped aside, as if sensing his presence.

"Where are we going?" Dr. Chen asked. "Where's the car?"

"Jeep. Not car," Karl said. "We'll get to the dig. First I have to get eyes on someone again."

"Who? Come on, you said you'd explain while we walked. We're walking. Spill."

Karl glanced at her face, saw eager curiosity overcoming travel fatigue. He liked that; the woman was game.

Karl navigated a blockage of a family of five digging through a suitcase to find the anodyne to mollify a bawling toddler. He cleared his throat. "Right. Zero one hundred this morning I made my rounds of the camp. I saw a car that didn't belong, idling along a trail. One man behind the wheel. Before I could approach, another man emerged from the trees, got in the car. They drove away. I had time to sprint to the car park, grab the Jeep. I followed. Thought about giving up after an hour or so, but they hit 307 and turned north. I had to pick you up at the airport anyway; no reason not to keep following. Turned out they were coming here."

Karl broke through a gaggle of garishly dressed middle-aged women taking group pictures, then slowed. Behind a moving screen of tourists, he saw a snack bar. Thirsty travelers stood two deep in a semicircle about the service window. Customers occupied each stool at the bar. Karl stopped.

"They parked," he continued. "Split up. One headed this

direction; the other entered Departures. I followed Mr. Departures. Couldn't get too close without spooking him or getting security on my ass. But I did get close enough to overhear his destination was JFK. For whatever that's worth."

"What about the other guy?" Dr. Chen asked.

"Over there," Karl said, jerking his chin at the snack bar. "The skinny guy in the baggy jeans and yellow Hawaiian shirt." Even as he spoke, the man in question leaned down and snatched up a compact carry-on bag resting against the stool next to him – a stool occupied by a travel-worn tourist paying more attention to his cell phone than his luggage. "Son of a bitch. You see that? Come on."

The skinny guy was up and moving, his near-empty bottle of Coke abandoned on the bar before him, the carry-on bag tucked under one bony arm. Wasn't much to the guy, maybe five feet seven tops, too-large clothing bagging and drooping about him. Large-frame sunglasses overwhelmed a light-skinned face, features possessing more of the Spanish than the locally common Mayan characteristics.

"What are we doing?" Dr. Chen asked between breaths as she struggled to keep up with Karl's longer strides. "Why don't you just alert security?"

"Baggage theft isn't my responsibility. Finding out what he was doing at our dig is."

Leaving the sidewalk with its concealing waves of tourists for the relatively empty expanse of parking lot, Karl slowed, letting his quarry create more separation. He recognized the man's car, a beat-up Peugeot coupe streaked with jungle mud. Karl veered away, moving fast toward the Jeep, a four-door model with a modest lift. He boosted Dr. Chen's suitcase into the back seat with no apparent effort. He held open the passenger door for her. To her credit, she appeared to have adopted his sense of urgency. She shrugged free of her backpack, handed it to him, and hustled in, hoisting her five feet and small change into the Jeep. He tossed the backpack after the suitcase and was in the driver's seat as she completed securing the seat belt harness.

Karl caught up with the Peugeot as it cleared the airport parking lot and headed north. He dropped back, allowed a taxi and a shuttle van to pull in front, limiting the chances of the Peugeot driver noticing he had a tail. The trick was to not let any other vehicles into the pursuit gap. The locals drove aggressively, indifferent to turn signals, lane markers, or any notion of safe following distance. Karl managed it skillfully; he had years of combative driving under his belt in places where the roads resembled more destruction derby arenas than public thoroughfares.

"So, Karl," Dr. Chen said, then paused, that opening gambit stalling. She cleared her throat. "Jim – I mean Professor Allison – sent you to pick me up?" Her right hand shifted constantly, searching for a firm handhold. "The dig is southwest of here, right? So aren't we going the wrong direction? Maybe you should just drive me to the dig site? Let this guy go?"

"Don't worry, Dr. Chen. I'll get you there." Karl braked, swerved, downshifted, and accelerated, clearing a rusting, dented truck loaded with water bottles, which had changed lanes without warning. "But picking up archaeologists at the airport isn't my primary mission."

"What is your primary mission?"

"Consider me a general-purpose troubleshooter. Site security is my remit. I see someone I don't know lurking outside, another stranger emerging from the dig site, I think —"

"Artifact theft," Dr. Chen interrupted. "Okay. I got you. But the one who got on the plane, he's probably the thief, the one carrying whatever it is that was stolen."

"Yeah, but maybe his driver can give us a clue. Who he was, what he stole. Where he's taking it."

"Wow. You take this responsibility seriously, don't you? Okay. Let's go get this bastard. The dig can wait."

Karl spared a glance at her, grinned. "That's the spirit, Dr. Chen."

"May. Please call me May. I'm already calling you Karl."

"Okay, May. Of course, down here you're more likely to hear me called by my given name, Carlos, rather than Karl."

"Well, how about that? You had me fooled. You don't... Your American accent is perfect."

"Probably because I'm American. Born and bred."

"Okay, I'm getting confused." May emitted an abbreviated *humph*. Then she clutched at Karl's leg with her left hand, fingers digging in like five tiny knives. "Look, Karl! He's turning."

"I see him," Karl said. He cut over into a nearly nonexistent gap in traffic, followed the Peugeot off the highway and onto a boulevard, now in Cancun proper, away from the linear commercial strip built up merely to serve traffic to and from the airport. The Jeep swayed, righted. Karl got a fix on the Peugeot, then let a taxi intervene, dropping back. The Peugeot turned again, north, then west again, moving farther away from the prime tourist areas.

As Karl took the westward turn, the Peugeot accelerated, the driver pulling around a couple of tourists on rented scooters and punching it hard. The Peugeot dwindled, then disappeared around a corner.

"Shit, he's made us," Karl said. He downshifted and applied steady pressure to the accelerator, RPMs climbing rapidly. He braked hard, took the corner on squealing tires, then stomped down on the gas pedal. The Peugeot again grew nearer through the windscreen.

"What do we do now?" May asked.

"The direct approach," Karl said.

The aging Peugeot's anemic four cylinders proved incapable of holding off the new Jeep's six, and Karl closed the gap in seconds. The Peugeot turned, then turned again, trending always west, Karl hanging on his tail. Traffic thinned as the two cars left the bars, restaurants, and souvenir shops farther and farther behind, entering an expanse of hardware stores and electronics retailers, auto repair and tire shops, taco and torta stands with weathered plastic chairs and torn vinyl awnings.

"Don't let him get away," May said, and Karl could almost sense her bouncing in the seat.

A battered pickup truck backed from a driveway into the

street a block ahead. The Peugeot cut to the left, slipping by the tailgate.

Karl nudged the Jeep to the right, popping two wheels onto the curb. He watched the truck driver's jaw drop in surprise as he squeezed the Jeep between the grille of the pickup and a window display of a Quinceañara specialty retailer. He dropped back onto the street.

The Peugeot driver was fighting the wheel, struggling to recover from his sudden maneuver. The car swerved right, then more sharply to the left as the driver overcorrected. The front bumper crumpled as the Peugeot struck the high curb almost head on. Metal scraped, then the tires jumped onto the sidewalk, and the car grated to a stop. The engine still revved, but the front tires had no purchase. The Peugeot was beached on two canted, mismatched sections of concrete sidewalk.

Karl stopped the Jeep behind the Peugeot before the driver gave reverse a shot. Karl looked about. The chase had ended in a narrow side street, in front of a chain-link fence fronting a closed – or perhaps defunct – restaurant. The painted menu out front was weather faded, advertising a variety of tacos, hamburgers, fish, and cold drinks. Corrugated metal covered the opening behind the counter. A single, filthy, blue plastic chair rested upended before a padlocked door.

Karl leapt from the Jeep. He wrenched open the rear door and retrieved heavy, long-handled bolt cutters from the back seat. The sound from the Peugeot altered, the driver working the transmission from drive to neutral. Before he could reach reverse, Karl jerked open the driver's side door. He raised the bolt cutters in a gesture that could be interpreted as menacing. That was the intent, anyway. The Peugeot driver certainly seemed to consider it minatory; he leaned far to the right, throwing his hands up before his face.

Karl reached in, turned the key to the off position. He left it in the ignition, since he couldn't extract it with the transmission still in the neutral position. Instead of worrying about that detail, Karl grabbed a fistful of Hawaiian shirt and yanked the luggage thief bodily from the Peugeot.

Karl maintained his grip on the floral-patterned fabric, keeping the skinny little guy off balance. He dragged him a couple of tottering steps, then flung him into the chain-link fence. Karl bounced the business end of the bolt cutters off the fence beside the thief's head. Terror froze the man in place. Karl plied the cutters on the padlock securing the gate. The lock clattered onto the filthy concrete.

"*Muévete*," he said, then followed the man inside the fence, the thief casting nervous glances over his shoulder at Karl.

Karl prodded him on with the bolt cutters, then snipped open the lock securing the door of the restaurant. The place was little more than a blockhouse of rebar, cinder blocks, and corrugated sheet iron. It held a rusting stove and a grill. Stains on the concrete floor indicated where a sink and a couple of refrigerators had once stood. A lone plastic chair remained, a long crack running through the seat. Three broken-paned windows and the open door provided enough light to tell the sad story of a failed business enterprise. Karl nudged the thief ahead of him.

"Too bad," Karl said. "I was so busy chasing your ass all over I never got breakfast. Could use a taco." He noted the incomprehension on the thief's face. No English? Or perhaps his English skills were simply too limited to process dry humor.

Karl heard the door pulling shut behind him and shot a glance over his shoulder. May stood, back to the door, eyes wide, fingers drumming on the doorknob. He flashed her what he hoped was a reassuring smile. Of course, she might take it for psychopathic glee. A thin line?

"*Sientaté*," Karl said, nodding at the chair. The thief complied, plopping down. The chair twisted, the crack in the seat threatening its structural integrity, but it held.

Karl offered the man a wide smile. He touched the hem of his own Hawaiian shirt, a dark red number sporting cream-colored hibiscus blossoms, then pointed at the thief's blousy yellow one.

"Nice shirt," he said, getting zero response. *No English, then. Confirmed. "Buenos dias. Como te llamas?"*

The thief said nothing, but his mouth pursed. Karl let his smile sag to a grim line. He slammed the head of the bolt cutters against the concrete floor between the thief's feet. The thief jumped.

"Enrique," the thief said. His Adam's apple bobbed. "*Me llamo* Enrique."

"*Bueno*, Enrique," Karl said. "*Me llamo El Jefe, comprendes?*"

The thief nodded.

Karl looked at May. "You following this so far?"

May nodded. "The simple stuff, yes. He's Enrique and you're the boss. My Spanish is rusty and never great to begin with. But I'm with you so far. But, uh, are you sure about this? This, interrogation?"

"Not my first interrogation, May. Wasn't my MOS, but I sat in on a few in Afghanistan."

"I don't doubt you. But I wasn't asking if you *could* do this. I was wondering if you *should*."

"Relax. Won't take long. We'll be on the way to the dig in no time." He returned his attention to Enrique.

Enrique, as Karl predicted, proved to be agreeably forthcoming. With his frightened eyes following every move of the bolt cutters, Enrique answered every question, elaborating without any prompting. He insisted that he was just the driver. He'd stolen the Peugeot. He knew the guy he took to the airport from a bar where he often fenced the items stolen from tourists. The bar was a hangout for lots of guys on the hustle. He'd picked up a few jobs there before. Didn't know the guy well, a man going by the name of Festo. Festo had hired Enrique to drive him out to the jungle, wait there while he took care of some business, then drive him to the airport.

"*Que negocio?*" Karl asked.

"*No se,*" Enrique said.

Karl repeated the question, tapping the floor around Enrique's toes with the bolt cutters.

Enrique ran off a string of Spanish. Karl nodded. He looked at May, who returned a quizzical look.

"Our friend Enrique says the only thing he got from Festo was that Festo was taking something to Mago D."

"Mago D?"

"Yep. Mago D. In NYC, apparently." Karl grinned. "Right, let's get on the road. Enrique, straighten up and fly right. Turn over a new leaf and walk the path of the righteous."

"*Que?*" asked Enrique.

A half dozen people stood near the Peugeot and the Jeep as Karl and May emerged. More approached, drawn to the spectacle. Distant lights and sirens suggested the imminent arrival of official inquiry. Karl shifted the bolt cutters to port arms. The onlookers shifted aside, opening a path to the Jeep. Karl held the door for May, offering a half bow. But once she was in, he wasted no time trotting around to the driver's side and starting the engine. He left twin streaks of rubber as he left Enrique and the stolen Peugeot to their fate.

———

May was silent as Karl made his way back to the highway, taking them south this time, back toward the airport and points farther on.

"That was an intense morning," she said at last. "You sure know how to show a lady a good time, Karl."

Karl glanced at the dashboard clock. "Early afternoon

now. Lunch?" From the corner of his eye, he could see May's forehead furrow. Calculating, he guessed."Look," said Karl, "this little adventure has set back the timetable. I doubt we could make K'aay-Boox today."

"K'aay-Boox?" May asked.

"One of the grad students deciphered an inscription a couple weeks back. K'aay-Boox. Professor Allison assigned it as the name of the site. My point is, the place is a ways off. So stopping to eat isn't going to be an insurmountable setback; we're already set back."

"Was it worth it?" May asked. "Did you accomplish what you needed with this ridiculous car chase and the third degree?"

"Hey, I'm hurt. I thought you were all in. You're part of the dig team now. Someone stole from *our* dig. I want to know what was stolen and who stole it. Kind of my job, May." Karl drummed his fingers on the steering wheel as a sort of emphatic punctuation. When he agreed to an undertaking, he performed the task. No shortcuts, no rationalizing his way out of inconvenient extra steps. He understood that his attitude might be construed as overzealous, but he didn't give a damn. "And yeah, to answer your question, it was worth it. I don't have all the answers, but I have a clue."

"Mago D in NYC. Big help," May said. "New York City doesn't narrow it down much. And Mago D? What is that, a rap name? Are we looking for a hip-hop star with a penchant for archaeology?"

Karl laughed. He was tired. Barring a short siesta yesterday afternoon, he'd been up for well over twenty-four hours. He was hungry. But the affaire d'Enrique had given him a boost. And he was enjoying the banter with May. Feisty. Though he probably shouldn't say that aloud.

"So," he said.

"Yes. All right. Let's eat. I slept through the food service on the plane. I'm hungry too. Haven't eaten since the layover in Houston."

Conversation picked up again once they'd gotten back on the road. Lunch had been quiet, May as narrowly focused on eating as Karl. The two had consumed a mountain of grilled flesh, Karl impressed that such a small woman could eat so much and that she'd not even hesitated at adding a couple of *lengua* tacos to the order. And she'd downed her ice-cold Tecate with gusto. A Tecate woman always earned points with Karl.

"Why aren't you sweating?" May had asked as they walked back to the Jeep.

"I am sweating," he answered, "just not as much as you." He flapped the hem of his Hawaiian shirt. "Loose clothing. Better for heat."

"I hear white clothing is good for heat."

"Yeah," Karl said, "white's not my color."

On the road, sipping coffee to go despite the heat, Karl asked, "So what brings you to our dig? You mentioned a layover in Houston. Where did you fly in from?" He wasn't all that curious, but despite the caffeine, fatigue was setting in. A full belly and a couple of cold *cervezas* didn't help. Conversation would help keep him alert.

"Portland. Took an airport shuttle up from Eugene.

Where I work – working on tenure, I suppose, while teaching archaeology to disinterested sophomores."

"University of Oregon, right? Not Oregon State?"

"Correct, Karl. You win a prize. The Beavers are about forty-five minutes away in Corvallis. And they didn't offer me a faculty position. So I'm a Duck."

Karl sipped his coffee. "You've known Professor Allison long?"

"He was my graduate advisor in Chattanooga."

"University of Tennessee?"

"You're good at this game, Karl. What's your alma mater?"

"The United States Army, ma'am. Graduated with honors."

"Oh. Sorry. Don't mean to sound surprised about it, but you come across as…well, as rather educated. Well read."

"I am well read. My mother saw to that. But we're still talking about you. You're the newcomer, you get grilled. Traditional, don't you know." Karl affected a passable British accent for the last sentence.

"Fair enough. Look, I don't know how much I should share."

"I'm just making conversation, May. Keeping awake. If it's too personal, stop me. I'm not going to pry."

"Thanks, Karl. But I might as well face it. I'm a talker. I'm going to talk. The thing is that Jim and I – well, when he asked me to fly down and assist on the dig, I wasn't sure whether his motive was purely because of my professional capability. Sorry, I'm not explaining this well."

"Take your time. Got plenty of it."

"Okay. See, we have…a past. Cliché, I know. Professor-student fling. Tawdry. Age difference. Not quite May-December. More May-September."

"May-September. I see what you did there. Been waiting years to use that one, haven't you, May?"

May punched his shoulder. "Come on, it was a good one. Worth the wait. Anyway, I decided to accept the invitation. See if there are any sparks remaining. And if not? Well, I've missed fieldwork, and from Jim's information, this seems like an exciting find. Is it exciting?"

Karl shrugged. "A lot of dirt. A lot of rock. A lot of jungle. I have just enough knowledge to be interested, not enough to be excited. I'm only the help, May, not one of you egghead experts."

May punched him again. "Egghead, am I?" But she was laughing while she spoke.

Late afternoon caught them as they reached Tulum.

"We need to head west from here," Karl said. "But most of it will be gravel roads or dirt track. Not the kind of thing you want to do at night. Trust me; I did it last night, and it sucked."

"Aren't they expecting us back today?"

Karl patted the center console. "I'll call on the sat phone, let them know we'll be late."

"Satellite phone? No cell coverage at the dig?"

Karl held his palm out flat and waggled his hand. "I wouldn't count on it. You'll occasionally see some people doing the Cell Signal Polka."

"Cell Signal Polka?" May laughed.

"Yeah. Hopping around, waving the phone, trying to get a solid signal. Sometimes you can even get a few uninterrupted moments if you find the right spot at the right time of day. But most people find it too aggravating and opt to wait for the sat phone. And given the kind of data you scientist types tend to send, a reliable signal is important."

"Fine. Hotel, then. Make the call. I could use a shower and room service before a month or so of roughing it. But separate rooms, Romeo."

Karl laughed. "Your loss, May. I was going to wash your back."

CHAPTER 2

The penthouse doorbell chimed, a funereal basso profundo. Dexicos Megistos did not deign to look up from the copy of *GQ* he was perusing from the wing-backed depths of his Eames chair.

A polite cough announced the presence of Dexicos' butler, Potter. "Sir," Potter said, "a *Señor* Festo Hidalgo requests a moment."

Dexicos glanced up from an article on the new cuts for autumn suit coats. Potter's face remained as blank and expressionless as ever; the big man, of some mixed African and Southeast Asian ancestry, possessed a gift for placidity and understatement. The butler's attire Dexicos had mandated suited him, classic and timeless.

"See him to the den," Dexicos said. "Decant a bottle of red. Something Chilean, I think. Or Australian. Use your judgment."

Dexicos waited until Potter glided from the room, then

rose with similar smoothness from the depths of the Eames chair, considering it a not bad effort for a man in his third millennium.

The sitting room windows overlooked Central Park, but Dexicos kept the blinds drawn, preferring to maintain his focus inward, a sentiment warranted as much by his justifiable self-regard as the ambiance of his penthouse sanctum. The sitting room altered annually, sometimes even seasonally, depending upon whether or not Dexicos concurred with the judgments of one of the interior design magazines that contributed to the glossy publications fanned across the glass top of the oak-framed coffee table. A trend toward minimalism had seen to the removal of a sectional leather couch, a sideboard, and a display hutch. Now only a second chair and a love seat in cream and chocolate joined his Eames chair.

There was also, of course, a full-length mirror. Dexicos Megistos – known by most of his current assemblage of flunkies and minions as either Dexter Magus or Mago D – paused to inspect himself. He straightened his waistcoat, thinking the subtle pinstripes accentuated his lean height and trim midsection. The charcoal slacks suggested the informality of the lord of the manor taking his ease while still projecting the requisite status and power of a man of his lofty, yet covert, position. He slicked back a stray lock of hair, the sidewalls graying but the top still black and luxuriant, the coiffure pomaded and combed back from a broad forehead.

Dexicos nodded his approval to himself, then padded down

the hall to the den. If the sitting room bowed to minimalism, the den served as its counterpoint. Curios and curiosities from seven continents and more than seven centuries festooned the walls and crammed the bookshelves that diminished what would otherwise have seemed a fair-sized room. Ornate, carved wooden masks of demonic or bestial aspect created a focal point opposite the entry. Beaded fetishes, ivory figurines of such antiquity as to be nearly featureless, and painted icons of forgotten saints sat in ranks on a shelf below a stretch of leather-bound volumes that would cause a rare-book dealer to swoon. Racked on another wall were ceremonial axes, sacrificial daggers – running the gamut from flint to bronze to modern alloys – and a small collection of spear points. Paintings, whose existence would startle art historians, hung where space allowed, certain masterpieces partially obscured by an array of crucifixes or a spreading sheaf of ostrich feathers.

It was too much to take in at once, a point in which Dexicos took some pride. And apparently his guest harbored the same opinion. He gazed about with unconcealed awe at the bewildering variety, ignoring the glass of wine Potter set before him.

"Thank you, Potter. That will be all," Dexicos said.

Potter nodded and departed. Dexicos focused his attention on the man seated in one of the deeply padded leather wingback chairs that flanked the tea table.

Festo Hidalgo appeared to be in his early thirties. Fit still, though on the cusp of letting himself go. Stubble-covered cheeks beginning to plump from good living. He wore a rumpled linen jacket over a yellowing, sweat-stained oxford, and khaki trousers. Dried mud crusted his leather brogues and darkened the knees of his trousers.

Dexicos made a note to tell Potter to vacuum once his guest left. Who knows what filth he'd tramped in?

"A bit of a dog's breakfast, I know," Dexicos said. "*Lo siento.*"

Hidalgo jerked, his entire body shifting spasmodically to face Dexicos. "*Señor* Magus. I did not see you there."

"I move in mysterious ways, Festo." Dexicos took the chair opposite.

Potter had poured two glasses. Dexicos picked one up, sniffed. The Australian. He would have gone with the Chilean, but he had told Potter to use his own judgment. *One can't do everything oneself.* He sipped. Bold and plumy. Good. But of course it would be, coming from his own cellars.

"Now, Festo, you've come a fair distance to see me. May I assume you have something for me?"

"*Sí, Señor* Magus." Festo patted a jacket pocket. "Was not easy. I hid in the jungle for a day, bugs crawling over me, before chance to take picture."

A picture. It had been too much to hope that this petty crook could get his hands on the actual artifact. No Indiana Jones here. Just a marginally competent hireling desperate to earn a peso. Dexicos offered a nod that suggested he'd expected no more.

He held out his hand. "The pictures, then. You know, of

course, that the highest figure I offered in recompense was for the article itself."

"Was hard, *Señor*," Festo whined. "I tried. Always too many people. Students, diggers, always there. Was risk to even get pictures."

"You bring artifacts, you receive artifact pay. You bring pictures, you get compensated correspondingly. Now give."

Festo retrieved the plastic, thumbnail-sized wafer of a digital camera's memory card. He hesitated, looked across the tea table at Dexicos. Dexicos narrowed his eyes, bringing his eyebrows close together. Festo's hand jerked across the table so rapidly he came within a fraction of an inch of upsetting the wineglasses.

Dexicos accepted the proffered wafer. "No case? Well, thank you. See Potter on the way out for your pay envelope. Wait." Dexicos drummed the manicured fingers of one hand atop the tea table. "Festo, should you wish to supplement that pay envelope, return to the site and perform a discreet reconnaissance. I will pay well for timely and reliable on-site intelligence. Now, you may go."

Festo left with less than dignified haste. Dexicos sipped his wine and pondered the card. If it held what he hoped… He smiled. The fun he could expect! The anthill he'd kick over!

Dexicos drained the rest of the glass, then retrieved a laptop computer from beneath a copy of *Hygromanteia*. He swigged Festo's untouched glass while he waited for the computer to churn fully awake. He thumbed the memory card into the proper slot. And…

"Potter," Dexicos said, voice raised only slightly above the conversational.

"Sir," Potter replied a moment later from the doorway.

"Summon Alexandros and Smith. I'll be in the office."

Dexicos was on his feet and in the hallway before Potter could even offer a deferential "Yes, sir."

Despite its impressive volume, the office could boast little furniture due to the sheer size of the desk occupying most of the square footage. The desk gleamed, a massive, polished expanse of burled walnut. It held only a telephone.

Dexicos leaned back against the firm tension of the high-tech, wheeled, swiveling office chair behind the desk. He liked the incongruity of the old-fashioned telephone, the handset with its brass earpiece and curved speaking horn resting in its cradle above the deep-bellied body that housed the telephone dial. Dexicos found pleasure in the precision and ritual of dialing the numbers that keypads could not replicate.

From memory, he began making calls.

"Brad, Dexter Magus. Buy jade. What? All of it. Stuff the portfolio. Put together some street teams, buy out the jewelry shops as well. What's that? Then stay late. Oh? Well, happy birthday."

"Kwan, Dexter Magus. Yes, I know what time it is. I need you to buy jade. The mines? No, I don't want a controlling interest. In fact, if I have any mine shares, sell them. But buy all the jade you can get your hands on. Yes, Kwan, I know it will drive the price up. Look, do I need to replace you? Fine. *Zài jiàn.*"

Thus, call after call, to brokers, factors, and money managers around the globe from London to Hong Kong. Not technically *his* brokers, factors, and money managers. In fact, the institutions employing them would be surprised to learn these financial professionals took instruction from someone who did not provide a regular paycheck. But they complied, even more readily than they did for their nominal employers – a globe-spanning collection of banks and investment firms – who now, unwittingly, had among them begun the process of cornering the jade market.

Dexicos presented a picture of contentment, reclined as far as the office chair would allow, fingers interlaced behind his head, when Alexandros and Smith appeared at the doorway. Alexandros rapped deferentially against the doorframe.

"Mr. Magus? You asked for us?"

Dexicos let the chair propel him upright. "Indeed I did. And you appear." He raised his right arm and flourished his hand theatrically. A bouquet of plastic roses thrust up from his right hand. A deck of cards sprayed from his left, littering the clean desktop.

Alexandros and Smith remained expressionless. Both were large men in expensive suits. Alexandros wore his thick, wavy hair slicked back, eyes hidden behind dark sunglasses even indoors, his features Levantine and impassive. Smith, black and smooth scalped – whether naturally or by choice, Dexicos neither knew nor cared – stood a couple of inches taller. The tailored Hugo Boss suit coats did little to hide physiques built by iron and anabolic steroids. But Dexicos had hired with brains as well as beef in mind, and both men were competent, independent thinkers he could task without the constant need to keep tabs on them or manage every aspect of the job.

Neither, however, possessed much of a sense of humor.

"Pack your bags, boys. We're going to Mexico," Dexicos said.

"Yes, sir," they replied, nearly in unison.

"Hold off on the bathing suits, though. This is a business trip. And, before you pack away your toothbrushes and sunscreen, I'll need you to arrange a crew of fixers on the ground."

"What's the job, boss?" Smith asked. "What skills do we need to recruit?"

"Excellent questions, Smith," Dexicos said. "I'd have led with 'where.' Mexico is a pretty big country. But, still, an excellent effort."

"Yes, sir," Smith said, betraying no more with his tone of voice than with his expression. "Where in Mexico shall we assemble the crew, Mr. Magus?"

"We're going to Cancun. *Señoritas* and piña coladas. So let's ensure our team can all speak Spanish this time? *Entiendes?*"

CHAPTER 3

"Look," said Alejandra Matamoros-Lopez in slow, very clearly enunciated Spanish, "the Gulf Cartel may be to the north and Los Zetas to the east, but they are not *here*. Not in this section of jungle." *These* indios. She couldn't be sure all of them spoke Spanish. Half the time all she heard from them was Mayan gobbledygook. Too many consonants. But a woman used what employees she could hire.

And what options did she have out here?

In shallow trenches hacked into thin, hard-packed soil cowered the physical plant of Alejandra's processing operation, tucked among the trees and beneath concealing tarp canopies in green and gray. Blue plastic barrels of solvents, yellow-tinged glass canisters of sulfuric acid, and yellow barrels of lye stood grouped in ranks beneath interlocking branches of ficus, persimmon, and willow trees. The leafy canopy protected against prying eyes in the sky. Seen from above, the jungle appeared a green, unbroken plain, the trees terminating at a uniform height, as if maintained by God's lawnmower (though the occasional palm tree thrust up higher, as if giving the deity the finger).

But Alejandra did not rely on trees alone for concealment. She'd discreetly brought in backhoes and tractors, digging deeply into the tough jungle soil. Interlocking dugout trench lines now stored bales of raw coca, Alejandra's strategy for competing with the big cartels. The big dogs primarily specialized in moving finished, packaged goods from producers in the South to the final consumers in *Los Estados Unidos*. They dealt in massive quantities, working economies of scale to their advantage. Alejandra couldn't match the prices per kilo offered by Los Zetas or the Knights Templar. But the leaves? Those she could get cheap. Within her trenches, beneath tarps of yellowing olive green, her army of chemists, packagers, couriers, and soldiers lived and worked, cooking up the final product. By processing herself, she saved the cost of buying the final product and thus could offer competitive prices. Narrowly, true. But with cost-conscious buyers, those margins made enough of a difference to matter.

Concealment. It all came down to hiding, really. If the enemy can't find you, he can't hurt you. Reasonable. How many people can you employ before concealment is no longer viable? That question grew increasingly important as successes mounted. Sales led to demand for larger deliveries. Larger deliveries required production of more product, which demanded more workers, more couriers, more security. But for now, Alejandra felt she was managing to maintain a low profile. Her organization was still small enough to conceal, small enough for her to personally vet each employee. So how had she let this stupid *puta* in? The sister of one of Alejandra's second cousin's brothers-in-law. Or something like that. A local, barely competent to purchase groceries, mix *masa*, and make tortillas. Barely.

She'd let the woman into her "office" (the space beneath an olive-green tarp holding a folding table and camp chair from which Alejandra ran her field operations) after Diego – her head of security and chief bodyguard – passed along the word that one of the cooks had seen something important in Las Crucitas. Diego now stood a respectful three paces away, his Bushmaster carbine slung at the ready across his expanse of chest. As always, he managed to look simultaneously bored and alert. Alejandra could understand the boredom. What could a barrel-chested, battle-hardened narco like Diego have to fear from a prematurely aged *indio* cook?

"*Sí, Señora,*" the woman was saying. "But I am sure I recognized him. He used to work for *mi tío* at the *llantería*. When I stopped seeing him there, I asked what happened to him. He was cute, you know? My uncle said he'd joined up with the Gulf Cartel. I know it was him driving that truck."

Alejandra's fingers tightened on the pearl and silver inlaid grips of her Sig Sauer P238. She kept the custom .380 pistol in a paddle holster at the small of her back. Her habit of clasping her hands behind her meant the weapon was always close to hand. "Did he see you?" Alejandra asked. She spoke evenly, calmly. But looking at this fat lump of a woman, with her thick ankles, coarse, plaited hair, and cheap, gaudy dress so inappropriate for the jungle, that red cloth practically a beacon... that such an uneducated peasant might jeopardize the entire operation was intolerable. Alexandra's operation. She was the *jefa*. And this woman's prattle bordered on disrespectful.

Alejandra took in a deep breath. She was letting this tortilla maker get under her skin.

The cook frowned at the question. "What, did I wave and chase the truck down the street?" she asked. "No. Do you think I'm stupid, *Señora*?"

That did it. No one spoke to Alejandra Matamoros-Lopez that way. The .380 was in Alejandra's fist and jammed beneath the cook's chin. "Yes, *puta*, I do think you're stupid. Worse, I think you're disrespectful."

The woman's eyes widened to a satisfying degree, insolence driven out by fear. That was what Alejandra needed to see. Without that fearful respect, how could a woman expect to maintain her control over an organization like this? If she had to bury another body in the jungle, she would. This stupid *puta* might serve Alejandra better as an example than as a cook.

The cook's mouth opened. "I..."

The ground trembled. Whatever the woman might have said remained unspoken. Alejandra spread both arms for balance as the earth shifted, swaying like a hammock. At least that removed the weapon from below the cook's head.

Alejandra disliked the thought of killing someone by accident. It would make her look foolish in front of Diego.

Sounds of devastation rose from the encampment. Alejandra could hear barrels toppling, tent poles snapping, tables collapsing, people screaming. Then a greater grinding and rumbling swelled to a crescendo, drowning out the lesser noises. Her camp desk toppled over, spilling documents to the seemingly animate ground. Guy wires and poles gave way. The tarp collapsed, enfolding Alejandra in its mildewed embrace.

She fought it, pushing at the heavy, clinging folds while the earth threatened to unbalance her, trying to throw her to the ground. Alejandra conjured the image of a grave-sized fissure opening at her feet and the tremor tossing her in, wrapped in a canvas shroud. She felt a scream rising from her knotted and pinched stomach. The earth ceased to move. Light from the morning sun returned as someone lifted the tarp from her: Diego, a look of concern altering his normally placid features.

"Alejandra, *estas bien?*" Diego asked.

Alejandra swallowed. She took a deep breath, holstered her pistol, smoothed down stray hairs the tarp had dislodged. Then she nodded. As Diego rolled away the tarp, she righted the folding table, then sat down on the camp chair.

"Let's hear the damages. Let the chiefs in to report." Her heart still pounded, the choking, engulfing burial within the tarp too recent. But she refused to let it show. *Sound calm, act calm, and they'll think you are calm. You are the boss; you can display no weakness.*

Initial damage reports alleviated her early concerns. A couple of overturned barrels spilling gasoline. A kitchen fire quickly doused. Scattered coca leaves. One broken arm. All tolerable, all remediable.

Then Hector arrived. One of Diego's lieutenants, Hector was earnest, serious, and reliable. He was related to Diego in some manner Alejandra hadn't bothered to trace, and looked up to the older man, emulating Diego's dress and manner. He even went so far as to adopt the same rifle.

"*Jefa*," he said, "the cenote tunnel has collapsed."

Shit. There was no easy fix to that. Her organization depended on secrecy, concealment. That included her delivery system. The tunnel system from the cenote was the indispensable first leg of that delivery system.

Deep sinkholes riddled the limestone bedrock of the Yucatan peninsula. These filled with water over the millennia. Water eroding soft limestone created linked tunnel complexes in some areas, most never explored. Alejandra had explored. The cenote within her camp served as more than a cooling pool to swim and bathe in. It also offered tunnel entrances. One of these tunnels exited several kilometers from camp, roadside. Alejandra had built a souvenir shop in front, a ramshackle affair suggesting an enterprise anticipating tourist traffic that had never materialized.

With the product emerging far from her camp and loaded into inconspicuous delivery trucks and vans, she could feel fairly confident she'd go unnoticed by the two large cartels battling to control the territory. And then, on to the cruise ships, where her network of cousins served aboard as pursers, cooks, maids, or in the laundries. After a luxury cruise, the goods would arrive in the States, where her purchasers would take delivery. Her cousins would take payment and deposit it in one of several US banks or return with the cash, whatever circumstances required.

"How bad?" Alejandra asked. "Can we dig it out?" Her *prima*, Maria Patricia, would be in port at Playa del Carmen on the *Grand Princess* in four days. She would be expecting the shipment.

"I don't think so, *Jefa*. We'd have to bring in heavy equipment. Backhoes, tractors." He shrugged. "Three, four weeks minimum."

Alejandra stood. "We don't have that much time. Let's take a look."

She led the men through the disarrayed encampment. It did not appear that any trees had fallen within the camp, though leaves and even complete branches littered the ground. Her people were already at work, righting toppled equipment, cleaning up spills, gathering fallen material and personal belongings. Good to see, but to Alejandra they looked frightfully exposed. Too open to aerial surveillance.

"Get the tarps back up. First priority," she said to Diego.

He nodded and peeled off, leaving her with Hector.

A dozen steps into deeper jungle, around a pile of stones possessing a regularity that suggested purpose, and down a ramp. The air grew increasingly humid with each step lower beneath the ground. Bare bulbs on a wire affixed to the cavern roof illuminated the pathway. The quake had not taken out the generator, *gracias a Dios*. Vines and tendril roots of the trees above clung to the porous rock walls. The ramp gave way to crude wooden stairs. They too remained intact.

So far so good. Perhaps the damage wasn't as bad as Hector had indicated.

The stairs switched back, once, twice. The final turn revealed the placid waters of the cenote, illuminated by both electric bulbs and the few shafts of sunlight managing to pierce through the layers of trees, undergrowth, earth, and limestone. The pool was roughly circular. A ledge allowed dry passage around roughly a third of it. At one time, five cavern mouths had opened off from the cenote – at least five above the surface. One of these stood at the far end of the ledge. Or it had before the quake. Now Alejandra could see only a mound of debris. The ground above the cavern had collapsed, stone and earth had slumped in to fill the newly open space, and now an impassable wall stood between Alejandra and the entrance to the tunnel through which she'd been accustomed to moving kilo upon kilo of product.

"Shit," Alejandra said. She fought back the urge to draw her pistol and unload the magazine into the offending obstruction. But she refused to show such petty emotion in front of Hector. "Hector, get some men down here with flashlights and ropes. Make sure they can swim. Get to exploring the other tunnels. Not just these four – any others close to camp they might know about. And then get into town, buy some inflatable rafts."

"Rafts?" Hector asked.

Alejandra gestured at the depths of the cenote. "Whatever we find, odds are it will involve water. Swimming over a few kilos at a time won't be too efficient, will it, Hector? We're going to find a new way out of here. And fast. *Muévete.*"

CHAPTER 4

Karl knocked on May's hotel door, paper cup of coffee in his other hand. "Morning," he said when she answered.

She accepted the proffered coffee with a smile. Karl noted with approval that May was freshly showered and dressed, with her suitcase packed and standing on its wheels by the door.

"Didn't need you to wash my back after all," May said. "Took some practice, but I figured it out all by myself." She took a sip of the coffee, but didn't entirely manage to hide her smile behind the cup.

"Pity. I'm famed for my back-scrubbing skills," Karl said. He reached by her and snatched up the suitcase. "Ready?"

"Just waiting on you, slowpoke."

The Jeep crawled free of the bohemian enclave of Tulum's hotel zone. Karl navigated onto 108, heading north-west, passing vans and buses full of tourists on their way to visit the ruins of Coba. He paid little attention to the scenery. He'd passed through so often over the last few months that it held scant interest for him. He kept quiet and let May enjoy the ride through the jungle. A wide, well-maintained highway cut through the dense ranks of trees, a wall of dull brown and green enlivened by colorful bursts of flowers. Every few miles the Jeep slowed at speed bumps to creep through interchangeable roadside towns, each with its stands displaying handicrafts remarkably similar to those of the last; each with cinder-block schools painted in primary colors occupied by uniformed children running about in pursuit of a soccer ball; each with mini-markets and tiny eateries offering *tortas* and *hamburguesas*.

After about an hour, Karl slowed. Despite all his trips to and from the dig, catching the turnoff from the highway still required his full attention. A dirt track – unencumbered by road sign or marker – slashed westward through the jungle.

"Gets a bit bumpy from here," Karl said. And it did. After a couple of miles, the track failed its seeming promise to lead the Jeep straight on to its final destination. Instead it narrowed, then forked, offering a choice of two rutted trails. Karl steered the Jeep onto the left-hand trail, the shock absorbers working hard to keep the jouncing and jostling to a minimum. This trail led to a maze of crisscrossing tracks cut through the jungle. Karl picked his turns unerringly.

"I'm already completely lost," May said.

"Yeah. Watch out for the Minotaur," Karl said. "First day I got here, I drove around for hours with a local, learning the ground. Still got lost three times during the next week."

Karl drove on, slowing to take it easy on May and whatever fragile items she might have stashed in her luggage. Without a passenger, he'd have cranked it up, fishtailing and flinging dirt.

The air smelled of dust overlaying a musty, vegetative smell like degraded and flaking paper, with occasional sweetly floral pockets. Karl knew well enough that soon the predominant odor would be sweat.

The trail widened.

"We're at the outskirts of the dig. Welcome to your new home, May," Karl said. "On your right you'll see the car park. Then the refuse dump – all garbage trucked out every Thursday. Beyond that on the left is Tent City, the chow hall, then the science tents and canopies. And a discreet distance farther…the dig. I'll drive you to Tent City. Don't feel like lugging your suitcase from the car park."

"Lazy ass," May said.

The trail became a broad dirt plaza, the right side filled with even rows of automobiles, mostly four-wheel-drive passenger vehicles along with a couple of old yellow school buses. Three beat-up big rigs with empty trailers attached hinted at the scope of the operation.

Past the car park, the trail narrowed again, curving around an outcropping of thick jungle. Beyond –

Karl swore. He stopped the Jeep. "Come on. Room assignment will have to wait."

The neat ranks of tents he'd left had become a jumbled

mess of canvas, nylon, and guy ropes. There were – or, rather, had been – thirty-five tents. Karl'd had plenty of time to count. Most were the temporary homes of archaeology students, the majority from Mexican universities, though about a half dozen American students cycled through from semester to semester. Other tents housed the support staff: cooks, heavy equipment operators, a nurse/paramedic. Dr. Allison occupied one of the nicer tents, Karl a much smaller. Though, given how much time he spent in the roomier, well-equipped exercise pavilion, he felt he almost had two tents. The nicest setup was reserved for visits from the bureaucrats of the National Institute of Anthropology and History, who descended periodically to ensure that no one absconded with relics. Karl always found their visits a personal and professional affront.

But now even that grand pavilion was a heap of fabric and jutting aluminum tent poles, like a good three-quarters of the rest. Debris had spilled from several of them, extending tongues of detritus from collapsed tent mouths – books, clothing, toiletries. Dried laceworks of foam decorated a few dented cans of Tecate that lay forlornly on the ground. *Damned shame.* At one end of a toppled aluminum shaft splayed the shattered remains of the satellite uplink dish. Only a few tents remained standing, unscathed by whatever disaster had struck.

Karl led May through the wreck of Tent City. A few students wandered dazedly about, a couple of them fruitlessly performing the Cell Signal Polka. He saw one he knew, a graduate student by the name of Judy Carrolton from New Mexico State. She was dragging a backpack from beneath the billows and waves of her collapsed tent.

"Judy," Karl said, "what the hell?"

Judy straightened up. She stood nearly eye-to-eye with Karl. A tall woman, sturdily built, wearing insect-resistant jeans, a long-sleeve shirt, and calf-high hiking boots. "Earthquake, Carlos." She skipped her usual extended rolling of the *R*, that in itself indicative of how rattled she was. "How'd you miss it? About a two-minute carnival ride on solid ground."

"I was on the road, ferrying Professor Chen. Didn't feel a thing."

"Hello, Professor Chen. Sorry we can't provide a better welcome. I'm Judy Carrolton. Professor Allison said you'd be coming." The two women shook hands in a rather perfunctory fashion, Karl interested that they even bothered under the circumstances.

"Any damage to the dig?" Karl asked.

"Don't know yet. I was here when the quake hit. Been doing damage control ever since. Why don't you ask Professor Allison?"

Karl was about to ask where the man was when he heard what Judy obviously already had – the swish and thwack of a stick through underbrush, the telltale sound of Jim Allison absently swinging his combination shooting stick and umbrella through the rare tangles of brush and sparse grass left in Tent City, the man going out of his way on the dry, stony soil of the camp to find stands of innocent growth to abuse.

Jim Allison retained a youthful, collegiate appearance even into his early forties. He wore stained khakis and a multi-pocketed bush vest. An orange ball cap with an embroidered T logo rested on the back of his head, brim jutting up at a ninety-degree angle.

Karl glanced at May to gauge her reaction. There was a tense expectation in her stance. He couldn't read it. Nerves? Hope? Fear? Karl couldn't help wishing her ultimate expression would be one of disappointment. Harsh, he supposed. Selfish, yes. But there it was.

Professor Allison was easier to read. The archaeologist looked worried and distracted. He reached the group and leaned on the folded handle of his walking stick, letting it take his weight. "May, good to see you. Wish it could be under more ideal circumstances."

"Jim, how are you?"

"Good question." Professor Allison straightened and swiped his walking stick back and forth like an irritated cat swishing its tail. He cleared his throat. "Let's catch up this evening after we evaluate the results of our little jostling. I can tell you that if the dig is good, then I'm good. So, in furtherance of that..." He swiveled, pointed his stick a couple of points west of due north. "Karl, I think the epicenter was that direction. Best guess is three, four miles thataway, in the deep stuff. See if it's close, eyeball the strength of it, if it's likely to have compromised the dig. I just got back from a peek at the ziggurat, didn't see any obvious signs of damage. But if the epicenter was too near, it might have created some instabilities. Don't want to risk a close inspection if the whole thing's likely to collapse on top of me or any of the kids."

"Already on it," Karl said and turned toward the Jeep.

As he hopped in, May climbed into the passenger seat. "I can see more of the area this way before getting my nose buried in the dig," she said.

Karl shrugged. He guessed the meeting with Jim Allison hadn't exactly gone as May anticipated, not met any of the scenarios she'd imagined. She might be joining Karl more as a distraction than for the reason she'd stated. Well, Karl would do his best to distract. It was only fair; she distracted him in all the right ways.

Karl started the Jeep and skirted the edge of the camp, picking up another jungle track. Beyond Tent City, he drove by a clearing gridded by twine and wooden stakes. Little flags poked up here and there, indicating some area of particular interest. The site appeared to have survived the quake relatively intact, although a cache of hand spades, brushes, and wire-bottomed sifting screens had come dislodged, strewing tools down onto the trail. Through gaps in the jungle beyond the clearing came glimpses of a truncated pyramidal heap of stone, reaching near the tops of the highest branches. Without stopping for a closer look, Karl couldn't tell how much damage the ruins of the ziggurat had suffered. Professor Allison had sounded relatively sanguine, and Karl hoped that he did so with good reason. The structure was the centerpiece of the dig, and Professor Allison would be devastated if the earthquake had demolished it. Karl didn't possess more than a passing interest in archaeology, but he'd been involved in the dig long enough to take a personal interest in the site, the findings, and the triumphs or disappointments of those who did care deeply about it.

May had shifted as far as her seatbelt allowed, staring past him at the glimpses of ruins. "Wow," she said. "Is there more?"

"It's a big site. Plenty more. Allison's got teams spread over a few square miles."

"Jim seems to place a lot of trust in you. What is it you do here, really? And how's a dirty-blond, corn-fed Midwestern type end up with a Mexican name like Carl?"

Karl chuckled. The driving required some attention, but it wasn't yet so technical that he couldn't hold up his end of a conversation.

"I fill my mead horn with tequila, May. My dad is a proud Norwegian by way of three generations of Minnesotans. But my mother is from Mexico City. A *chilanga* from 'Day Effay,' as she likes to say."

"An international love story. How romantic."

"You don't know the half of it. They met in the Olympics. Dad was a shot-putter. Says he barely made the team. But hell, an Olympian is an Olympian. Mom was on the springboard team for Mexico. Pretty good. Ended up a few tenths of a point out of bronze. They fell in love. Mom moved to the US, became a Classics teacher at a community college in Idaho. Dad managed the marketing department for a manufactured homes builder."

"Okay. I guess that explains the name."

"Yeah. It was one the folks could agree on. Mom called

me Carlitos. Dad liked the sound of Karl, with the sort of pan-Nordic/Germanic meaning of 'Freeman.' Or, when we were roughhousing in the yard, he'd call me his Housecarl."

"So what brings Karl, the Mexican Viking, from Idaho to the Yucatan jungle?"

Karl brought the Jeep to a crawl at an intersection, picked the trail going most directly north.

"Enlisted out of high school. Did a few tours in various vacation paradises. Afterwards I worked as a bodyguard for VIPs in the Middle East, for a military contracting company. Didn't like the lack of autonomy. Don't much care to have my activities and movements constantly dictated by someone else's agenda."

"That must have made the army a barrel of laughs."

"There's a reason I didn't re-enlist again. Special ops wasn't so bad as far as that goes. But still…What's the term the kids are using now? Agency? I felt a lack of agency. So I went solo. Currently the solo gig is guide/troubleshooter/security for Jim Allison's bug-infested jungle extravaganza."

"How is 'security' different from 'bodyguard'?"

"Jim consults me on proceedings. I help direct the day's activities instead of the day's activities directing me. Allows me at least a modicum of 'agency.'"

"Don't like to be tied down, want to be your own boss?"

"Yes, I'm a walking cliché," Karl said, sparing a moment to offer May a grin. "Look, I have nothing but respect for anyone who holds down a steady job. Like my old man. That sort of stability is what makes the world work. Allows people like you and me to gad about the globe, shoveling up remnants of the past. So cheers to the hardworking entrepreneurs and the nine-to-fivers who work for them. Cheers to what they've created. I'm happy to take advantage of it. But I don't intend to join in."

"You're shooting for what, then? Independently wealthy? International playboy? Man of leisure?"

"Why not all of the above? Though 'leisure' sounds a bit dull."

Karl slowed the Jeep to a crawl. The quantity of fallen branches and leaves shaken free of their moorings grew increasingly thick, and the track became correspondingly more difficult to follow. The Jeep crept over a toppled sapling, then another a dozen yards farther. The thickness of the next fallen tree proved a more daunting obstacle. Not far beyond that, two sizeable trunks had toppled one atop the other, effectively blocking the trail.

Karl shut off the engine. "'All truly great thoughts are conceived by walking,'" he said.

"Huh?" May said.

"Nietzsche."

"Oh. Meaning we're on foot from here?"

"Yep. Hold on." Karl leaned across the Jeep's cabin, popped open the glove compartment, and retrieved a canister of insect repellent. "Douse yourself." He handed the bug spray to May. While she was busy fogging herself, he rummaged around behind the front seats until he found his cased jungle knife, its curved, blackened blade half-kukri, half-machete.

"Nietzsche," May said in between spritzes. "Wasn't he that nihilist? Or Nazi? Why Nietzsche?"

Karl chuckled. "Guess you were too busy in archaeology classes to study philosophy." He dismounted the Jeep. "That Nazi claim is bullshit, same as the anarchist stuff. But it's a common misconception." He accepted the insect repellent from May and absently doused himself while he surveyed the scenery. The trees rose about like the bones of giants browned by age. They grew in stands and copses, with gaps and narrow glades here and there between the clusters. From above, Karl knew, the canopy would appear uniform, unbroken. But on the ground, the growth distribution belied that. The jungle here was not in the same league with the tropical density that could be found not too far south. Compared to those southern jungles, this growth pattern with the widely spaced boles and relatively thin undergrowth was practically a city park. But comparisons couldn't improve the visibility.

It took a moment to sift the specific from the general, to see the trees from the forest. But with a deliberate shifting of focus, Karl began to see where limbs had fallen in greater profusion. Then beyond, where trunks had cracked and started to topple, to be propped up by neighbors. Looked at more closely, an entire section of forest appeared like so many drunken sailors, holding each other up at various angles.

"Okay, Plato. What did Nietzsche say?" May asked.

"What? Oh. I'm not a philosophy lecturer," Karl said, temporarily returning his focus back to May. "Nutshell: he posited that we should dispense with the older modes of morality and look for new ones. Not abandon morality entirely. He wasn't proposing some Aleister Crowley 'Do What Thou Wilt' lifestyle. He was looking for something new."

"Do you buy into that?"

Karl shrugged. "Can't say I agree with him. I figure over the course of human history, all models of morality have been tried at one point or another. Nothing new under the sun, right? But I like to read Nietzsche to remind myself to remain flexible. Keep an open mind."

May grunted a "huh" and let the subject drop.

"That way," Karl said, gesturing with his knife. He tossed the bug spray into the Jeep, then fastened the knife sheath to his belt. "I think the epicenter is that direction. Let's go see if the quake has shaken anything loose badly enough to concern Professor Allison."

"Or me," May said.

"Right you are," Karl said, not the least abashed at her mild rebuke.

Karl led in as near a straight line as possible along the path of increasing damage. The heat, sweat, and profusion of insects increased with each step. He broke out the machete a couple of times to clear obstructions, but this terrain was relatively tame in comparison to some of the bush he'd traversed while still in uniform. The occasional glance over his shoulder showed that May was having little difficulty keeping up.

The path of destruction dropped down into a fold of

ground, back up, then carried on over the brow of a low rise. Karl froze as his head cleared the crest of the slope. Without looking behind him, he lifted an admonishing hand and hissed a warning. People milled through the remnants of some sort of encampment. A sizeable encampment, not a recreational sprawl of colorful pup tents, but an organized bivouac. Not quite the scale of Professor Allison's scientific expedition, but of nearly the same order. The quake had toppled tent poles, collapsed tarpaulins, and – was that camouflage netting?

"What?" whispered May.

"Keep your voice down," Karl whispered back. "I'm guessing narcos. Some sort of cartel operation." He watched two men wrestling a fifty-five-gallon steel drum upright. Several more struggled to erect a partially buckled tent.

"Let me see," May hissed. She crept up next to him, fallen branches and dry underbrush crackling beneath her. Karl winced at the noise.

"Come on, let's go," Karl said. This camp looked to have borne the brunt of the earthquake. As near as he could figure, it lay several klicks beyond the bounds of the archaeologists' site. That the two groups had never previously encountered each other seemed evidence enough of that. But still…

If this was the greatest extent of the quake damage, Karl could report back reassuring news about the earthquake question to Professor Allison – right before he reported this revelation. *Fucking narcos*. Shit, at the very least Allison would need to hire more security. Might need to work his

National Institute of Anthropology and History contacts to bring in the army. Or might need to pack up and go before everyone got shot.

"Oh," May said. "How many of them do you think there are? Do they live out here?"

"Come on, May. Not the time for sightseeing." A camp this size would have security. The earthquake would probably disrupt any regular patrols, but Karl didn't like risking May on probabilities.

"Okay," May said. She slipped back, making less noise with this movement. A quick study.

CHAPTER 5

Bark and dirt erupted from the trunk of a tree above Karl's head almost simultaneously with the report of a rifle. Two riflemen scrambled southward along the ridgeline toward May and Karl. Decidedly nonmilitary. Both wore T-shirts and cargo shorts, though of differing colors. One was in flip-flops, the other in high-top Pumas. Each carried an AK or some sort of tricked-out SKS. Karl couldn't be sure at a glance.

Karl's reaction to gunfire was as much instinctual as it was the result of training and experience. He propelled himself backward, down the slope, following then passing May. He grabbed her wrist with his left hand. His right pushed aside the hem of his shirt and found the grip of the .38 Smith & Wesson snub nose in the paddle holster at his back. He tugged it free.

"Move," he said.

She moved. Moved pretty good, too. She didn't freeze,

didn't drop to the ground and crawl, didn't try some ridiculous tree-to-tree serpentine rigmarole. She simply bent slightly at the waist and ran. Karl let go of her wrist and dropped behind, letting her take the lead.

Two more shots indicated the narcos hadn't lost interest. Karl performed a running pirouette, brought up the .38 as he spun, then thought better of it. He caught the merest glimpse of one of them through the trees. A wild pistol shot would provide no deterrence in the circumstances. Karl completed his three-sixty and kept running. He'd cleared away the worst of the obstructions on the way in with his jungle knife, so the two of them were able to make pretty good time.

Another round cracked overhead, then another.

"Shit, shit," May said. Then kept repeating it over the next hundred yards.

Another shot, this one passing nowhere nearby. The Jeep came in sight. Another shot sounded, but the noise came through less crisply, as if the shooter was no longer aiming in even the general direction of May and Karl.

May flung herself into the Jeep. Karl holstered the .38 and dug out the keys.

"Come on," May said.

Karl lifted an eyebrow. "In a hurry?" But he fired up the Jeep as he said it. "Buckle up." A pity he had to run. But he was outgunned here, and his objective was only reconnaissance. Besides, he had no business putting May at risk merely for the personal satisfaction of fighting back.

He put his foot down, spun the wheel, and threw the

Jeep into a bounding, careening flight back down the trail. Gunfire followed, rounds tearing through leaves and branches or smacking into tree trunks above the Jeep. Karl figured the riflemen were firing blind, trying to aim by sound and relying on luck. He grinned, letting himself enjoy the moment.

Karl slowed after the first bend in the trail. Puncturing a tire or high centering the Jeep was a more immediate danger than the gunmen. He spared a glance at May. She looked flushed, frightened. But not in shock, not panicked. Kept her head in a crisis. Good. There seemed to be more and more to like about May Chen. He flashed her a smile.

The gunfire ceased. Karl eased up even more on the throttle, done with risk taking for the moment.

"They were shooting at us," May said. "What the hell was that all about? And you have a gun. Why do you have a gun? How do you have a gun? This is Mexico. Not New Mexico. Okay, I'm talking too much. Sorry. I've never been shot at before."

"First time? You handled it like a pro, May." Karl offered her a congratulatory pat on the knee. "The gun? Well, I've got dual citizenship, so I'm also Mexican. Mexico has highly restrictive gun laws, but there are certain limited classes of firearms a citizen can own."

That was true as far as it went. Karl left it there, let her assume that meant he was legally authorized to carry. He wasn't. As a citizen, so long as he jumped through certain bureaucratic hoops, he could keep a .38 at home. But for a man without a fixed abode, "home" was a problematic concept.

"Why didn't you shoot back?"

"With this? Thing's got a barrel shorter than my thumb. Can't hit shit with it past seven yards at the range. Running through the woods, shooting behind me? I might as well toss bullets over my shoulder. And narcos or not, I'm not in the habit of shooting people I don't absolutely have to. Besides, this way I don't have to clean the gun tonight."

"Okay. Makes sense. So what do we do now?"

"Report back to Professor Allison. He has to know his dig is only a few miles from a cartel camp."

"What will he do? What can he do?"

"Fight or flight, I suppose. Beef up security and speed up the dig. Call in the authorities. Hope the local police or military aren't on this cartel's payroll. Or pull up stakes, go home, and publish his findings."

"Or come back next year. No, there won't be a next year. Some other university or organization will risk it if we leave." May sat silently for the next half mile as Karl drove them back toward the site. "I just got here. No way am I going to pack up and go home."

They talked about May's work and teaching load during the drive back. Karl figured it would keep May from dwelling on the recent excitement. She'd handled herself with aplomb, true, but getting shot at is still getting shot at no matter how cool one is under fire. By the time they reached the dig, Karl felt he could find his way around Eugene without much assistance.

Karl had hoped to allow May a few moments to unpack and get acquainted with her tent. But Professor Jim Allison met the Jeep at the car park as Karl pulled in.

"Leave it, May, leave it," Allison said as May reached for her backpack. "All hands on deck. You too, Karl. I want to get the camp in order before sunset."

"Jim," Karl said, "you're gonna want to hear –"

"Later, Karl. I shouldn't have sent you two out scouting. The quake scrambled my brains. Lost my priorities. Priority one: shelter. We can talk about whatever you found once we get the tents up again."

"But –"

Professor Allison was already walking, May trotting alongside to keep up with his hurried, walking-stick-assisted stride. She looked over her shoulder at Karl, giving him a helpless shrug.

"Shit," Karl said. He hopped out of the Jeep, adjusted the seat of pistol and jungle knife, and followed.

Tent City was resuming its old shape. The trio joined a team of twenty-somethings – most wearing T-shirts or ball caps bearing university logos – raising the center pole of the dining pavilion. Erecting tents was a matter of muscle memory for Karl. He couldn't begin to calculate the number of shelter halves, personal tents, and large general-purpose tents he'd helped set up in any number of countries and weather conditions.

Eventually he found himself hammering in a tent peg next to Professor Allison. "Jim," he said, "while I've got you here…I understand your priorities, but maybe this should not be your biggest concern right now."

Professor Allison was listening, without much choice as he was committed to holding a pole in position while May and one of the Mexican undergrad students slotted it into a canvas sleeve. Karl figured he'd take the opportunity to inform the professor of the pressing news.

"You've got narcos sitting on your doorstep. They aren't going to be happy with neighbors."

Professor Allison blinked at Karl. He pushed back his hat with his free hand and ran his fingers through thinning hair. "Narcos? What do you mean?"

"I mean narcotraffickers. You've got a coca operation a few miles away. If they didn't know about your dig before, I'm pretty sure they will soon."

Professor Allison blinked at him. He puffed up his cheeks, then blew out a long breath. "I suppose you've got a point, Karl. We should speed up the dig. I'd like to get the preliminaries out of the way before the rainy season anyway."

"Not sure you're getting it, Jim," Karl said.

"Jim," May said, "you really ought to listen to him. I don't like the idea of packing up and leaving. I haven't even *unpacked* yet. But we just got shot at." She made pistols with her fingers. "Bang! Bang! We got chased through the woods by guys with guns."

May might want to stand her ground, but she certainly sounded to Karl as if she were advocating withdrawal. Maybe some feminine tactical maneuvering there, good old-fashioned reverse psychology: the male authority figure unable to accept the advice of a woman. *Does that even work anymore?*

"Okay, okay. Let me think about it. Should I call the *federales*? Wait, call them how? The dish is smashed; we've got no reliable commo. Okay, revised question: Should I drive to the nearest town with a cell phone tower and call the *federales*?"

Karl finished hammering in the spike. He stood and stretched his back. "Maybe," he said, "but if the local cops are on the payroll of these narcos, they'll just find an excuse to kick us off the dig. Or perhaps just bury us here."

"The army?" Professor Allison asked, then answered his own question. "Same deal as the police, I suppose."

Karl nodded. He considered the problem, the terrain; estimated the capabilities of this unknown OpFor and the known capabilities of the archaeologists. Might he have overestimated the immediacy of the threat?

"Look, there's no way you can clear out tonight. Too many people to move. I don't see the narcos finding us and organizing an assault in just one day. The fact that they haven't come across us yet argues in our favor." He tugged at his belt, where the weight of gun and knife was causing some sag. "Suggestion: Tomorrow I go into town and work my contacts, try to find out if we can trust local law enforcement – at least as far as this pack of narcos goes. Of course, that assumes we can figure out which cartel we're dealing with."

"What do you mean?" May asked.

"You've got at least a couple different organizations fighting over this territory," Karl said. "Local police might be clean, might be in the pay of one cartel, or might even be on the take from both sides. Same goes with the military. All kinds of potential scenarios. If we decide to ask for protection rather than bailing, it would behoove us to know which scenario obtains."

"I'd rather not run," Professor Allison said. "If we leave, another university will snake in, taking advantage of all of our preliminary fieldwork."

"Probably with a full security team, too," Karl said.

"On the other hand," Professor Allison said, as if he hadn't heard Karl, "the safety of all of these people is my responsibility."

"Mine too," Karl said, almost growling the words. He did not like this situation. He felt torn. He wanted to get these people to safety. But at the same time he felt possessive of the site, of the work these people had done. He didn't want to abandon it.

"Doubt I'll get much sleep tonight," Professor Allison said. "Right. Tomorrow, Karl, you head to civilization, see what you can find out. I'll bring May up to speed, operating under the assumption that you'll come back with good news."

"More assumptions," Karl said. "Outstanding."

The clock in the bottom corner of Dexicos Megistos' laptop computer read 3:02 a.m. Propped up against two pillows, swathed in a crimson silk dressing gown that shifted easily across the 1200-thread count Egyptian cotton sheets, Dexicos sipped at a porcelain cup of rosehip tea laced with cognac. His other hand tapped at the keyboard and manipulated the touchpad. Three o'clock in the morning meant nothing to Dexicos. He slept little, seldom more than twenty or thirty minutes a day. Though there were times, perhaps twice a century, when he'd go under for up to a month, emerging gaunt and dehydrated yet mentally invigorated.

An icon on the computer screen flashed, notifying Dexicos of an incoming video call. Dexicos sipped from the cup – Chinese, twelfth century – then clicked on the icon. The face of Festo Hidalgo, lit a wan yellow and green, appeared. From the image wobble, Dexicos figured Festo was using a cell phone. And judging from the flickering, intermittent quality, Festo must be at the outer limits of cellular reception.

"*Señor* Magus?" asked Festo.

"In the flesh, Festo," Dexicos said.

The image shifted, stabilized. Festo must have rested his hand on something, steadying it. Dexicos took a second, then recognized it as the inside of a car. Festo was in the passenger seat, evidently with his hand propped against the dashboard. Dexicos couldn't make out the model of the car, only that it was aging and poorly maintained. A movement suggested that someone occupied the driver's seat.

"Have you something to report?" Dexicos asked. "Or is this purely a social call?"

"Much to report, *Señor*," Festo said. He swatted at something the cell phone video was incapable of picking up, some jungle insect infiltrating the car, attracted to the light from the cell phone. "*Dos cosas, supongo.* I don't know which to tell first."

"Dealer's choice," Dexicos said. "Or flip a coin. Do not rush yourself. I've got all night. What's left of it, anyway."

"Okay. *Pues*…first thing is these archaeologists are not alone here."

"Oh? Company other than yourself?"

"*Sí*. Narcos. In the jungle, a few kilometers away. Was an earthquake here this morning. Stirred up everyone. *Como hormigas*. No trouble yet, but I think you want to know this, yes?"

"Yes. Well done, Festo. What else have you for me?"

"This one here has something to tell you." The cell phone imagery traversed the interior of the car in a nauseating swoop. The image wavered, then focused on the man in the driver's seat. Despite the poor video quality, Dexicos could make out dissolute and undernourished features. The oversized shirt accentuated a furtive, mustelid quality. The man couldn't look directly into the lens for more than a second, as his eyes constantly shifted and leapt. "This is Enrique. He drove me to the dig and back to the airport." Festo switched to Spanish. "Enrique, tell him what happened after you dropped me at the airport."

Enrique swallowed, the Adam's apple a grayish bobbing shadow. He stammered.

"Go on, Enrique," Dexicos said, his Spanish betraying occasional hints of archaic Castilian. "I'm a captive audience."

"A man from the diggings followed us to the airport. I stayed at the airport for a while, got a drink, and picked up a loose suitcase someone had abandoned. The man from the diggings followed me when I drove away. I tried to lose him, but he chased me down."

"Just one man?"

"There were two. One was a woman. And the man, he was big. A big gringo. He threatened me with bolt cutters. Beat me."

"He beat you? Perhaps it is an artifact of the poor connection, but you do not appear much bruised or battered to me."

"Well, not in the face. I did not want to tell him anything, but he forced me. I had no choice."

"I see. So I must assume the site administrator is aware of outside interest. Festo, you are correct. That is of interest." The cell phone returned to capture Festo's face, upon which was clearly etched relief and satisfaction. "Tell me, Festo, are you paying so little to your driver that he has to supplement his income with petty luggage theft?"

Enrique's voice came from out of frame. "That's right. He barely pays enough to fill the tank. With all these extra risks and the beatings, I deserve more."

Dexicos *tsked* sympathetically. "Festo, see that the driver gets all he has coming to him."

The image shook. Dexicos had trouble making out the widening eyes of Festo. Then the picture steadied. Festo nodded. The image tumbled, rotating from the ceiling of the car, flashing by the baggy-clothed driver, then coming to a stop with a view of the driver's waist and hips and the torn fabric of the driver's seat. Dexicos assumed the cell phone had wedged itself somewhere within the center console.

Enrique's lower torso twisted, and a shadow fell across the image.

"Festo, *que estas haciendo?*" Enrique asked, his voice rising in panicked shrill.

"*No!*"

The leg twitched as the "no" became a scream. The scream dropped to a gasping gurgle, and the leg twitches slowed, then ceased.

The image moved again, providing a brief glimpse of

Enrique's body slumped against the seat, his head lolling back from a gashed-open neck, his oversized shirt soaked with some dark stain, the fabric conforming now to the contours of his narrow chest. Festo filled the image, wiping spots from his face with a hand that still held a dripping knife.

"I think, *Señor*, Enrique got all he had coming to him."

"Excellent, Festo. You show surprising initiative. Let's see if you can show some more. I'll be coming down to oversee this matter personally. Hire a suitable vehicle. Something larger than that mechanical excrescence you are currently occupying. Two gentlemen, by the names of Alexandros and Smith, will be in contact with you."

Dexicos ended the call without waiting for a response. His impending excursion looked to have grown more interesting. Good. His thin lips drew back in a tight smile. At the very least, the trip would not bore him.

CHAPTER 7

Karl saluted May with his coffee cup as she shuffled, yawning, into the dining tent. Sans makeup, with her hair in a ponytail dangling from the back of a baseball cap, she still looked good. The hint of dark circles under her eyes only added to the overall look, a sort of disheveled morning chic. She loaded her breakfast tray with fruit and a plate of *huevos con chorizo* and took a seat next to Karl.

"Did you sleep well?" he asked.

"Back in the field, in a tent, lying on a cot under mosquito netting, an exciting new find to explore, trigger-happy drug gang next door – I slept like a baby. Okay, no. I slept fitfully. I need caffeine."

Karl rose to fetch her a cup. As he returned, Professor Allison joined them. Karl noticed that while Professor Allison seated himself next to May, he maintained a standard separation, not scooching his chair in close to her. Karl held no ill will toward Jim Allison, but he couldn't help but feel heartened by this further evidence that May's arrival hadn't struck any romantic sparks.

Professor Allison didn't offer any personal chitchat, instead launching immediately into his tale of the dig. Karl had heard it all before: How a combination of intense Google map viewing and expensive Lidar flights had suggested an uninvestigated settlement here, presumably Mayan. How seismic activity had dropped the settlement – town, city, religious or administrative center, or whatever – into the limestone caverns below, doing relatively little structural damage and squirreling the site away, preventing discovery until now.

Karl poured a second cup of coffee, then followed May and Professor Allison from the chow tent as the tale shifted into the tour. He figured he'd drive to the coast once he'd finished this cup. Start at Tulum, then work his way north to Cancun, wringing what intel he could from his network of informants: old Special Ops buddies now running dive shops, military contractors edging into the shadier side of mercenary work, a few outright criminals. Karl knew a lot of people. He listened, didn't judge – at least not out loud – and was always willing to stand a round or two of drinks. People confided in him, and he did his best to ensure no one paid a price for doing so. At least, no one who didn't have it coming.

Karl caught up with the other two as they reached the main clearing. He stopped to allow May to take in the upper third of the ziggurat poking up from the cenote into which it had plunged. The upper tier had toppled off, the massive blocks still wedged between the sloping steps of the pyramid and the lip of the cenote. The ziggurat was the showpiece of the dig, but it wasn't the sole point of interest. Roped-off areas extended from the main clearing where sections of the site that had not fallen through cracks were being surveyed and cataloged. Little flags proclaimed significant finds, though many of these had been dislodged by the earthquake and shifted by errant breezes far from the finds they were meant to mark.

The site had grown during Karl's tenure. He knew the archaeologists were excited by the extent of the find. But while he found the individual ruins impressive enough, he didn't grasp the scope of the entire location. The fallen stone blocks, the extant walls, and mostly complete buildings were still largely separated by stretches of jungle. And many of the finds were partially – or completely – underground. The site remained piecemeal, pieces of a puzzle still jumbled up in the box. He couldn't see the finished picture yet.

Professor Allison apparently could. "I believe it was more a ritual site than a functioning metropolis," he was telling May. "The proportion of shrines and temples to dwellings and storehouses is higher than we see regionally. And look here." A rectangular pediment reached by a wide stairway of chipped stone blocks held a peaked structure, looking to Karl like an A-Frame from a ski lodge built of stone rather than wooden shingles, but always referred to by Professor Allison as a "corbeled arch." "Note how robust these walls are. We measured it; the walls are twice as thick as the space left within. Not typical, not practical. This was built for display rather than functionality. Good thing for us, too; the construction method allowed some of the structures to survive drops they probably wouldn't have otherwise. You'll see those later."

Karl stood impassively while the other two halted, though he wanted nothing more than for Professor Allison to get on with the nickel tour – the potential threat from the cartel only grew while the professor held forth. Yet he felt a compulsion to accompany May through the dog and pony show, a protective urge. Or was it an unwillingness to leave her alone with Jim Allison? He told himself he wasn't nursing the java. And that he wasn't personally interested in whether or not Professor Allison tried to rekindle his former relationship with May.

He figured he'd stick with her at the very least until he'd finished his second cup.

Allison moved them along, too eager to show off everything to linger at any particular location. They reached the ziggurat. A wooden barrier followed the circumference of the cenote, preventing accidental tumbles into the depths. Months' worth of footsteps had worn a path to the entryway. The ends of the barrier overlapped, creating a switchback entry in lieu of a gate.

Karl looked up at the truncated tip of the pyramid jutting from the hole in the ground like the gabled roof of a house submerged to the eaves in a flood, a sight half desperate, half defiant. He tried to see it as May might, with academic rigor. Examining the weathering of the stone, the damage caused by roots growing between gaps in the stones. Trying to decipher meaning from the eroded bas-relief images chiseled into the stair risers. Attempting to see it as individual components providing windows into a lost culture, offering clues to real, flesh and blood people. But he couldn't. No matter how many times he saw it – or any of the ruins hacked free from their jungle concealment – he still couldn't view it with detachment, always experiencing a frisson of awe, an ineffable, almost religious reverence for the admixture of antiquity and mystery. He glanced at May, at her tilted jaw, lips slightly parted, the one eye visible from his vantage point glinting. No cold academic detachment there. Not yet.

Karl followed the other two along the path to the lip of the cenote. A landing of sturdy planks led onto a wooden staircase descending in a series of switchbacks toward the water far below. Naked bulbs on a wire stapled to the damp limestone wall of the pit illuminated the descent as sunlight gave way to the cenote's shadows. The bulbs provided plenty of light.

Karl had visited enough cenotes in the Yucatan peninsula to be used to the humidity. Most of those required clambering down slick, confined stairways built against vine-draped, naked stone before expanding to a reservoir of cool water within a vast, echoing chamber. But here the bulk of the ziggurat filled the cenote, like a cork pushed down through the neck of a bottle. The effect was claustrophobic. The sloping face of the pyramid grew closer, the space tightening as he descended.

The stair ended at a ledge rising three feet above the dark, placid water. If he wished, Karl could reach out to touch the cool, rough stone of the ziggurat. May did, nearly toppling over the ledge as she misjudged the distance. Karl curled a hand over her shoulder, steadying her.

"Don't gaze too long into the abyss," he said.

She shot him a quirked smile, half relieved thanks, half irritation. "This is amazing," she said, turning back to Professor Allison. "I mean, I've seen the pictures you sent, Jim. But to see it in person…Have you sent down divers?"

"Not yet. Still working mostly dry foot. I've got a tentative commitment from ECU, but not until next spring."

May glanced at Karl.

"East Carolina University," he said. "Pirates."

"Man's got a gift," May said.

The ledge curved around nearly a quarter of the cenote, the string of bare light bulbs illuminating its length. The stairway terminated at one end of the ledge. At the other end, a wooden footbridge crossed the pool to the lowest dry level of the ziggurat.

May took a few steps toward the bridge.

"Wait," Jim said. "You can clamber over the pyramid to your heart's content. But I've got more to show you first." He gestured away from the pool, at a spot about midway along the ledge. A wire branched off from the main string of lights, dropping down the wall, then disappearing within a rough-edged semicircular opening. A glimmer of light indicated the opening was more than a mere depression in the cenote wall.

Professor Allison led the way, dropping to a crouch to duck walk through the opening. May and Karl followed, Karl brushing the top of his head against the arch of the tunnel entry. The string of light bulbs lit a narrow, tubular passage. It had been swept clean of debris, but the floor remained uneven, the footing awkward, that awkwardness enhanced by the unnatural gait of a duck walk. The tunnel curved to the right, beginning to expand as it did. Within another twenty yards, May could walk upright. Ten yards farther on, so could Professor Allison. Karl remained confined at either a slight crouch or with his neck bowed.

A few yards later, a side passage opened on the right. Allison led into this one. It, thankfully, had a ceiling height varying from six to seven feet, though it was narrow, occasionally requiring Karl to edge through sideways. After a minute or so, the passage plunged down. Temporary wooden stairs augmented the natural stair steps of the tunnel. The walls beaded wetly, dampness growing as the passage descended until the walls were sheeted with moisture, and a miniature rill collected the runoff and trickled down the center of the corridor.

A minute later, the passage, now at a liminal phase between passage and shaft, opened up into a low-ceilinged, cramped chamber. Regular, linear features in the soil of the ceiling suggested cut stone. Bare limestone patches showed here and there from the walls of damp earth. Frills of root ends laced through the dirt, populated by creeping beetles. The wall opposite the passageway sloped steeply up. Two stone steps lay bare, swept clean. The entire wall was carefully gridded with twine. Boreholes and squared-off, excavated sections were marked with color-coded flags.

"This is something new to Mesoamerican archaeology," Professor Allison said, the man incapable of turning off his lecturing tone, even when conversing with colleagues. "This chamber is largely undisturbed. It predates the seismic event that buried the city. Meaning the inhabitants excavated a tunnel complex around, and probably below, the ziggurat."

"How far down are we?" May asked.

"Nearly one hundred and fifty feet below the surface. Even supposing they followed natural channels and tunnels, this represents an extraordinary effort. And this, this place, this chamber, must have been of supreme importance. Ritual, political, or religious. Or, most likely, all three."

A shelf, table, or altar stone jutted from the angle between the sloping wall and the left-hand side of the chamber. The surface of the shelf was clean enough for surgery, or at least clean enough to eat off. Incised in its surface was an elaborate depiction of a variety of deities involved in some esoteric activity involving a collection of abstract objects. Karl wasn't clear on it. He still had trouble differentiating one god's image from another. Though he did enjoy correcting condescending grad students' pronunciation when they tried, once again, to explain the imagery to him. His mother, while from all appearances possessing barely a trace of Aztec, Mayan, Toltec, or Olmec blood, was inordinately proud of Mexico's Mesoamerican past and, thus, her heritage. She'd ensured he'd grown up with ghoulish tales of Mictlan and Xibalba, just as his dad had embellished Karl's childhood with tales of the Aesir and Vanir.

Wooden pallets provided wobbly but dry access across the muddy floor. Karl followed the other two toward the altar stone, the pallets rocking and clattering beneath his feet. A glint of plastic on the gritty, mud-daubed surface of a pallet caught his eye. He bent down and picked up a tiny clamshell case of the type used to hold digital camera memory cards, then joined the other two before the altar.

A selection of artifacts rested atop the shelf. An effigy vessel of bone-hued stone. Ceremonial, anthropomorphic axe-heads of chipped flint. Jadeite stelae in the likenesses of the gods. A porphyry bowl. A bone flute. A selection of bead necklaces.

Professor Allison picked up an item, a jade dagger. Its hilt took the form of some sort of beast. Its blade gleamed: a green, serpentine, six-inch length. "This is perhaps the finest piece we've uncovered so far. Look. The handle, I believe, depicts a were-jaguar. And the blade is Kukulkan himself."

"Extraordinary," May said. She examined the dagger, then swept her gaze across the shelf of artifacts. "Would you say anything is missing? After the adventure Karl and I had leaving the airport…"

Karl held up the plastic clamshell case. "Perhaps nothing was stolen after all. Were you taking pictures the other day, Jim?"

"What? No. Do you see any light stands or scale bars? We took preliminary images of each object upon excavation, but those are usually taken *in situ*, with tablet computers, not digital cameras."

"I'm thinking you might need to publish something ASAP if you don't want to get scooped. Someone's got photos. But Jim, that's not really your biggest concern right now." Karl had, by this point, finished his coffee and figured he couldn't procrastinate any longer.

"I know, Karl. The sooner you get to town, the sooner I can decide what to do."

May spoke up. She was making a circuit of the chamber, tapping on the walls, prodding at the stone and earth. "Even without that scary crap, Jim, you might consider bringing in structural engineers for a consultation before continuing excavations. We're still not sure what instabilities the earthquake might have caused."

She pushed against the wall in emphasis. A section of limestone about three feet wide and six feet tall gave way, collapsing into the unknown beyond. May went with it, her startled gasp following a fraction of a second later from the darkness.

CHAPTER 8

Alejandra savored the tacos. The local salsa took getting used to, consisting primarily of lime and chile pepper. Too thin for her tastes – sufficiently *picante*, sure, but she preferred a thicker consistency. Still, it was growing on her. She wiped her chin with a paper napkin, then took a sip of tamarind-flavored soda. She exhaled slowly, eyes narrowing in pleasure. This was a working lunch, but there was no reason Alejandra shouldn't enjoy it. She was *La Jefa*, after all, and perquisites accompany power.

The roadside taco stand didn't have much to recommend it. Other than the *cochinita pibil*. And the location. The restaurant was isolated, yet near enough to both her jungle operation and the coastal cities to serve as a rendezvous.

Alejandra could have stayed at her production facility, helping clean up from the earthquake, or leading one of the exploration parties looking for another subterranean smuggling route. But her people were competent enough for that. Someone had to consider and establish contingencies. So here she was, waiting for Fernando.

Fernando was her cousin. Or a sort of cousin anyway. Alejandra had tried a couple of times to work out the consanguinity but had given it up, hopelessly tangled in the family tree. The point was that Fernando might provide a makeshift, onetime-only transport option. He lived in Cancun and drove a truck for a water company, delivering water cooler bottles and collecting the empties. Alejandra figured she could stash product in the center of the truck, masked by the water bottles, then arrange for Fernando to deliver a load of water to the *Grand Princess*. She didn't like it. Too many unknowns. Too many aspects she couldn't control. But she couldn't afford to screw up this shipment and miss the payday. If her soldiers couldn't find a concealed route to the usual exchange site, Alejandra wanted to have a backup.

Alejandra shifted on the backless barstool, growing impatient. The pearl-inlaid pistol grip rubbed reassuringly at the small of her back. She picked up the remaining half of a taco, then set it down. She had no appetite left.

A mechanical growl reached her ears, the sound increasing to a rumble. A truck appeared from the bend about a half mile down the road. Alejandra took another sip of her soda as she watched the truck approach. It slowed as it neared the roadside dirt and gravel crescent that served as the taco stand's parking lot. The load in the back resolved from lumpy sine waves to stacked nineteen-liter water bottles rising to a peak. It had to be Fernando.

Alejandra rose from the barstool. She turned to order two more drinks. Now was not the time for stinginess. She needed a favor, and it was time for charm and pleasantry.

When she turned back, she saw two men emerging from the parked truck. *Two?* Fernando had said nothing about a co-driver. Fernando must be the one on the right: short, in blue jeans and a T-shirt straining over a trucker's belly, Atlante F.C. ball cap pulled down low over his eyes.

Fernando's companion presented another picture entirely. He wasn't a tall man, but next to Fernando, his trim, erect figure created the illusion of height. He wore all black, his pants some sort of tough fabric, reinforced at the knees, and his unseasonable jacket sprouted more pockets and loops than seemed necessary. There was something particularly military about his bearing. He too wore a ball cap, his all black, sans logo. Mirrored sunglasses concealed his eyes.

Fernando had sold her out. *Fucking Zetas*. Had to be. Ex-military, the bunch of them. And didn't they like to strut about like a bunch of *pinches* peacocks.

Alejandra moved. The .380 was in her hand, and she was scooting, bent over, behind the counter before the Zeta had come five feet. The boy and the woman – presumably the boy's mother – behind the counter saw her pistol and raised their hands high. Alejandra ignored them. Behind the counter, with its smoking grill and containers full of meat and vegetables, lay the cinder-block back wall of the taco stand, painted a bright blue. Between two whining, rattling refrigerators was the back door. Alejandra opened it and slipped through just as the front door opened.

As she pushed the door to behind her and started to rise, a burst of gunfire punched a sequence of holes through the door panel right above her head. She shifted the vertical movement into horizontal, diving to her right behind rusting drums filled with rubbish and discarded scraps of food. A cloud of insects rose, buzzing their annoyance at her disturbing their feast.

Alejandra scrambled to her feet. The door slammed against the wall as it was kicked open. Without looking, Alejandra raised the pistol behind her and squeezed off a couple of rounds in what she hoped was the right direction. Her feet scrabbled for purchase as she began her sprint toward the parking lot. Black leather pumps perhaps hadn't been the ideal choice of footwear, no matter how good they looked with her Vera Wang suit.

She rounded the corner, hoping the Zeta hadn't doubled back fast enough to catch her at the front. He hadn't. Instead she barreled into Fernando. His eyes widened beneath the brim of his ball cap. Alejandra did recognize him from some distant family function, though she couldn't place the year or the event. His arms clutched at her. He called over her head, "I've got —"

Alejandra placed a single round under his chin. Fernando's head snapped back. A pulpy spout of red burst from the top of his hat. His hands dropped from her arms. Alejandra pushed him away, leapt over the falling body, and ran.

Another short burst clipped the corner of the taco stand. Alejandra felt a sting as a chip of cement shrapnel from the cinder block tore through the shoulder of her jacket.

Pinche cabrón. This is a Vera Wang.

The parking lot held only the water truck, a rusty Ford pickup truck, and Alejandra's Toyota Land Cruiser. She'd allowed enough grime and mud to build up on it to create an appearance of age and wear and tear. Cheap camouflage, a magician's misdirection to distract from the true worth of the vehicle and the likely corresponding wealth of the driver. When traveling without Diego and one or two other bodyguards, Alejandra was nearly as subject to kidnapping as the next wealthy woman in Mexico. Nearly: she was armed and, as Fernando's still warm corpse could attest, willing to shoot.

Head lowered, arms pistoning, and with a silent prayer to the Virgin of Guadalupe that her pumps wouldn't slip in the gravel, Alejandra sprinted for the Toyota. The chatter of fully automatic fire sounded behind her as she neared the shelter of the water truck. Gravel and ricocheting bullets erupted behind her and stuttered off to her right.

Alejandra rounded the bumper of the truck, grabbing one of the stanchions restraining the stack of water bottles to help her make the turn. Two of the bottles burst above her head, punctured by bullets, and she ducked under twin streams of water. She risked a glance back toward the taco stand as she passed the cabin of the water truck. Through one filthy window – the driver's side window had been rolled down or was missing entirely – she saw the Zeta ejecting a spent magazine from a submachine gun, a Heckler & Koch MP5, Alejandra thought.

Taking advantage of the brief window of safety, Alejandra crossed the open ground to the Toyota. The thought of risking a shot at the Zeta while he reloaded suggested itself, but Alejandra dismissed it immediately. The distance was too great for her .380. The caliber and barrel length of the compact Sig Sauer were not conducive to accuracy at that distance. She'd need something heavier to give her a decent chance of success. A full-size .45 or a .357. But those were hard to conceal, heavy, and ruined the lines of her clothes. Besides, despite Diego's encouragement, she never put in enough time at target practice to be comfortable with such a shot.

So instead, she threw open the door of the Land Cruiser and clambered in, tossing her pistol onto the passenger seat as she did. She tugged the door shut with her left hand while fumbling the key into the ignition with her right. *Push button ignition*, Alejandra thought. *My next car will have push button ignition.*

The Toyota fired up, and Alejandra threw it into drive. The Land Cruiser jounced over the line of head-sized boulders that delineated the boundary of the parking lot, in and out of the roadside runoff ditch, then up onto the road itself. The Toyota's suspension took it all in stride, merely sliding Alejandra's ass around on the leather seat.

The rear window shattered. Submachine gun rounds buried themselves in the headrests of the rear passenger bench. Alejandra let out a scream and slewed the Toyota left and right. She bit down on her terror, straightened out the wheel, and stomped down on the accelerator. *Missed me, pendejo.*

Alejandra glanced at the rearview mirror. The taco stand was rapidly receding. The trim figure of the Zeta was clambering into the cab of the water truck. *Fine, let's see him catch me.* Then she swore. She realized she'd driven west, instinctively following the route back to camp. She should have headed east, leading the Zeta away from her operation.

A side road beckoned to her right, a dirt track cutting through the jungle. Alejandra braked hard and snapped the Toyota into a juddering slide. When the nose of the Land Cruiser faced the mouth of the side road, she punched it, sending the Toyota bouncing and leaping down the track. "Try to keep up with this, asshole," she said. She doubted the water truck had four-wheel drive. And the way the jungle canopy began closing overhead within the first quarter mile of the track, she doubted there would be room for that large a truck much longer.

Alejandra eased off the accelerator past the first bend. The four-wheel drive might give her an advantage over the Zeta, but the Toyota wasn't a tank. If she tangled with a tree, the tree would win. Clear thinking, strategy, patience, circumspection. These were the virtues upon which she'd built her organization. Her temper, she knew, constantly threatened to undermine these virtues. So lifting off the gas was as much a deliberate act of will as it was a sensible response to driving conditions.

Her father would have approved, Alejandra thought.

He'd been a great proponent of the cautious, deliberate approach. Even with respect to risky endeavors. "Manage the risk," he'd say, sitting at the kitchen table, working out the logistics of slipping a boatload of marijuana past the US Coast Guard.

The descendant of a long line of Veracruz fisherman, Fermin Matamoros was a pioneer of Mexico's drug-smuggling history. As he'd explained to Alejandra, he was irritated by the Colombians reaping all the rewards. All those cocaine cowboys flying small planes north were stealing opportunities that should belong to Mexicans. After all, Mexico bordered the States. Colombia – where the fuck was Colombia, anyway? Fermin had taken inspiration from his own grandfather, who used to load his rickety fishing boat with cases of rum and tequila, then with running lights extinguished, hazard the run to the Texas stretch of the Gulf Coast. If the old man could do it during the Americans' idiotic era of Prohibition with a leaky tub stinking of grouper, why couldn't Fermin? But do it carefully. Learn a lesson from those flash Colombians, flaunting their cash in Miami, thumbing their noses at the *federales*, then getting sent to jail or gunned down.

If only Fermin had fully embraced that philosophy of discretion. He'd clung to it long enough to amass a modest fortune. But Alejandra's father hadn't been able to achieve an equilibrium between wealth and circumspection. His extravagant expenditures eventually brought unwanted attention. And while he'd made a pile, the pile wasn't big enough to bribe his way out of trouble. He'd died in a prison brawl after five years behind bars.

Alejandra had no intention of going out like that. Her father had taught her well, even if he hadn't been able to follow his own instruction. Once she'd earned her millions, she'd quietly disappear. She understood the draw of a hacienda in the country, *Doña* Alejandra lording it over the *peones*. But she doubted that sort of hubris would end well. Shouting "here I am" to former rivals, to the authorities, to the envious, to the larcenous – the desperate, heavily armed larcenous. No. Alejandra would slip away to the Caribbean, find an island with incurious banks, and while away her remaining decades on a beach, cold drink near at hand.

If, that is, she could elude this fucking Zeta. *World's slowest car chase*, Alejandra thought.

CHAPTER 9

"May?" Professor Allison asked, his tone rising from querulous to panicked within a single syllable.

Karl was already moving, not thinking, merely reacting. His boots hammered across the pallet flooring. The newly opened fissure in the wall through which May had fallen was about three feet wide and six tall, an irregular, jagged oblong. Karl barely slowed as he reached the opening. He slapped his left hand against the edge of the fissure, checking his speed at the last moment, but still maintaining enough momentum to plunge his torso through the gap, right hand extended and flailing in the hopes of grasping… something. Anything: an arm, a shirtsleeve, a ponytail. His fingers encountered nothing.

Karl could see nothing. The space felt vast. Dark and cavernous. A chill breeze reached him from somewhere below. It smelled of damp stone and earth. He pulled himself out, employing his hips as much as his left arm. A bare bulb on the wire circling the treasure chamber was within easy reach. Karl grabbed the wire and yanked, sending several staples rocketing about the chamber. He ducked back inside the fissure, holding the light dangling before him.

A vast, irregular gallery opened, a linear expanse ending at a wall perhaps fifteen feet in front of him, but stretching on either side beyond the extent of the light bulb's wavering globe of illumination. Limestone capped the gallery about six feet overhead, but below it dropped away into darkness. Immediately beneath the opening through which Karl leaned ran a narrow ledge, maybe a foot wide. To his left it narrowed to nothing. To his right it widened to a broad, level platform, a space about five feet square. Even Karl's cursory, peripheral glimpse suggested it had been worked by tools. But that didn't command Karl's attention. Instead, he looked down.

Karl gazed into the abyss and saw May. Relief surged through him.

Two hands gripped the lip of the narrow ledge. Two hands belonging to May Chen. Her pale face, tilted back to stare up into Karl's, bore a look of grim determination. Her feet still scrambled for some sort of purchase. Fragments of limestone broke off beneath the soles of her boots, falling away into the darkness below.

Karl's relief began to ebb. May's hold looked precarious and was getting worse by the second. He let the wire holding the light bulb go and reached down and out in the darkness to grasp one of May's wrists.

"I've got you," he said.

Her fingers wrapped around his wrist. "Good," May said, her voice tight. "I'd like to get out of this hole now." The last few words came rushed, rising to a hiccuping giggle.

"Do you see her?" Professor Allison asked from behind Karl.

Karl grunted. "Got her. Can't see her." Then he heaved. May didn't weigh much, Karl figuring maybe a buck ten. But dangling at the end of his right arm while he lay sprawled halfway through a hole, she felt a hell of a lot heavier. He could hear her boot soles scratching against the wall of the cleft. That effort helped some. She rose a few inches. Karl was able to set his own feet against the base of the outside of the wall, transferring some of the strain from arm and shoulder down through his back and hips.

He felt something at his back, then recognized it as Professor Allison hooking his fingers through the back of his belt. The .38 in its holster dug into him, adding to the general discomfort. But the assistance was worth the pain. Karl drew May up a few more inches, able to lean back a ways. He shifted his weight, taking up more of the strain on his left side, gaining leverage with his left hand against the edge of the hole.

From there May rose more smoothly. Karl's torso was now halfway back into the treasure chamber. His eyes had adjusted enough now to vaguely make out May. Her other hand was flat atop the ledge, and she was swinging up a knee. Placing almost his full weight on the left edge of the hole, Karl heaved one more time. He felt the stone give way beneath his weight, but kept pulling until May knelt on the ledge, gasping.

"You have her?" Professor Allison asked.

"Yeah, Jim," Karl said, "I've got her." The professor obviously couldn't see around Karl's bulk, so he restrained his instinctive sarcasm. Besides, he was still too intent on May to have enjoyed it. "Get some light in here, would you?"

Once again the bare light bulb lit up a portion of the slot cavern. May knelt in the same spot, shaking. When Karl wrapped his arms around her, she leaned into him without hesitation, breathing heavily. She wasn't crying, wasn't whimpering. Just shaking. And the shaking subsided to trembling.

Safe. And, Karl noticed, she felt good in his arms. Karl let her compose herself, patient, unspeaking. He occupied the time checking out the newly exposed space, taking his attention from May before his thoughts turned the embrace into something awkward. The widened area to his right intrigued him.

"Jim," he said, "poke your head in here. Look to your right."

Professor Allison thrust the light farther inside, following with his torso, rather cramping the gap in the wall. The wide area struck Karl as a sort of observation platform, a half-assed mezzanine. Regularly shaped, apparently manmade objects, cluttered the platform, mostly near the wall. Depressions in the wall suggested windows, observation ports, or spy holes. At the far end of the platform, near the limits of the light bulb's wavering glow, the platform took a sharp, ninety-degree turn, becoming a bridge arching over the crevasse. At the far end of the bridge, a deeper area of shadow hinted at a doorway in the opposite wall of the crevasse.

"Well now," Professor Allison said, "this place grows ever more intriguing."

"Let me see," May said.

Karl pulled her through the gap. May wiggled out of Karl's embrace, her curiosity driving away the vestiges of shock. Karl stepped through the gap, replacing May on the ledge to allow room for all three of them to rubberneck. She turned, took in the find, and whistled. "We can't cut and run now, Jim," she said. "We have got to preserve this site, start cataloguing. And exploring." She turned back to Karl. "And you, shouldn't you be on your way to Playa or Cancun?"

All business now, huh? Karl couldn't help but admire her professional dedication. "Kind of hard to save your ass here *and* drive. But, yeah. I'll hit the road as soon as we get you back to Tent City."

May didn't appear to hear him. "We need security. If your contacts don't give you any good news, maybe you ought to see about hiring private guards? Could be a show of force would be enough to keep the narcos away."

Karl wasn't so sure about that, but he said, "Could be. Come on, let's get you back to Tent City. Get another cup of coffee in you; then you and Jim can strategize your spelunking expedition."

Karl grasped the edge of the gap with both hands and pulled, intending to propel himself back inside to join the other two. Instead, the weakened limestone crumbled beneath his fingers and, unbalanced, Karl tumbled back off the ledge into darkness.

CHAPTER 10

Karl flailed, desperate to get a hand or finger on anything to arrest his fall. He kicked a wall. That spun his plunging form ninety degrees, but failed to otherwise affect his drop. No light glimmered in the crevasse, the darkness utterly stygian. Karl had no fear of heights. He'd jumped from all manner of aircraft, at all manner of elevations. But he knew then how far below him lay the landing and roughly how long it would take. Here, in the blackness, he knew nothing other than that the fall would end at some point, and he wasn't going to enjoy the landing any more than he did the drop.

It wasn't fear he experienced so much as regret. He'd signed on for a job. And if he couldn't finish it because of something as stupid as this…

The chill of the water took Karl by surprise. It felt as if he'd hit solid ground and his bones and internal organs had shattered and burst upwards away from a somehow intact and still falling spine and brain.

But that was only the chill of the water, striking gelid and unexpected. And that realization triggered a second: He couldn't have fallen too far if he'd survived hitting the surface without breaking bones or losing consciousness. Fall from high enough and hitting water might as well be hitting concrete. *Terminal velocity is a bitch.*

Karl plunged into the water over his head and kept descending. Night jumps from a helo moving low and slow over the ocean had taught him how to curl his legs and arrest his descent. He rose gently to the surface, threw his head back, and gulped in a humid breath of air. He could see nothing above, no glimmer of light from where he'd fallen.

"I am a heavy drop falling out of the dark cloud," Karl muttered.

He was treading water – cool water, but not as chill as the initial impact had suggested – in total darkness, alone. "Fuck," Karl said loudly, then waited for echoes.

The profanity was enough to express his displeasure, vent incipient panic. It also served to tell him that the body of water into which he'd plunged was in a relatively enclosed space, nowhere near the size of the ziggurat cenote. Probably near it in space, though. Odds were the ziggurat cenote and wherever Karl had found himself constituted parts of the same system and connected some-how. That was an encouraging thought.

Karl took a couple of calming breaths, shifted onto his back, and floated. He felt a sluggish current. He didn't fight it, instead letting it carry him where it would. He wondered how far it had already carried him, if his movement underwater during the initial immersion had already carried him out of range of whatever light Professor Allison and May Chen might be using right now in an attempt to locate him. He couldn't hear them calling, so he might already have passed by sufficient baffles to disrupt sound. Of course, his hearing wasn't what it had been a decade ago. A hundred thousand rounds sent downrange, numerous explosions, the hammering of engines in enclosed spaces – armored personnel carriers, C-130s, and helicopters – had done a number on his ears. It was possible that Jim's and May's calls would be audible to most. But he couldn't worry about that.

Karl's shoulder nudged something solid. He reached out a hand, felt his fingers trailing a stone wall. He reached up, felt wall, wall, wall, then nothing. He lowered his hand until it made contact again, curled his fingers and clutched at something, arresting his drift.

He wished he could see. He wished he'd brought along a pocket LED flashlight at minimum. But Karl had prepared for a journey to the coastal cities, not for spelunking. He shouldn't be floating about in this underground fun ride right now. He should be on the road, preparing to see contacts who might know something about the local narco threat. He should be doing his fucking job.

He remembered his cell phone. It was usually an afterthought in this land of the Cell Signal Polka, but he carried it still. *Routine is a masterful force.* Maintaining his grip on whatever he'd caught onto with his right hand, he dug his phone out of the front pocket of his jeans with his left. He didn't expect a signal down here, but it would provide light.

It did not. The fall, or the water, or both had done for the electronics, leaving the phone nothing but an inert rectangle of plastic.

Karl slipped the phone back into his pocket, more out of habit than anything. He tested his weight against whatever it was he'd grasped with his other hand. He guessed it was simply the lip of a break in the crevasse wall. Whatever, it held. Unlike that treacherous bit of limestone back in the treasure cavern. He heaved himself out of the water, probing ahead of him with his free hand. There was an open space before him and some sort of rough, irregular floor. Karl dragged himself onto the floor, catching one of the buttons of his Hawaiian shirt on the lip of the ledge and feeling it tear free. His belt buckle caught briefly, but he arched his hips and tightened his abs, freeing it.

Karl rose gingerly to a knee, one hand raised above him to test for a low ceiling. He felt nothing. Saw nothing. He pondered a moment. Should he sit and await rescue? That idea lasted all of a half second. He could wait when the mission called for it. But right now the mission was the rescue, and he figured he was the best man for the job.

Hands probing before him, testing the footing of each step before committing his full weight, Karl moved forward into the darkness, away from the water-filled crevasse. After a dozen steps over a corrugated, wavy floor that challenged his balance at every pace, he encountered another wall before him.

Dead end? He didn't want to turn back and hope the water led him out. He mentally flipped a coin then turned left, following the wall. Eight paces later the wall ended. Karl felt at its edge, discovering it only about a foot thick, a sort of internal sheetrock providing part of the architecture of this particular pit of Xibalba. So he followed it back the other way, this time on the opposite side of the wall. A dozen measured steps later, a blade of light cut across his path.

Light!

Motes drifted through the slanting shaft of light, a shaft that originated above Karl and to his left. He couldn't judge how high up the opening was. Either it was rather small and relatively close, or twenty to thirty feet up and relatively large. It didn't illuminate more than the floor and a section of the wall on his right.

Still, it was light. Karl stepped into the shaft and inspected himself, looking for blood, any cuts he might have missed. He seemed intact. He drew his .38, snapped open the cylinder, and removed the rounds. Karl didn't have anything to dry them on, but this dunking shouldn't ruin the immediate effectiveness of either the piece or the ammunition. He'd give the pistol a thorough cleaning as soon as he had a chance. He settled for blowing through each chamber and rolling each .38 +P round between thumb and forefinger, then replacing them.

Feeling a bit better for the light and taking some

measure of control over his own affairs, Karl pressed on. He re-entered darkness. His probing hand encountered another obstruction a few paces farther. In the left extremity of his peripheral vision, he thought he glimpsed a bright glint. It might be nothing but a trick of the eye, but left was as good a direction as any.

Karl edged along the obstruction: a high shelf, the end of the cavern, another baffle wall, or something else entirely. The glint grew to a glow, illuminating the end of the obstruction. Another wall. Rounding the corner, Karl saw another shaft of light, high up. And beyond that another. The light showed a corridor or passageway. Humps and protrusions from the floor, as well as a meandering, nonlinear character suggested it was a natural passage. On the other hand, Karl saw striations in the wall that might have been tool marks. But he didn't stop to inspect them. Archaeology was Professor Allison's job.

At the limits of the illumination of the second light shaft, Karl thought he saw the hint of a third. And – was that? Yes. He heard something. Distant voices. A search party? Professor Allison's crew had explored the site pretty well. Perhaps they knew something of this catacomb, at least an entrance to it, and were operating under the assumption that Karl had survived his fall and might make his way in this direction.

"Hey!" Karl called. "Over here!"

The voices stopped. The dim, diffuse end of a flashlight beam swept weakly over him. Then the familiar red bloom of a muzzle flash, followed by the crack of a rifle shot. Bits of limestone erupted near his feet. Shards slapped against the fabric of his damp jeans.

Karl dropped and rolled to his left, into the shelter of one of the knobby protrusions that made navigating the passageway such a treat. He rose to a crouch and drew his pistol.

Fucking narcos. A .38 snub nose wasn't much gun for a firefight with cartel soldiers armed with rifles. At least one rifle. Still, he was Karl Thorson. These narco scrubs were about to learn not to fuck with their betters.

Karl explored the extent of his protection with his left hand. The stone hummock was a kidney-bean shape, about knee high at the high ends and about three feet long. It ended about two feet from the left-hand wall of the passage. Karl wormed into the gap, a tight fit, hunkered down, with the pistol resting on one bulbous side of the kidney bean and held in a firm, two-handed grip.

"Shoot, move, communicate" fell short as a combat mantra for this tactical situation. Karl had no one with whom to communicate. Even with his eyes adjusting to use the faint light behind him, he could make out no cover other than that which he already occupied, so there was really nowhere to move. All that left was "shoot." He was outgunned here. But they had to come to him. If they came bunched up, rushing him, he liked his chances.

They didn't come bunched up. Instead one narco took the lead, a second followed about ten paces behind, providing cover, and the third stayed put. Two flashlight beams neared, one ahead and to one side of the other, while a third waited, dim and distant, wobbling a trifle but otherwise still.

The trick to surviving a gunfight was to remain calm. Unfortunately, the human body's programmed response to a threat was the precise opposite. It wanted to ramp up the nerves, dump adrenaline into the system, attack screaming and flailing, or run like hell. None of that helped aiming. A couple of methods helped overcome the fight-or-flight response. One was familiarization, a thorough immersion in stress in an attempt to desensitize the nervous system, convince it that this scary shit was no threat at all.

The second was repetition of the tasks likely to be required in a fight, hammer them into muscle memory so those actions could be performed almost unconsciously, undermining the fight-or-flight instinct's attempt to hijack the brain.

Karl was well versed in both methods.

The flashlight beam of the point man swept the corridor like a metronome, nearing with each step the narco took. Karl watched it from the corner of his eye, avoiding taking the beam directly in the face and ruining his night vision. When it came close enough that he could hear the crunch of the narco's tennis-shoe soles on the loose debris littering the floor, Karl began timing the light sweep. Right: one-one thousand, two-one thousand. Left. The narco reached pistol range. One-one thousand, two-one thousand. The beam swept to the right.

Karl squeezed the trigger, the stubby barrel pointed at an area just left of the source of the light. The crack of the .38

was followed by a grunt of surprise. The flashlight beam rose, sweeping the ceiling of the corridor, then down the left-hand wall, finally focusing a white, unwavering circle of brightness on a curving juncture of wall and floor.

The trailing narco failed to freeze in shock, failed to call his partner's name in a fatal second of panic. Instead he opened up in Karl's general direction, sending semiautomatic rifle fire downrange as fast as he could squeeze the trigger. Karl pushed away from his spot between boulder and wall. Bullets slammed into the boulder before him, ricocheted from the wall above and to his side. Dropping to his belly, he low crawled to the other side of the boulder, away from the wall.

The muzzle flashes and the beam of the flashlight lined up vertically, suggesting the narco either had a tactical light slotted to an auxiliary rail beneath the barrel of his rifle, or he'd duct-taped on a flashlight. Either worked. At the same time, it gave Karl something to aim for. The light fucked up his night vision, but he squeezed two rounds directly into it.

The narco screamed. The rifle clattered to the floor. Karl moved, rising to his feet and sprinting toward the light, which still pointed roughly toward him. The narco was still screaming. Karl ignored him, dropping to a knee and snatching up the rifle, leaving his .38 in its place. He reversed it, snapped it up to his shoulder, and shone the beam down the corridor toward where he assumed the third narco would be.

The fucker was already running away.

Karl didn't know the rifle, didn't know the model, the

caliber, or the configuration. Neither did he have enough light to use the sights. Hell, he couldn't even see the sights. But with the flashlight beam marking his target, he felt reasonably confident about placing a round or two somewhere in the vicinity of center mass. So long as he did so in the next couple of seconds before the narco fled out of range.

Karl placed the stock against his cheek, found the curve of the trigger with the fleshy, first joint of his forefinger, began to squeeze…and something grabbed his ankle and yanked, pulling him off balance.

The rifle fired, sending a round into the ceiling. Karl maintained his grip on the rifle with his right hand. He snapped his left down in an attempt to maintain balance and to remain upright. His open palm came down on the shoulder of the narco clutching at his ankle, the man still screaming. The scream now held as much rage and primal violence as it did pain from the gunshot. The difference was subtle, but apparent to a man who'd heard as many screams as Karl. The timbre deepened, took on more guttural characteristics.

Karl wanted to bring the rifle around, get a two-handed grip, and slam the buttstock into the narco's face. But he was slightly off balance and needed his left hand to prevent him from sprawling on his ass. If he ended up flat on his back, he risked letting the narco swarm over him. He lunged forward, pushing off his right foot and, to a lesser extent, from his left hand pressing against the narco's shoulder. He tore free from the man's grip and stumbled, fighting for balance. His foot caught on a stone or raised protuberance of the floor, and he tumbled forward, landing on hands and knees. The rifle clattered away from him.

Karl sensed the leap of the narco. Whether he'd heard a pained intake of breath, the scuff of sole against floor, or felt air currents shift before the man's moving bulk, he couldn't say. He just sensed the form coming at him in the dark from behind. The rifle was out of reach, somewhere in the dark. So was his pistol. His knife was still cased at his belt.

Fine.

Karl rolled to his left. A hand grazed his side right before he heard the impact of flesh on stone and the resultant grunt of pain and frustration. Karl allowed the narco no time to recover. He rolled back to his right and kept going, up on top of the narco, grappling for position and control. After a few moments of straining and cursing in two languages, Karl was astride the narco. The narco had wriggled onto his side, so the seat was narrow and boney. Karl had a grip on one arm with which the narco was attempting to fend him off, rather weakly. The grip was sticky, somewhat slippery, so Karl figured his bullet had struck the man's arm. The man was frantically bucking and squirming, trying to get out from underneath, or at least move onto his back, bring his other arm into play and fight from a more stable position. But Karl locked in his legs and held on. With his free hand, in a moment between bucks, Karl got hold of his knife, snapped free the restraining strap, and tugged it free of the sheath.

The struggle ended a second later, the knife driven through the narco's neck up to the hilt.

Karl scrambled up. He yanked loose the knife, the blade seemingly reluctant to leave the bed of muscle and cartilage. He couldn't spend time cleaning up, instead sticking the wet blade back into its sheath. He stopped to retrieve the rifle, splashed the light around behind him for a moment until he sighted his pistol, the weapon lying near the boulder behind which he'd taken refuge. The glimpse of the boulder suggested to Karl more the sculptural than the natural, the tunnel now appearing as much artifice as the work of water and geological forces, the whole suffused with the weight of time. But he didn't have time to play scientist. He snatched up the pistol, then took off after the last narco, fumbling the .38 back into the paddle holster as he trotted on. Karl would prefer an outright sprint, but the narrow beam of the flashlight failed to illuminate the floor well enough to inspire confidence in the footing.

The last narco was probably retracing his own path, so in theory he had the advantage of familiarity with the terrain. But given that he was using the same light source, Karl doubted the man was moving much faster than he was. Without a thorough examination, he couldn't be sure, but Karl's impression was of an unbroken tunnel or hallway, with no splits, intersections, or branches. So he pushed on, moving as fast as he dared. Within half a minute he heard the regular pat-pat of footsteps before him. Within another half minute he could see the bobbing, darting shaft of a flashlight.

A moment later Karl was glad of his turn of speed, for the light ahead vanished – but not before he caught a flicker to the left. He shone the light affixed to the rifle in that direction and saw a gap in the wall he would likely have missed without the telltale flicker from the last narco's light. The gap was an oval, maybe two feet wide and four high, set about waist high in the wall, its sides irregular, but smoothed by time. Karl wormed his way inside and found himself at the bottom of a chimney. A gleam of sunlight beckoned high above.

A serpentine waggle disrupted the distant glimmer. *Snake*, Karl thought before recognizing it for the shimmy of a rope, its gyrations already lessening. A climber's rope. Karl darted the flashlight beam around the chimney until he located the terminal end of the rope, its motion now almost still. The narco hadn't pulled it up after him. Perhaps he was waiting at the surface for Karl to follow, planning to cut the rope once Karl neared the top. Or put a bullet in his head once it appeared above ground.

Karl located the rifle's sling, draped it around his neck, grasped the rope, and began to climb. He looped the rope around his leg as he ascended, his muscles remembering rope work without any conscious instruction.

Karl's hair ruffled in a stray breeze as he at length reached the end of the rope, the long climb allowing his eyes to adjust to the increasing light. The yellow and blue nylon curved over the edge and out of sight, on to some anchoring point. Karl removed one hand from the rope, found purchase for it on the lip of the chimney top, then repeated the exercise with the other. He took a steadying breath and let the rope slither from its coil around his right leg, leaving himself dangling by his hands. Then, with an explosive effort, he heaved his torso free of the hole, out of the underworld, into the sunlight.

No one shot him.

He did see movement in the trees ahead of him. Karl hauled himself up, onto the surface. The rope was anchored about the base of a ficus tree, about three feet from the lip of the hole. A dozen yards beyond, disappearing into the jungle, was the retreating form of the narco.

Karl took a moment to mark his position, fixing landmarks in his memory, absently flicking off the flashlight at the end of the rifle as he did so. He recognized none of the scenery, had no idea where this hole sat in relation to the dig site. His only point of reference thus was this spot, where the unwary could take a fatal header into the dark.

He moved out after the narco, unslinging the rifle as he went. After his trek through the tunnels, the exertion of the fight, and the climb up the rope, his clothes had nearly dried. The Yucatan sun got to work on what dampness remained – a nearly futile task given the humidity of the Yucatan jungle. Insects zeroed in on the new, intriguing target. Karl ignored them, concentrating on pushing through the trees with as much silence as he could manage, keeping higher branches from whipping into his face and preventing the rifle – a Taurus ART556, he noted – and sling from snagging in the lower branches and sparse undergrowth.

Voices from his right drew Karl's attention. He stopped,

went down to one knee behind a cluster of willows. A trio of narcos emerged, one after another, from beneath the tangled roots of an ancient ficus that apparently concealed another entrance to the subterranean world. Karl listened intently. From what he gathered, the three men were disappointed. Their search had failed to locate a new route. A new route from where to where, they didn't say.

Once dusted off, they passed around a canteen, then moved off in the direction the narco Karl was tracking had gone. Given that Karl was at this point worried he'd lost the narco, this proved convenient. He got back to his feet and continued on, following them, but maintaining his distance.

Ten minutes later Karl slowed his steps, sounds of activity growing nearer: the hum of voices, the clatter of tools and moving objects. He sank to his knees, propped the rifle on his forearms, and commenced a low crawl. If he was nearing the narco encampment again, he could expect sentries, perhaps even tripwires.

Karl wormed his way up a slight rise. Easing between two flowering shrubs, he took in the narco camp below. He sniffed, getting a whiff of gasoline and pungent chemicals. The camp appeared pretty squared away, though he saw signs that the narcos were still recovering from the previous day's earthquake. A gang of men were draping a dingy green tarpaulin over a wooden frame. Another man was adding a stacked armload of bent and broken timber, aluminum tent poles, and plastic rods to a depot of debris.

The entirety exhibited an orderliness that Karl couldn't help but admire. Whoever ran this outfit possessed outstanding organizational skills and the ability to impose discipline.

Casting his gaze as far as he could, Karl thought he could see the spot where he and May had encountered the encampment yesterday. It lay on the opposite side of the camp. If he wanted to hoof it back through the trails to the dig, he'd have to cross through the camp or make a wide detour.

Walking right through the middle of this camp/processing facility was right out. Suicidal. Karl didn't fancy circling about either. In addition to the risk of getting lost, he had to worry about encountering pickets, booby traps, or more groups of narcos searching for this new route of theirs, whatever that was.

That left one slightly less horrible option: retracing his steps – and his swimming strokes. Back underground.

Karl eased from his observation post with a patient, silent reverse low crawl until he found a sheltered spot to turn around. Then, moving with as much speed as he could consistent with stealth, he returned the way he'd come until he spotted the landmarks denoting the chimney entrance to the underworld.

He removed the rope from its anchor point and retied it in a quick-release knot. Dangerous, yes, but he hadn't brought along climbing gear. Karl tested his weight against the knot, then lowered himself down into the hole. At the bottom, he tugged to free the rope, then blew out a relieved breath as it came slithering down in the darkness around him.

Karl coiled the rope by feel, saving the flashlight battery. He secured the rope over his shoulder and under the opposite arm, then thumbed the flashlight button, lighting his way.

Again he felt the weight of antiquity and noted what might be evidence of tool marks in the corridor. How extensive was the system of underground passages in Professor Allison's ruined city? What had they been used for? What deeds had occurred here in the dark or beneath the flickering light of torches?

The bodies of the two narcos still sprawled where Karl had left them, in congealing puddles of blood. Karl rifled through their pockets, extracting the basic climbing gear they'd packed. On the body of the narco whose rifle Karl had appropriated, Karl found one spare magazine. He field-stripped the rifle of the other narco (a poorly maintained, Chinese-made SKS), pocketing the bolt. A mini-light was taped to the forestock.

Karl checked that the light worked, splashing its beam on the boulder behind which he'd sheltered during the firefight. The boulder gave him the creeps, its amorphous bulbous form somehow suggestive of something amphibian and alien. Karl switched the mini-light off, cut it free of the SKS, and dropped it into the breast pocket of his shirt.

That done, Karl made his way back to the water.

The channel of dark water appeared smaller in the light than Karl's imagination had made it. Still, it measured a good dozen feet side to side, stretched out of reach of the flashlight's beam in either direction, and rose at least thirty feet overhead.

Karl beamed the light upstream, hoping for a glimpse of the gap through which he'd tumbled into the sluggish, subterranean river. No dice. He grunted, more in resignation than disappointment. He seldom bothered hoping for the best. He didn't hope much at all; so much time wasted that could more profitably be spent on planning and preparation.

Karl tugged off his boots, tied the laces together, and slung them around his neck. He slid the flashlight off the accessory rack of the rifle, then gripped it between his teeth. Awkward, but manageable. Then he eased into the water, letting his body adjust to avoid expending the energy loss that would accompany a cold shock.

Keeping his head above water and the flashlight beam tracking high along the opposite wall, Karl began a deliberate dog paddle. With the flashlight forcing his jaws open, the resistance of the Taurus behind him, the assorted bulky objects in his pockets and the climbing rope coiled around him dragging him down, and the gentle, but constant current of the water pushing against him, the swim demanded Karl's full concentration and more effort than he'd anticipated.

At first the light showed him only the water-smoothed channel, essentially featureless, relieved here and there by the darting motion of insects dazzled by the unexpected brilliance disturbing their stygian home. Then he saw depressions in the wall, regular in form and spacing. Karl puzzled at them. Apertures of some sort. Windows? He lacked context and scale, but he thought them too small. Maybe gaps where something had once been, support beams for walkways or bridges perhaps.

If Professor Allison's expedition survived the narcos, the team would go nuts down here. If Karl managed to find his way out to tell them, that is.

Karl's legs began to tire. He maintained his conditioning in the exercise pavilion at Tent City. But this pentathlon of swimming, climbing, shooting, hiking, and hand-to-hand fighting tested the limits of fitness his workout routine allowed.

He kicked himself toward the wall. At this angle he might miss seeing the opening above, but at least he'd be able to place a hand against the stone and rest a bit. Karl's head jerked with the greater motion, the flashlight beam drawing crazed lines and arcs across the face of the wall. He almost missed it, just another obsidian-dark spot in the field of black temporarily interrupted by the streak of light. But the light had crossed over that black spot. Or so he thought.

Karl turned his kick into an eggbeater stroke, holding himself against the current and sweeping the beam in a search pattern around the area he thought the black spot lay.

There. A narrow, irregular rectangle near the top of the tunnel. Holding his light as steadily as his clenched teeth allowed, he could make out depth, dimension in the rectangle. That had to be it; the spot from which he'd fallen.

He resumed kicking, reaching the wall beneath. Now came the hard part.

Karl's experience included a bit of climbing. But he

lacked the free climber's physique, the long, sinewy muscles, the ideal balance of light weight and strength. Karl's build consisted of blocky slabs of muscle. Useful for moving heavy things around, but not optimally suited for bodyweight exercises. The wall stretching above him had been smoothed by eons of water, absent any obvious projections or cracks into which he could insert hands or feet. It looked a difficult free climb, perhaps even impossible.

But he did have what he'd looted from the narcos. The climbing rope, the handful of pitons, the carabiners, the hammers. Decent-quality apparatus for serious mountaineering – or spelunking. He considered the climbing equipment and the passing mention he'd heard of a new route. And he added in where he'd encountered the narcos. All that added up to an underground drug-smuggling route. The earthquake must have damaged it, sending the soldiers out searching for a replacement. That suited Karl well enough as he examined the sheer wall above him, sweeping the flashlight beam in a careful search pattern, looking for a climbing route; he needed the narcos' climbing gear.

Limestone is a soft stone. Karl hammered in the first piton like a nail into a pine board. Easy, other than the fact that he had to hold himself in position against the current with only his legs, twice having to swim back upstream when he'd slipped free. But once it was in place, he had an anchor. He hitched one end of the rope around his waist and secured it to the piton. If he fell, he'd have at least this starting point in place. And the piton would serve as a foothold while he probed for the next hold.

Unfortunately, the narcos hadn't carried enough pitons for Karl to simply drive a series of them up the face of the wall. He still needed to find handholds, some irregularities in the surface.

No point in delaying, waiting for the chilling water to sap his energy. Karl grasped the piton in one hand and heaved himself up, groping for a spot of shadow his flashlight had cast that might represent an indentation or projection. His fingers felt a diagonal ridge projecting perhaps an inch from the flat of the wall.

And then his fingers slipped. He splashed back into the river.

Karl took a breath through his nostrils, cast the light between his teeth at the area, gathered himself, and tried again. His fingers encountered the ridge, the tendons and knuckles tightened, and he held on. Then he pulled himself from the water. Transitioning a foot onto the piton in place of his hand resulted in trod-on fingers, and only the need to keep the flashlight in his mouth prevented a burst of profanity. But he did it.

Keeping himself flat against the wall, he straightened, feeling with his free hand for another hold. He found a gap he could fit a finger in. Enough for a trained free climber, someone fifty pounds lighter than Karl, dry, properly equipped, and with a bag of rosin to coat his fingers in. Not much good for Karl. But it did provide a spot for Karl to wedge a piton in one-handed. That in place, he retrieved the hammer, tapped gently until he was sure the piton was securely set, then drove it in with as much strength as he could apply without leaning back.

Karl secured the rope to the second piton and continued up. And up. He fell. Twice. The second time his weight tore free the top piton, about three-quarters of the way up, and he was forced to redo a painstaking maneuver. But he persevered.

What choice did he have?

Karl neared the top. His jaw ached from holding the light in place. His forearm tendons screamed, and his shoulders and hips protested. He leaned against the wall, one foot resting on a ledge – if a projecting nub of wall about one inch wide could be considered a ledge. He could see a decent handhold about three feet up and to his right. A sweep of the light showed a bulge in the rock a bit below that, a decent place for his foot. From there, he thought he could reach the top by hammering in his last remaining piton as high above him as he could reach.

Karl studied the route for a minute, then leaned and stretched for the handhold. As his fingers brushed against it, he felt the rifle sling catch on an unseen protrusion. He wriggled, trying to free himself, but he could not move far enough back from the wall face to do it without precipitating himself backwards and into the drink.

Karl grunted, pushed off the handhold with the fingers of his right hand, returning to his previous position. Gingerly, he unslung the rifle with his right hand. Trusting to his foothold and the weight of his body leaning against the wall, he let go of his hold with his left and transferred the rifle from right hand to left. He slipped the sling up his wrist, regained the hold with his left, and let the rifle dangle.

Then he tried again for the new hold. He lost another button from his Hawaiian shirt, but the cloth gave enough to get him by the protrusion. Karl's fingers found a secure grip on a handhold. Then he stretched his right leg out for the next foothold, his flexibility pushed to his limits. Satisfied the position would hold him, Karl pushed off with his left foot, straightening. As he did, the rifle slid from his left wrist. He grabbed at it, the fingers of his left hand closing briefly on the barrel before it slipped free. A splash announced the rifle meeting the river below.

He opened his mouth to swear. And the flashlight tumbled out, the beam somersaulting a couple of times before disappearing into the water.

Karl fought down irritation. He was almost to the top. *Almost* did shit for him. He could be irritated once safely sprawled out on a horizontal surface.

He fished the mini-light out from his shirt pocket. He worked his jaw for a moment, giving it a rest. Then he flicked on the light, placed it between his teeth, and returned to the climb.

He'd read the route correctly. Two more moves had the ledge beneath his fingers. Karl chinned himself up and rolled onto the ledge. Its narrow, one-foot width felt luxuriously broad. He lay on his side, eyes closed, gasping.

When Karl opened his eyes, he realized he no longer needed the mini-light. The treasure chamber lay just beyond the crack that led to the ledge. And light spilled from the crack, emanating from the electric bulbs that illuminated the treasure chamber.

And he could hear something. Activity of some sort and muttering voices. Karl got to his feet and stuck his head through the gap.

The treasure chamber floor was littered. Karl saw partially inflated rubber rafts, accordion foot pumps, ropes, hardhats with fixed lights, backpacks, blankets, and first aid kits. A half dozen members of the dig crew were pumping air into rafts, checking ropes, and inventorying backpack contents. May and Professor Allison were consulting a hand-drawn map.

Karl stepped into the chamber.

"Can I help?" he asked.

CHAPTER 11

The Gulfstream touched down, with a barely perceptible jounce, in Cancun at 3 p.m. local time. Dexicos Megistos finished sipping his glass of chilled Gewürztraminer as the jet taxied to the private terminal. He wondered if the leather seats retained the ideal balance of plush comfort and lumbar support. That the idea crossed his mind suggested they did not. Perhaps it was time to purchase a new jet. This one was, after all, nearly a decade old. Something to consider.

The customs official departed. Dexicos watched him through the window while he pocketed his passport. A relatively new development, the passport. Yet how many had he already been through? Under how many names? Issued by — or forged in the name of – how many countries?

Three black SUVs pulled up on the tarmac as Dexicos gazed out the window, memories of recent centuries trickling idly through his mind.

Enough navel-gazing. Time to work.

Dexicos deplaned, Potter at his heels carrying the matched leather luggage custom made in Florence. Dexicos carried only a single briefcase, also of hand-tooled Italian leather. The SUVs emptied as Dexicos descended the stairs, the SUV passengers lining up in formation in what Dexicos assumed was for most of them an unconscious remnant of military indoctrination. For the others, probably habitual blending with the herd, the protective camouflage of anonymity.

Willing to pursue the military image, Dexicos paced the rank, inspecting the troops. His crew reminded him of one of those racially diverse street gangs from bad 1980s police procedurals. But in his case the mixture served a function other than prophylactic deflection of accusing scolds crying "racism." He had sufficient locals to allow for certain contingencies and to make up the language defects of the less proficient Spanish speakers.

Alexandros and Smith bookended the formation. They had changed suits for field garb, wearing khaki cargo pants and dark polo shirts, the shirts tight enough to display the results of countless hours in the gymnasium. Dark sunglasses hid their eyes. Each man had a large black duffel bag resting on the tarmac beside him.

Dexicos couldn't complain about the crew of hitters and fixers Smith and Alexandros had assembled in such a short time, though he would if it suited him. All eleven appeared competent, most with the indefinable quality that suggested an extensive military background. Half of them possessed complexions that indicated that military experience might be from here in Mexico or from some nearby Central American country. Most were heavily tattooed. Some of the tattoos hinted at criminal affiliations supplanting military. All of them wore variations on Alexandros' and Smith's getups, a sort of mufti that Dexicos dubbed "paramilitary casual." All either carried oversized bags or bore heavy backpacks.

"Gentlemen," Dexicos said, addressing the group as a whole. He was nearer to Smith's side of the formation. "Are they briefed?" he asked Smith.

"Best we could, sir," Smith said.

Dexicos turned back to the formation. He held one hand behind his back, keeping a firm grip on the briefcase in the other. Then he strode in a mock-military fashion to face the center of the rank. The men were sweating beneath the tropical afternoon sun. Dexicos himself remained dry, his own tropical-weight suit of cream-colored linen, tailored for him in Hong Kong, betrayed not a single spot of dampness. He'd dealt with greater heat, with greater temperature extremes than any of these mayflies. In addition to simple familiarity alleviating any discomfort, he'd long since developed the ability to regulate his own internal body temperature no matter the exterior conditions.

Facing them, Dexicos asked, *"Tienen suficientes carabinas y pistoles?"* He gauged the response time. The widening eyes of gradual comprehension pegged those weak in Spanish. Only a couple. Scarred, tattooed, and muscular the both of them. He'd have to ensure that Smith and Alexandro paired off each of these with a native speaker.

"We are here to recover an item." Dexicos tested English comprehension this time. Excellent response across the rank. "An item of some value to me, though of little monetary value to anyone else: collector, museum, or university. Bear that in mind should you determine that your wages are insufficient. Stealing from me would be, at the least, unprofitable.

"You already know Alexandros and Smith. They will provide direction, answer questions, and see to your reimbursement. You should not be required to ask me anything. Indeed, the less personal interaction we have, the happier we will all be. But if I issue an order, I expect you to obey unhesitatingly."

One of the thugs with limited Spanish – tall, gangly, rope-muscled, with spiky-cut blond hair – frowned.

"Yes? You have a question?" Dexicos asked, his voice mild. Inviting, even.

The thug stepped forward. His clothing was new, the creases still evident, though perspiration was hard at work smoothing out weave and fabric. "Yeah. What kind of orders?"

No "sir." Posture not as erect as the others. Muscles probably prison grown rather than from military service. Though Dexicos considered that a distinction without much difference.

Dexicos moved to stand before the thug. They were nearly of a height. Dexicos was shorter, but appeared taller than he truly was, the effect of the sheer intensity of his presence, his narrow frame, and two-inch lifts in his bespoke shoes.

Dexicos looked the thug in eye. "Make me a sandwich, bitch."

The crew sniggered at this. All, that is, except the blond thug. His thoughts were clearly expressed by a twisting of his features, the bunching of his fists. And the sudden step forward he took, the cocking of an arm preparatory to a punch.

Smith and Alexandros were already in motion. But Dexicos had no need of their protection. He gestured, and an electronic stun gun, a plastic and metal rectangle with two protruding darts, appeared in his hand. Dexicos jabbed the stun gun into the thug's midsection before he could complete his roundhouse, and triggered it. The effect was immediate and satisfying. The thug flopped to the tarmac and continued spasming.

Simple sleight of hand, of course. A stage magician's flourish combined with a spring-loaded release. Dexicos could have done worse with actual sorcery. He could have summoned up a creature with the sole purpose of hunting down and devouring the thug. He could have instilled debilitating nightmares of gradually increasing intensity, driving the man mad. He could have boiled the thug from the inside. The options were endless. But such required time. This simple, mundane demonstration of power should suffice for this lot.

"Does anyone else have a question?" Dexicos asked. No one replied. "*Entonces*, let's go get my artifact."

Dexicos walked to the lead vehicle. Potter was somehow there before him, opening the rear passenger-side door of the Cadillac Escalade. Dexicos placed the briefcase on the buff-colored leather bucket seat beside him. The rear hatch opened, and Dexicos listened to Potter load the luggage. He could hear Smith issuing orders. Dexicos assumed Alexandros was dealing with the electrocuted thug while Smith assigned the rest of the crew to the SUVs. Details for which he paid Alexandros and Smith handsomely and didn't bother himself with.

Potter climbed into the rear row of the Escalade, occupying one of the bucket seats. Even this maneuver he handled with quiet grace. The front doors opened. Alexandros hauled himself into the driver's seat. One of the crew, possibly a local, got into the front passenger seat, a trim, black carbine now slung across his chest. Alexandros turned the key, bringing the Cadillac to throaty, growling life. He cleared his throat. "Sir? Straight to the dig?"

"No, Alexandros, I prefer heading immediately to the beach for sun and *cerveza*. Would you like me to rub suntan lotion on your back for you? You could buy me a friendship bracelet from one of those picturesque beach vendors, perhaps one of those adorable moppets you can't help but think ought to be in school." Dexicos sighed. "Of course we're going straight to the dig. I guess Smith is the smart one. I'd always suspected."

Alexandros gave no sign of taking offense. He shifted

into gear and began to drive. "Right, sir. And when we arrive, how shall I deploy the men? What is the objective?"

"You've seen the pictures. The dagger is the objective. I want no delays. Go directly to this treasure chamber where Festo snapped his surreptitious shots. Get the artifact." Dexicos retrieved the briefcase and set it in his lap. "After that, I don't much care. The boys can take what they want, break what they want. Have fun, so long as I receive the dagger intact."

Dexicos opened the case. Bright, clean implements gleamed inside, each secured within a precise receptacle cut from the foam that lined the interior.

The gunman in the front passenger seat pivoted as far as his position would allow. As he hadn't bothered with a seatbelt, his position allowed considerable range of motion. He looked curiously at the case.

"See anything you like?" Dexicos asked.

"My *tio* Bernardo is a *brujo* in Oaxaca," the man said. "He uses a spreader like that when he reads the chicken intestines." The man pointed at one of the devices in the case.

"Charming," Dexicos said.

"Of course, *mi tio*'s was made of copper. That looks like pure *plata*." The man craned his head for a closer look. "Lots of blades in there. And we're getting a dagger. Something to do with a sacrifice? We need to cut out a heart or something?"

"No, my curious, chattering friend. There is a ritual involved to evoke the powers of the artifact. But not blood magic. I can understand why you might think that. During my earliest visits to the region, the rituals conducted tended toward the sanguine. Downright savage, you might say." Dexicos leaned back. His eyelids drooped. The eyes moved beneath them as if seeing something none of the others in the Cadillac could. The temperature in the SUV's cabin seemed to drop even lower than what the laboring air conditioning managed, and the light dimmed as if a bank of clouds had occluded the sun. "The Serpent Stairs turned to cascades of blood. Obsidian blades grew dull, or chipped and broke from breaking through so many rib cages. Hills of discarded hearts, those at the top still feebly twitching, darkened, sheeted with flies. The priest-kings conjured dark entelechies, cementing their own power and exerting their will against their neighbors. The clash of arms consumed thousands. Black sorcery entombed cities."

Dexicos opened his eyes again. "It was an exciting time to visit, the Middle Kingdom having grown tedious." The cabin temperature rose again to the merely chill, and the Yucatan sun once again flooded the Cadillac's interior.

The gunman blinked, cleared his throat. Dexicos watched unease fight machismo in his face. Machismo won. "When was this?" the gunman asked, both arms wrapped around the headrest of the front passenger seat to lock himself in his twisted position.

The words did not emerge as casually as Dexicos imagined the gunman wished.

"Oh, about a century or so after the Ptolemies enthroned themselves in Alexandria."

"They didn't teach us about any visits here prior to Cortez," the man said. "No trips from Egypt. Nothing before the birth of *Jesu Cristo*."

"What is your name?" Dexicos asked, focusing on the gunman. He seldom expected to find an educated man among his armed flunkies. This one appeared to have at least some grasp of history. At least, conventional history.

"Omar. Omar de la Cruz."

"Well, Omar de la Cruz, 'they' teach what they know. And they know very little. Those with gifts and powers have traversed the globe for millennia, exchanging knowledge, engaging in challenges, feuding, playing games of dominance, staving off boredom. The evidence is there for those who choose to see it. The connections, the similarities, the 'coincidences.' Ask your *tio*. If he has even a touch of the gift, he'll have some sense of the truth. Or do not ask him. What you believe is of no consequence." Dexicos plucked an item from his case, a sliver of amber in which was encased an insect notable for its size as much as the brilliant colors of its wings and the deep emerald of its thorax. He held it to his eye, allowing the attraction of the focus to open his senses to the supernatural. Dexicos directed the lens at the gunman. He felt nothing out of the ordinary. Omar held no hidden depths. Another hired gun, nothing more. Overeducated for a trigger puller, perhaps. Skeptical, a trifle discourteous. But nothing special. Still, the examination itself, the exercise – a sort of magical limbering up – rejuvenated and relaxed Dexicos, placed him in a reflective, talkative mood.

"Turn around," Alexandros said to Omar. "Leave the boss alone."

"No, Alexandros. Let him be. He asks more intelligent questions than you've managed so far today." Dexicos rubbed his thumb in circles about the amber sliver, appreciating the smoothness, considering the millennia that had passed since this hapless insect had found itself entrapped. "The journeys are easier now," Dexicos said. "Around the globe in forty-eight hours. But even then trips from Alexandria to Tulum, or Alexandria to Beijing, or Alexandria to a certain no-longer-extant city in the heart of Australia were not uncommon – if not precisely routine.

"The first time I saw the dagger was during my second visit to Mesoamerica. My embassy was traveling from Coba to Tikal. The litter carrying our hosts bobbed along next to mine. I fell into conversation with the Jaguar priest of Coba. He told me he'd neglected to bring along guest-gifts. He produced the dagger and performed a ritual. A ritual I paid close attention to. So, I can assure you, Omar, the ritual is bloodless. The embassy itself, however, was not so lucky. Certain misunderstandings occurred, leading to war between Coba and Tikal, which proved rather amusing. For me, at least; I imagine the casualties and prisoners on both sides found it less so."

"That's a good story," Omar said. "But it could use some details."

"You'll have to wait for my memoirs," Dexicos said. "Check the bookstores sometime in the next dozen centuries."

Omar laughed. "I will, *jefe*. So, the instruments in the case…?"

"Not for the ritual, no." Dexicos replaced the chip of amber. He ran his finger over blades, wands, rings, crystals, coins, and other assorted artifacts from a variety of civilizations and centuries. "These tools are precautionary, in the event we run into opposition that you and the rest of the crew are unable to handle." From the upper right corner of the case, Dexicos plucked a corkscrew. "Also, for lunch. Potter, if you would be so kind as to hand me a bottle."

CHAPTER 12

Alejandra looked at the backs of her hands, satisfying herself they weren't shaking. Then she emerged with studied calm from the bullet-riddled, trail-dented Land Cruiser, parked in the "executive lot" – a secluded, tree-canopied area a kilometer from the camp. She risked no more than two vehicles there, moving everyone in and out through the cenote tunnel. Or, rather, had done so. She'd have to figure out something soon. Her people weren't long going to tolerate virtual imprisonment in the middle of the fucking jungle.

The 4x4 hissed and ticked, the engine cooling after its labors. An unwelcome heat source in the middle of tropical afternoon, the jungle already oppressive.

Diego was waiting for her, expressionless as usual. Dark glasses hid his eyes, but from the slight movements of his head, Alejandra could tell he was scanning the trail behind her. One hand clutched the grip of his rifle; the other curled about the forestock.

"Alejandra," he asked, "are you hurt?" His tone suggested a deferential concern.

"Me? No. But the car? It needs a priest. Fine, I wanted a new one anyway. I like the Range Rover Evoque. Too flashy, I know. Could I get away with a Lexus?" She'd beat the Land Rover to shit. Alejandra had not shied away from scraping paint against tree trunks, slamming tires at speed into deep potholes, or pushing through brush between trails, risking unseen snags and boulders.

"What happened?" They were already moving along the trail to the camp, Diego a pace behind.

"Los Zetas. The meet was a setup. *El pendejo de* Fernando fucking sold me out."

"I'll put out a contract. How much for the head?"

"Save the money, Diego. I handled it."

Alejandra could imagine the grin on Diego's face as he said, "You're the *jefa, Jefa*," then, "What about Los Zetas?"

"I lost the one following me. Lured him north, then doubled back." Alejandra felt the memories attempting to rise up and overwhelm her, the desperate chances, the bumper glancing off tree trunks, the shattering of headlights, the occasional bursts of gunfire when the Zeta soldier drew close enough. Then finding the trail spur fifty meters around a sharp bend, right where she'd remembered it, hoping she'd built enough of a lead to duck in before the Zeta rounded the corner. Cutting the engine, sitting with her pistol gripped in white knuckles, praying the Zeta would drive by, wouldn't see her. She couldn't let the ghost of that terror shroud her, affect her decision-making. She couldn't let it show on her face. "I lost him," she said again, with a firm finality. "But we have to stay sharp. They know we are in the region. I'll need you to recruit some more soldiers after we make this delivery."

"*Si, Jefa.* You've got one of your soldiers in your office, waiting to report."

"Oh? Did we find a new route?"

"I don't know," Diego said. "I don't know if there are any other routes."

"Well, let's find out," Alejandra said, rounding a clump of ficus and entering the camp.

Diego had performed a competent job returning the camp to functionality. Tarps again concealed the location from prying eyes in the sky. Stacks and bundles of unsalvageable materials made up a sizeable refuse depot in a newly dug pit, also covered by a tarp. Alejandra's employees were once more converting coca leaves to paste and paste to blocks of powder.

Alejandra's office looked to her identical to its pre-quake appearance. One of her soldiers waited for her beneath the olive drab tarpaulin. He stood as she entered, almost knocking over the camp chair as he rose. She recognized him, though she couldn't recall his name. He wore cargo shorts, low hiking boots, and a black T-shirt promoting a *Los Tigres del Norte* concert from a time when this kid couldn't have been more than ten. The clothes clung limply to his body, as if on the cusp of sun-dried. Lank, damp hair drooped over his eyes. His rifle, a cheap AK-47, eccentrically modded, leaned against the back of the camp chair.

Alejandra glanced over her shoulder at Diego. "Arturo," Diego said. "I sent him out with Carlos El Rojo and Miguelito."

Alejandra sank into her camp chair behind the rickety desk. "Okay, Arturo. What do you have to report?"

Arturo made fists with both hands, then cracked his knuckles. "El Rojo and Miguelito are dead, *Jefa*." He uttered the words with a flat lack of intonation, as if letting her know they were running low on diesel for the generators.

Arturo is a cold one. Shitty taste in guns and clothes, maybe, but a good tool for dirty work.

"*Que paso?*" Alejandra asked. "How did they die?" She made a note to ask who Miguelito was. She remembered El Rojo, one of Diego's more trusted gunhands.

"We were exploring a cave entrance Miguelito and I knew about. Diego assigned El Rojo to lead us."

"Where is this cave?" Alejandra asked. She shifted some papers from atop a map.

Arturo leaned over, jabbed a finger at a spot near the camp.

"Only a couple of kilometers, *Jefa*. We brought rope and climbing gear. The entrance is a shaft, straight down. At the bottom is a tunnel. Humid. I could smell water. We followed the tunnel."

"How big? Wide enough to move product? Rafts?"

"*Si, Jefa*. Smooth, straight. Plenty of room."

Alejandra grunted her satisfaction. Promising. "So what happened? A fall? An aftershock?"

"No, *Jefa*. We met someone coming the other way. Must have been one of those tomb raiders from the ruins. Miguelito took a shot at him. But the *cabrón* shot back."

"The archaeologists are packing?"

"This one was. We went for him. He killed Miguelito and El Rojo. I got away."

So, cold, but with a healthy respect for his own skin. Even better. Tools that didn't understand their own worth were usually wasted.

A respectful cough announced another visitor. Alejandra glanced that way. Waiting behind Diego's shoulder was Hector.

"Come in, Hector. Back from town?"

Hector entered, stepping deferentially around Diego and eyeing Arturo. "Yes. I've got a truck bed full of rafts, paddles, and foot pumps."

"Good. Arturo, I want you to take Hector to the tunnel. Hector, bring a raft. How many men can your rafts hold?"

"I bought a selection. The largest can hold six."

Alejandra leaned back into the canvas of the camp chair, feeling it creak and stretch. God, she was tired of cheap, rickety furniture and outdoor living. But with Los Zetas hunting for her, this was not the time to risk any ostentation. She had to keep her head down, stick with the plan.

"Okay. Bring that one. Pick four soldiers. Armed. Take ropes, lights, climbing gear. Arturo may have found our new route. Trouble is it might lead through the old ruins. We might need to chase off those college kids. And at least one of them is armed. Scout a route, but try to keep quiet. No shooting if you can avoid it."

"Chase off the college kids?" Diego asked. He raised an eyebrow.

Alejandra shrugged. "Might be too many to kill and bury. Scaring them away might be prudent. We'll make a decision once Hector returns." She made a show of focusing her attention on the papers scattered over her desk. "You've got your instructions. Go."

CHAPTER 13

K arl was nearly dry by the time he returned to his tent, helped solicitously by Professor Allison, May Chen, and a rotating squadron of the archaeology students who'd been gathered in the treasure chamber, preparing a search and rescue operation. All were eager to assist whether he needed their help or not. He did not. In fact – with the single exception of the *Universidad Iberoamericana* co-ed who'd retrieved a sandwich for him from the mess tent – their assistance was more an inconvenience than an aid. Still, he didn't object. There was nothing objectionable to May pressing close against his side, "supporting" him.

Having the crowd see him back to his tent accomplished two things, as far as Karl could figure. First, it gave him time to think, allowing them to believe him too knackered to tell his story. Second, and perhaps more importantly, it got the lot of them back above ground, away from the risk of running into more spelunking narcos.

His tent felt comforting, familiar, after his trek through the depths. But Karl fought the feeling down, considering it dangerous and illusory. Time, he felt, ran short. The safety of these people – his responsibility – was in jeopardy. No matter how cozy and inviting the tent looked. He'd lived in smaller accommodations, usually sharing them. This tent felt positively roomy compared to, say, a shelter half, or a goat pen topped with a handful of branches for a roof, said goat pen shared with three other men and a dozen goats. Here he had space for a cot, a footlocker, a duffel bag, back-pack, and a wooden crate containing a dozen paperbacks: novels (primarily classics recommended by his mother), a couple of popular histories, a pocket Shakespeare, *Don Quixote* (in the original Spanish), and a battered copy of *Thus Spoke Zarathustra*. He also counted among his riches a modest collection of toiletries and, resting atop the crate, a table lamp with an extension cord running out through the tent flap.

Karl allowed himself to slump onto his cot. He glanced up at Professor Allison, who turned and shooed away the faces clustering about the tent flap.

"Go on, you rubberneckers. You'll hear all about it later," the professor said. He waited until only he, May, and Karl remained, then said, "So, spill. What happened?"

Karl placed his elbows on his knees and leaned forward, resting his face in his cupped palms. "Jim, you need to clear your people out. Break camp and evacuate. ASAFP."

"What?" asked Professor Allison.

"Narcos over the hill was bad enough. I should have pushed you harder to leave this morning. Now they are in the tunnels."

"What tunnels?"

"You've got some sort of tunnel complex down there. Looked worked to me, artificial, not natural. Not completely, anyway. At least one exit leads out within a couple klicks of the narco camp."

"Really?" Professor Allison blinked. His jaw actually fell open before he snapped it shut and blinked a couple more times. "This site is even more important than I thought. May, we have to get teams down mapping. Right away. Maybe we can borrow a ground-penetrating radar from UADY."

"Jim," May said, "Karl said we've got narcotics traffickers in the tunnels. They aren't ants. We can't spray them and sweep up the bodies."

"Well, yes. Okay, first things first. Karl, as soon as you've rested, get to the coast, like you planned. Work your contacts. Get us some more guards. Secure the site. Then we can start exploring."

"It's too late for that, Jim," Karl said. "It's only a matter of time before they reach the cenote and take care of your inconvenient students."

"Well, why would they? They haven't so far." Professor Allison began pacing the length of the tent. Three paces, turn. Three paces, turn. He sounded petulant to Karl, a child scrambling for reasons he should be allowed to stay up late, throwing each one at the wall in hopes it would stick.

"They know you are here now, for one reason," Karl said, his tone even, matter-of-fact, each word enunciated distinctly. "For another, I imagine they want to kill me."

"What?" Professor Allison asked. He stopped pacing.

May mouthed, "Kill you?"

"Ran into three of them down there. They took a shot at me. We tangled. One of them got away. I couldn't catch him before he got back to their camp. They were looking for something in the tunnels. No reason to think they plan on stopping until they find it. And now they probably want to find me as well."

"What the hell did you do that for?" Professor Allison asked. "Why didn't you just leave them alone?"

Karl straightened. "I would have been happy to. They fired at me. Not the other way around. Look, Jim, if you have a problem with me defending my own life, we can have a personal talk about that. Not employer-employee. Just you and me. But right now we've got the lives of everyone in this camp to consider. We need to evacuate."

"Karl, Goddamnit, this dig is important." Professor Allison took off his hat, ran one hand through his hair. "Do you have any idea –" He stopped, shot a glance at May.

"Does he have any idea how important this is to your career?" May asked. "Is that what you mean?"

Karl watched Allison's internal conflict manifest in his changing expressions. He understood how much the professor had invested in this expedition. He had some inkling how important it was as a historical and archaeological find. He knew it represented tremendous intellectual value and probably tremendous monetary value. This was the sort of discovery that could make a reputation, establish a legacy, forge a certain academic immortality.

"The kids," said Karl.

Professor Allison's face sagged; his shoulders slumped. "I know. I know. They are my responsibility, even more so than yours. I brought them out here. Their safety is my priority. Not...not my reputation."

May moved in and placed a comforting hand against the small of Professor Allison's back. Karl turned away, allowing them the moment, but hoping it was merely a kindly, collegial gesture on May's part and not something more intimate. He worked the paddle holster containing the .38 from his waistband. Bending, he allowed a chain to slip from inside his shirt, granting access to the padlock key hanging from the chain. This he inserted into the lock that clasped shut his footlocker. From inside he dug out a cleaning kit and a bottle of solvent/lubricant. He also retrieved a .45 automatic, tucked into its holster, the entire package wrapped in a belt.

Karl hadn't precisely lied to May about Mexico's gun laws. He hadn't been entirely forthcoming either. Under certain circumstances he, as a Mexican citizen, did have the legal ability to own a .38-caliber pistol. Tucking it under his shirt and toting it about, however, would have violated his permit – had he bothered to apply for a permit in the first place.

The .45 was another matter entirely, not even remotely within the legally permitted range of weapons. Karl, however, practiced an ironclad philosophy anent laws to which he had not personally acquiesced: if said law interfered with his interests, he considered compliance optional. And any law that compelled him to trust his own personal safety to police officers decidedly interfered with his interests. Especially given police officers who might or might not be within any helpful distance. Or who might be as likely to side with the party threatening harm as with Karl. He'd been to plenty of countries where the latter was commonplace, if not the default. And the former was universal.

So Karl removed the sodden leather belt and slipped the new one bearing the .45 through the belt loops on his pants, added the jungle knife to the load, then tugged the tail of his Hawaiian shirt over the whole. The still damp shirt printed a bit, but Karl figured he could get away with it if no one was looking for the gun. The cheap-ass .45 hadn't been his first choice. But he'd taken Jim Allison's job offer on short notice. He'd had to relocate out to the dig right away. The best pistols he'd been able to find within the course of a single evening were a .38 S&W and a Hi-Point .45 ACP. Both of which he'd overpaid for. The Smith was worth the money. The Hi-Point he hoped he wouldn't need to rely on.

At least it's in black. The black-market gun dealer had tried to sell him a piece in some hideous desert camouflage pattern.

Karl shoved an extra magazine into his back pocket.

Then he picked up the cleaning kit and the .38, getting to work on the powder fouling and the water spotting. He deliberately ignored Professors Allison and Chen, the eyes of both of whom he could feel boring into him.

"Is there any more in your arsenal I should be aware of?" Professor Allison asked.

"Sadly, no. A couple of peashooters ain't ideal for taking on a drug gang. The best weapon against an enemy is another enemy, but I'll have to settle for a Saturday Night Special and a backup piece."

"Did he just quote Nietzsche?" Professor Allison asked Professor Chen.

"He does that," May said. "I haven't decided yet if it's endearing or annoying."

"Okay. Fine. Karl, you continue preparing for a show-down at the OK Corral. May and I will start the evacuation."

"I know it's a disappointment, Jim," May said. "But with angry narco-traffickers next door…"

"I'm sold, May," Professor Allison said. "I know I'm going to regret this, but –"

"Pardon me," someone asked in English, the voice cultured but the accent unplaceable, "am I interrupting?"

CHAPTER 14

A dapper, trim figure in a well-cut tropical-weight suit stood framed in the tent's entrance. He stooped to enter, a tall man, graying a touch but maintaining, if not a youthful appearance, a certain agelessness. Karl couldn't place the background. Was there something of the Middle Eastern about him? Or perhaps Eastern European? Or Basque? It didn't matter, Karl supposed, but the sense of abnormality nagged him.

The stranger swaggered in as if he'd just leased the place, surprised to see the previous tenants hadn't yet vacated. A mass of humanity followed, threatening to exceed the tent's occupancy capacity. Three of them looked a type Karl knew well: military contractors. They wore the uniform: tight polo shirts, khakis or cargo pants, ballistic sunglasses slung on lanyards across developed pectorals. All three toted rifles or carbines, high-end semiautomatics chambered for 5.56. Behind, moving with impressive grace for his bulk and the tight quarters, came a man incongruously attired as a butler and carrying a briefcase. And behind him slunk one more, a man Karl recognized.

Karl sat up, scooting in front of the .38 in the distant hope it had gone unseen.

"I beg you to pardon the intrusion," the dapper gentleman said. He offered a slight bow. "Circumstances prevented my telephoning ahead."

"What do you want?" Professor Allison asked, half-belligerent, half bewildered. "Who are you?"

"Mago D from NYC, I presume," Karl said.

The intruder shifted to face Karl, an eloquent eyebrow lifting in query. "My fame precedes me in an unexpected fashion." Without taking his eyes from Karl, he tilted his head enough to utter a command over his shoulder. "Alexandros, be so kind as to remove the snub nose pistol from the cot this gentleman is reposed upon."

One of the mercs stepped forward. He probably measured a couple of inches taller than Karl and massed a bit more. Karl figured him for Greek, maybe southern Italian in origin, and probably in his early forties. Karl assumed he could take him if it came to blows. But three of them would present a problem. And it wouldn't do to underestimate the other three men, that butler especially. Besides, May and the boss were too likely to become casualties in a mass brouhaha in the confines of the tent.

So Karl shifted aside, exposing the Smith & Wesson. Alexandros, stone-faced, scooped it up. Karl noted he maintained his distance and kept positive control of the Heckler and Koch AR-15-style carbine slung across his chest. The MR556, Karl guessed. Collapsible stock folded, red-dot sight attached to the top of the equipment rail, tactical light beneath. Not an amateur, this one, but an experienced operator.

"It is a trifle awkward to discover myself known by the unfortunate street sobriquet of Mago D," the intruder continued, a man Karl presumed was enamored of the sound of his own voice. "It does cast something of a pall over 'Allow me to introduce myself.'" He waved his hand in a dismissive gesture. "So be it. I am Dexter Magus. Not, I'm afraid, at your service." Magus redirected his attention to Professor Allison. "You are, I presume, Professor James Allison. I must regretfully require you to be at *my* service."

"This day keeps getting better," Professor Allison said. "What is it you want, Mr. Magus?"

Karl cleared his throat. Violence still did not recommend itself, but he could at least begin sowing dissension and mistrust. "Oh, I think I can make a guess at what Mago D is after. Some high-quality snapshots brought him down here. Isn't that right, Festo?" Karl asked the man hovering about the tent entrance. "How was your flight to New York?"

Magus hoisted the eyebrow again, then pivoted to face the tent flap. "*Señor* Hidalgo, do you know this man?"

"No, *Señor*," Festo answered. He squirmed, looking tempted to turn and bolt, yet too obviously terrified of Magus to move. "I mean, I have seen him. He is, I don't know, like the guard. Always patrolling the site. I could not get in for the pictures until I was sure he was somewhere else. I guess he's the one followed us to the airport."

"How's Enrique, Festo?" Karl asked. The response displayed on Festo's face suggested – *what? Guilt?*

"What are you doing, Karl?" Professor Allison asked. "This isn't the time to piss people off."

Karl closed his eyes, huffed a sigh, then opened them again. *Do I tell you how to do your job?*

"Karl," Magus said, "was attempting to seed doubt and divisiveness, Professor Allison. He was also hoping you not use his name; an anonymous opponent can be more formidable."

Professor Allison grimaced, crestfallen. May looked ready to kick him in the shin.

Magus continued, "But, Karl, allow me to answer your question on behalf of my hired minion. Enrique is faring poorly. So poorly, in fact, that I fear he has taken the dark road to the unknown. It seems he was overly communicative. Our friend Festo is wiser, hence his reticence."

"What do you want?" Karl asked. He let a note of defeat inform the question. He remained sitting, unthreatening. The intruders had, so far as they knew, disarmed him. Let them believe him neutralized.

"Good. To business. I want merely a single specimen. Professor Allison, you have uncovered so much, one artifact is little to ask. We'll then let you return to your unearthing the past. So long as you cooperate, that is. As you can see, I've not come to negotiate. And these three armed gentlemen are not the extent of my persuasiveness."

"How many did you bring?" Karl asked.

Dexter Magus chuckled. "Enough. Currently the rest of my merry band are rounding up the graduate students, cooks, maintenance personnel, drivers, etc."

"Please, we'll do as you ask," Professor Allison said. "Just don't hurt any of them."

"Any pain or death that ensues is entirely up to you, Professor."

"That's a lot of hostages to keep an eye on, Magus," Karl said. "Be kind of like corralling kittens."

"He's not entirely wrong," said Alexandros. "You get a big enough group, especially young people, you're going to get a few wannabe heroes."

"Once you shoot those, Alexandros, I believe the rest will be sufficiently discouraged," Magus said.

"Or maybe you stir up a stampede," Karl said. "Or alert a passing tour bus. Gunshots carry."

"Did you have a suggestion, Karl? Or are you simply stalling? There is no rescue coming. The cavalry is not waiting over the hill."

"Hey, Mago D, you're in charge here. Nobody is coming to save us. I get that. I want to keep everyone safe; it's my job. If that means helping you complete your heist faster, more smoothly, then yeah, I'll make a suggestion."

"Which is? Ticktock," Magus said, tapping his wrist.

"Load up everyone in whatever vehicles you can find in the car park. Then they're confined, easy to keep an eye on. And, if you're going to be in and out as fast as you say, why not send them to town? If they aren't here, you won't have to worry about any heroes. Frees up the rest of your boys to look for stragglers."

"Except for the part about letting them drive off, I like it, sir," Alexandros said.

Karl maintained a neutral expression. Staging everyone in the vans, trucks, and passenger cars meant an easier evacuation when the narcos arrived. Getting them on the road had been too much to hope for. But asking for more than he was willing to settle for had always struck Karl as a sensible bargaining tactic. Of course, he might have just caged them for ease of execution, so many proverbial fish in a barrel.

"Fine. Omar, go inform Smith," Magus said. "Then rejoin us. We'll be on the way to the ziggurat."

One of the gunmen nodded, a lanky youth, fit, but carrying less bulk than the other two. He ducked out of the tent.

"Now then, if you would lead the way, Professor," Magus said. "Please accompany us, miss," he said to May, then, addressing Karl, "And you, Karl, if you would be so kind as to precede Alexandros by three or four paces, lest there be some sort of unfortunate misunderstanding."

Karl kept both hands up, arms bent at the elbows and away from his body as he rose with exaggerated care.

The butler reached for May's elbow, his manner solicitous.

She slapped at his hand like a kitten swiping a paw at a Saint Bernard. "Hands off, Lurch."

The butler took it with the same patient indifference one

would expect from a Saint Bernard. "After you, miss," he said with utter placidity.

Karl took up the penultimate position in the procession winding through Tent City and on to the dig proper. Professor Allison led the way with Dexter Magus at his side. The unnamed gunman followed, keeping an eye on Allison. Festo trudged after, his hands in his pockets, his head, pigeon-like, on an erratic swivel. Then came May and the butler, Karl, and, – a judicious few steps behind, weapon at the ready – Alexandros.

Karl walked as erect as possible, hoping to keep the fabric of his still-drying shirt draped loosely. A pro like Alexandros would notice the telltale outline of a weapon if his attention was drawn to it. But having taken the .38, Alexandros might well assume he'd disarmed Karl. And the man must have a lot more on his mind, running this circus under the gaze of a ringmaster like Dexter Magus. Karl almost felt sorry for the mercenary. Almost.

Tent City felt like a ghost town. A canvas and nylon ghost town. Karl cast a guilty glance at the equipment in the gymnasium tent. Given his swimming/climbing/fighting earlier that day, the guilt derived more from the habits formed by daily structured workouts than from any physiological need for exercise.

They passed through the cleared excavation sites. The westering sun lent the scene a numinous air of melancholy, blurring sharp edges and creating shadowy hints of mystery. Karl could see Dexter Magus gesturing as he carried on some effusive monologue. Omar caught up with them as they reached the cenote, stoppered by its ziggurat, the parade bunching up as they descended the stairs.

"Earthquakes do catastrophically devalue a neighborhood," Magus was saying as Karl reached earshot at the edge of the cenote. "I hardly recognize the place. But, over that way, I imagine." He led off toward the treasure chamber with assurance, wending through the subterranean passages with the familiarity of a frequent visitor.

The treasure chamber looked worse for wear. All the people passing through in preparation for the unnecessary rescue of Karl had churned up the damp earth and coated the pallet flooring with muddy shoe prints. But the altar stone or display shelf – whatever it was – remained pristine, its treasures still proudly displayed.

The group clustered inside. Alexandros, Karl noted, took up position by the entry and Omar by the gap in the wall near the display shelf. The other gunman, a heavily tattooed blond, stayed within two paces of Magus. Decent security for a three-man team, Karl thought, though he would have posted one man outside the entry.

Given the confined space of the treasure chamber, Karl figured his edging closer to Magus presented no suspicious aspect. People group in tight spaces, especially if the walls are damp. And groups of people play hell with clean lines of fire.

"This is all you've uncovered?" Magus asked Professor Allison. "I really must let you get back to work. This city boasted vast wealth and truly exquisite relics. Still, I should not complain. You did dig up the one item that tickled my fancy."

Professor Allison shook his head. "You're a gifted conman, Mr. Magus. No offense intended. But you almost convince me you visited K'aay-Boox in its heyday."

"That truth is often less than compelling is one of humanity's great tragedies," Magus said. "I find that tends to work to my favor. Now, where is it? Ahhh, there is my beauty." He gestured at the collection of artifacts assembled on the altar. "My were-jaguar. Do you know what you have in that dagger, Professor Allison?"

The professor shrugged. "An exquisite example of Classical-era workmanship?"

"Superficial, Professor. I expect better from you. No. What you have is an inexhaustible source of wealth – if used properly."

"How so?" May asked. "It is a nice piece. It would fetch a handsome price on the market. Every textbook on Mesoamerica will want a picture. It would make any traveling museum exhibit. But that wouldn't add up to much. Certainly not inexhaustible wealth."

"No, my dear," Magus said. "But as Carl Jung once said to me, 'The thing itself merely veils a universe of possibilities.' Of course, Carl was baked to a brittle crispness at the time, so his statement leaves room for interpretation." Magus smiled, as if receiving acclaim from an attentive audience. "To answer your question, dear lady, the Jade Dagger is an enchanted artifact, a rarity known among the cognoscenti as a Replicator. An extremely specific example, resonant with jade only."

No one spoke. Karl could see Professor Allison compressing his lips. May turned her head away from Magus, allowing Karl to see her fighting back a contemptuous laugh.

"They scoff, don't they, Omar?" Magus said. "Your *tio* Bernardo wouldn't. It is a simple enough process. No ritual sacrifice involved, no – blood magic." Karl thought he detected a hint of deception in the words, a hesitation and a slight tightening of the lips. Magus pushed on. "I'll not need Potter to hand me the case with my tools of the trade for this bit of legerdemain. One merely grasps the dagger, places a bit of jade against the blade, exerts a measure of will, and speaks 'yax tun' three times. Jade will then manifest next to the Jade Dagger and continue to do so for as long as the wielder wills it."

"Inexhaustible wealth," Omar said. "All that jade to sell. Nice."

"Or," Magus said, "one could convince certain parties to corner the jade market beforehand, investing entire fortunes. Then, reclined in a comfortable Eames chair, sipping a fruit-forward burgundy, one could at his leisure create an absurdly vast pile of jade…"

"Completely devaluing the market," said Karl. "To what purpose?"

"Ah, a grasp of economics," Magus said. "How pleasant to discover an educated man within the guise of a lumpen security guard. To what purpose? Why, chaos. Beautiful chaos. Certain banking houses overinvested in jade will collapse. Others will fall, not so much like dominoes but like trees in a landslide – haphazardly. The worldwide financial and political consequences will be gloriously entertaining."

"I don't understand," Professor Allison said. "Stipulating that all this magic rigmarole is real, what is the point of causing a financial crisis?"

"I just told you. Weren't you listening? It will be gloriously entertaining. I realize this is difficult for you mayflies to understand. Your lives are so fleeting, you have no time to truly comprehend ennui. I have walked this planet for millennia."

Professor Allison cleared his throat.

"Scoff if you will, Professor. Your lack of belief does not change the fact. And the fact is boredom. For me, the point of life, other than to continue to live, is to stave off boredom."

"What," asked May, "you don't want to rule the world like any self-respecting second-rate megalomaniac?"

"No, dear child," Magus said, and offered May an indulgent smile. "I do not want to rule the world. I have done that, or at least a decent chunk of it. I found it entirely too much work. The constant demands for my attention, the need to make decisions about absolutely everything, no matter how petty. Exhausting. No, if you could ever reach my age, you'd gain much more pleasure from, ahh…stirring up shit and watching the results."

"Like kicking over an anthill," Karl said. He realized he

truly did not want Mago D to kick over whatever particular anthill he had in mind. Whether the man was delusional, or possessed even a fraction of the power he hinted at, he was clearly dangerous. A danger to the dig. A danger to May. Perhaps – if Mago D wasn't a complete bullshit artist – a danger to the world.

"Indeed," Magus said. "You appear to understand the impulse."

"I understand you are a sadistic psycho," Karl said. And he moved.

The prospect of death sweetened the moment, but slowed him not the least. The treasure chamber was not a large room. May Chen, Professor Allison, Festo, the butler – *Potter?* – masked the sight lines of the three gunmen. None of them could get a clear shot so long as Karl moved fast.

And Karl did move fast, pumping his arms like a sprinter out of the blocks for the few steps it took him to blow past Magus and reach the altar. He scooped up the Jade Dagger, braced his foot against the side of the altar, and pushed off, redirecting himself toward Omar without losing much speed.

A shot boomed, the noise amplified within the confined space. Karl felt the disruption in the air as the bullet passed overhead to bury itself into dirt and limestone. Whether Magus' bodyguard or Alexandros had pulled the trigger, Karl didn't know. Omar was still bringing his rifle to bear when Karl hit him in a flying tackle.

Omar went ass first through the gap in the treasure chamber wall, Karl's arms wrapped around his hips, Karl's face pressed into his chest, the forestock and barrel of the rifle digging into Karl's clavicle. As Karl felt Omar over-balance, he slipped his arms free, groping up for the rifle's buttstock and barrel. Somehow Omar avoided the most probable outcome of Karl's attack: that is, butt on the far side of the opening, knees bent over the ragged lip, feet still inside the chamber. Instead Omar offered an incompletely adroit display of agility. The lower edge of the gap caught one leg, eliminating one point of contact. But Omar managed to hop and kick his other leg enough to clear the lip, bringing it down on the far side. That, however, failed to provide a stable enough platform for him to regain his balance. Instead it let him keep upright just enough for Karl to drive him, hopping and staggering, across the narrow ledge beyond the treasure chamber and over the precipice.

Karl tried to get a firm grip on the rifle, in the desperate hope of wrenching it free of the combat sling. But he ran out of time, letting go after he'd passed through the fissure. He stumbled and nearly followed Omar off the edge of the cliff. He could make out the man's dim form falling. He lost sight of him before Omar's shocked bellowing ceased, smothered by the cold waters below.

Karl swiveled to his right, his heels digging divots in the thin soil. He moved. As soon as the ledge widened sufficiently, he dropped to hands and knees, scrambling on all fours as he went, only rising back to his full height after he'd cleared the line of sight from within the treasure chamber. Hands extended before him, he ran along the platform, making for the narrow stone bridge he recalled from his equally unwelcome visit earlier that day.

His palms slammed into the wall at the end of the platform. Meaning the span over the subterranean river should be immediately to his left. If, that is, his memory of the geography was correct. The feeble light emanating from within the treasure chamber was suggestive but not definitive. The grayish band disappearing into the dark might be the bridge or it might be a trick of pallid light and meager shadow. Karl considered dropping again to hands and knees, essaying a cautious probe and equally cautious crossing.

To become wise, one must wish *to have certain experiences and run, as it were, into their gaping jaws.* Karl headed for what he hoped was the bridge in an all-out sprint.

Fucking Nietzsche, he thought.

CHAPTER 15

Dexicos Megistos had, centuries ago, ceased allowing events to surprise him. At least in the sense of the unexpected shocking him into temporary lack of volition or decision. Karl's move had been unforeseen, yes. But even as the garish Hawaiian shirt vanished through the narrow fissure in the wall, Dexicos was already formulating his response while also nurturing a burgeoning antipathy toward this meddling night watchman.

Alexandros shoved through the knot in the middle of the treasure chamber. Dexicos held up a restraining hand. He'd lost a third of his immediate security detachment in the last couple of seconds. It behooved him to husband his resources.

"Wait, Alexandros," he said. "I want you here." He grabbed the shoulder of the gunman at his side, the man's carbine smoking from his errant wing shot. "You – what's your name?"

"Snyder, sir. Ex-Marine Recon –"

"I asked your name, not your CV. Duck your head through there. Report." Dexicos didn't wait for the man to respond. "Alexandros, you're with me. Festo, keep an eye on our guests."

Festo offered a look in response that betokened as much exasperation as fear. The man wasn't armed, after all. Well, except for a knife. But the small Eurasian woman and the archaeologist couldn't know that. Control and manipulation depended as much upon disinformation as overt power.

Meanwhile Snyder poked the barrel of his carbine through the gap in the wall, triggering the flashlight racked onto the equipment rail. He followed with his head. From the motion of his back, the mercenary was sweeping the beam back and forth, then down. He flicked the flashlight off as he returned to Dexicos.

"Sir, I'm pretty sure we lost Omar," Snyder said. "There's a stream or a river about twenty feet down. But I think the other guy kept his feet. There are fresh marks on the ledge, and there's a kind of bridge over the water. I can't be sure, but I think I saw someone on the far side."

"There is more speculation than observation in that report. It will, nonetheless, have to suffice as intelligence." Dexicos stroked his chin. "Right. Snyder, I want you to pursue Karl. Kill him if you like. It makes little difference to me. But above all, retrieve the Jade Dagger. Oh, and please don't let him disarm you." He waved Snyder on. "Potter, please hand me the case. I have a mission for you."

Potter gave up the briefcase and waited, hands clasped behind his back, for his instructions. Snyder returned to the fissure and stepped through the gap into the darkness beyond.

Alexandros spoke up before Dexicos could issue his orders to Potter. "Sir, perhaps you should send me. Snyder might have been a Marine, I don't know. But Recon? Not a chance. This guy, Karl, I got a feeling about him. He seems to know his business. He isn't a minimum-wage security guard taking an easy gig in Mexico like a vacation. The man's an operator. He'll take down Snyder."

"Perhaps, Alexandros. And perhaps you should shut up," Dexicos said. "You *are* more skilled than Snyder. That is why I want you close rather than our ersatz Marine." Dexicos sighed. "Let me be clear, Alexandros. If you second-guess my orders again, I will leave you staked out here for the ants. Have you ever watched a million or so ants strip a body down to the bones? A fascinating spectacle, I can assure you."

Dexicos turned his attention from Alexandros without waiting for a reply. The help must know its place: Alexandros could be replaced. Dexicos had replaced hundreds of Alexandroses over the centuries.

"Now, Potter. A manhunt through the catacombs of K'aay-Boox will require more boots underground than Snyder's two. Instruct Smith to leave a single guard to watch the prisoners. Smith is to report here with the rest of the men immediately. Please escort them back here with all dispatch."

Potter said, "Very good, sir," but there was an unspoken question in his acquiescence.

"Of course one man is insufficient, Potter. Don't you begin to second-guess me as well. These buses full of archaeology students are of tertiary importance at best. By the time they can reach any responsive authority, we'll have completed our business and vacated. The guard is not to exert himself unduly. Now, off with you."

Potter offered the slightest of nods and left, moving with a grace that left the pallet flooring unmoved.

"Thank you, Mr. Magus," the woman said. "They're just kids, most of them."

"Hmmm?" Dexicos said. "They are an inconvenience is what they are. They can flee to the T-shirt shops of Cancun or be mowed down by whatever trigger-happy guard Smith sticks with babysitting duty. I do not care."

Dexicos dismissed her from his attention as well. He had no doubts regarding Alexandros' ability to prevent any mischief from the two captives. He hoisted the briefcase and settled it atop the altar stone, sweeping aside the display of artifacts. Professor Allison's dismayed gasp left him unmoved. The years had not been kind to the altar. It retained none of the numinous, blood-soaked energy he remembered from his last visit to K'aay-Boox, no power for Dexicos to tap into. But the exercise he intended to perform did not promise to tax his own reserves; he need not draw upon any eldritch batteries or natural concentrations of magic.

Dexicos thumbed open the latches holding shut the

briefcase and opened it. He considered the contents, evaluating possibilities.

The catacombs had shifted. The wear and tear of the centuries had likely closed some ways and perhaps opened others. Not enough by itself to confound someone familiar with the place. But the massive geological shifts that had undermined K'aay-Boox's majestic structures – including, Dexicos supposed, the tremor that had occurred the other day – must have altered the passageways almost beyond recognition. He could not rely on his memory of the turnings and twistings, the intersections, spy holes and murder holes. And assuredly there were many that his hosts had not felt obligated to share with him.

Dexicos retained clear memories of his first visit to K'aay-Boox, when the central palace/temple complex axed through the jungle like an amorphous, growing beast still finding its shape. He remembered sharing architectural ideas from the necropolises of Memphis and Thebes, and noting novel construction methods and engineering concepts to take back to the Middle Kingdom with him. The city had reached nearly its final size and configuration by the time he'd returned for a second visit. The increase in knowledge and power of the sorcerer-priests of K'aay-Boox had grown commensurately with the sprawl and complexity of the city beneath the city, the sorcerous might and the labyrinthine complexity reinforcing each other in a sort of magical feedback loop.

That very complexity indicated that Karl could potentially elude Snyder indefinitely. In fact, he could likely avoid capture by the entire force of mercenaries at Dexicos' disposal. Dexicos determined it in his best interests to draw upon other resources.

The contents of the briefcase eased his task somewhat. He could make do with scrounged raw material, but doing so would require more time and greater expenditures of his personal store of energy. Dexicos pondered his options, then settled upon a lens of scratched, time-yellowed glass about the size of a Kennedy half-dollar. He held it up to his eye, allowing the light from one of the bare electric bulbs to pass through the lens. A shadow writhed within the murky, light-distorting glass.

"Still with us," Dexicos said, careful to avoid naming the entity trapped inside the ancient quartz lattice. He thought of the atelier of the lens grinder and amateur alchemist where he'd first encountered this particular curiosity. Amsterdam, Dexicos thought. Or was it Bruges? Something Hanseatic, or nearby at any rate, sometime in the mid-sixteenth century. "Well, of course. Where else could you go? Perhaps you'd enjoy a brief parole, a chance to stretch your – appendages."

The art of summoning lay in coercion, willpower, and knowledge, all driven through a focus. Dexicos held ample reserves of all three mental requisites. And he held a focus, a focus that possessed the additional convenience of already containing a trapped creature of unimaginable age, a native of a long-dead world circling strange stars. After an inter-minable voyage through the dark spaces of the void, it had fallen into the gravity well of Earth, where with a cold, inhuman malice, it had raged across continents, seeking whom it might devour. Until confined, entrapped, and enslaved by one of Dexicos' peers. Its prison was passed around, traded, lost, and rediscovered over the centuries, the nature of its bondage and the physical structure of the prison undergoing alterations and upgrades until it reached its final form in the workshop of the unfortunate Hans – unfortunate in that he'd shown off his prize to Dexicos Megistos, a mage of vastly greater age, skill, and covetousness.

"Festo," Dexicos said, "come here, please."

"*Señor?*" Festo asked, stepping up beside Dexicos, though leaving a respectful distance. His voice trembled.

"Your knife, if you please, Festo." Dexicos held out his hand, palm up. He kept his eyes on the lens, not glancing at Festo. He waited; nothing. He cleared his throat. The hilt of an opened clasp knife slapped into his palm. Dexicos closed his fingers around it. He turned to face Festo and smiled. With the hand holding the lens, he grabbed Festo by the wrist. A quick slash of the knife opened a gash in Festo's forearm. "Thank you, Festo," he said. "Put some pressure on that, would you?"

Festo emitted a startled scream that grew as the pain hit.

"Oh, do be quiet, Festo," Dexicos said. He let a note of irritation enter his voice. "I require a degree of silence if I am to concentrate."

The woman approached Festo, tugging a bandanna from a pocket. Dexicos left her to her ministrations, dismissing the entire scene. He moved to stand before the fissure leading from the treasure chamber, out to what had once been a less-than-secret observation platform. In fact, he'd once stood out there, watching an initiation ceremony through one of the spy holes.

Dexicos held the lens out before him. He scraped some of Festo's blood from the knife blade onto the lens. He built an image of Karl in his mind, examined it, then added the sound of Karl's voice. "Seek," Dexicos said. "Kill." He concentrated on the Jade Dagger, constructing a mental model of it in exacting detail. "Fetch. Return before sunrise or suffer the consequences."

Then Dexicos poured his will through the lens and whispered a Name and a Command.

The nebulous form within the lens swam and swirled. Then it vanished, leaving behind merely an aged circle of polished glass. Upon the unlit floor of the observation platform, Something took shape. Dexicos caught only an impression of size, of a mass built up of slim angularity rather than solid bulk. And he caught a whiff of the smell, a metallic pong overlaying a rancid, oily reek.

The figure appeared to unfold, stretching and expanding. With a skittering of multiple pointed feet, it moved, disappearing in the direction of the bridge.

"That," said Dexicos, "is that. My money is not on Snyder."

The bridge held. Karl's sense of direction held, as did the traction of the soles of his boots. He did not plummet off the edge. But his memory of the doorway on the far side proved faulty. He hit the wall at a jog; it could have been worse, but it still hurt. His left fist struck first, providing enough time for him to turn his hip, causing his thigh to slam into the limestone instead of his knee. He bit back an Urdu profanity, trying to ignore the lance of pain shooting up from his knuckles. He felt around with his undamaged arm, searching to his left for the opening, wondering if he should risk a light, hoping he'd find an empty space instead of the flat stone.

Fuck it, he thought. He dug the mini-light from a pocket and flashed a quick strobe at the wall. He'd missed by about six inches to the right. Chancing another quick glimmer of light, Karl took a peek through the doorway. Escaping Magus only to drop into a pit would be a shitty trade-off.

The lintel reached to about his mid forehead. Karl stooped to look. The flicker of light offered a glimpse of a hallway running with geometrical perfection straight before him, with the suggestion of an intersecting passage at the limit of the mini-light's range. At Karl's feet was, thank God, more solid floor. Overlaying the flooring was centuries of dust, grit, insect carcasses, bat dung, and bits of crumbled stone. The walls and ceiling held the remains of carved tiles, few intact, suggesting the origin of the stone fragments on the floor.

So much for stealth.

Karl turned off the light and entered the hallway, taking each trotting step on the balls of his feet. The floor crunched beneath him at each footfall – Karl wondered what priceless bits of Mayan artwork he was grinding to gravel beneath his feet, what stories the tiles could have told Professors Chen and Allison – but he at least moved more quietly that way than if he'd taken full, rolling steps. The tingling in his fingers subsided. It seemed he hadn't seriously damaged his hand. He straightened and bent the digits a few times, loosening them up.

Karl reckoned he'd gone about halfway toward the crossing hallway when he heard footsteps behind him. A glimmer of light brushed the hallway. One or more of Magus' goons. Probably still on the bridge, his gun-mounted tactical light sweeping for targets. Karl would offer one hell of a target, without cover in the middle of the hallway.

This archaeological expedition, this site, the people performing the excavations, analysis, and preservation; the people laundering their clothes, cooking their dinners, and providing all the other essential camp services – all were Karl's charges. Their safety was his responsibility, his job. Getting the hell out of Dodge did not reach the top ten of his list of options. And he couldn't attempt any sort of rescue while in constant evasion mode. Yet here he was, running. What other choice did he have? He could pull the .45, try to shoot it out. But he didn't care for the odds. Sure, Karl's mini-light could go some way to offset the visibility advantage of the rail-mounted tac-light. Yet at this range, the longer gun had the advantage. Meaning he'd probably lose said shoot-out. That sort of loss wasn't followed by handshakes and rote mumblings of "good game." That sort of loss meant you were dead. Karl definitely could not engage in any hostage-rescuing, May Chen-impressing heroics if he were dead.

So he ran. Karl let the fingertips of his left hand brush against the wall until they located the cross passage. He started to his left, then reconsidered and darted across the open hallway, entering the right-hand stretch of the cross passage. His earlier drift down the subterranean river and his trek down the open corridor toward the shoot-out with the narcos hinted that the left-hand stretch might terminate sooner than he'd consider ideal. Of course, it was only an impression, an ill-informed guess at the layout of this ancient labyrinth. At best an instinct. But if he had only his instincts to rely upon, what other choice did he have?

What next? An ambush? Any experienced operator would suspect something like that at the first blind spot.

Karl shielded the mini-light with his hand and flicked it on, examining the passage ahead of him and looking for opportunities.

The tiled walls looked more intact down this stretch of passage. Animal-headed, human-shaped figures in profile stood in a queue, engaged in activities that conveyed nothing to Karl. A few stelae stood at intervals of three or four paces. Others – most, Karl figured – had toppled and cracked. The floor remained paved with the detritus of centuries, much like the previous hallway, but without the noisy grit of fallen wall tiles.

Far ahead Karl saw blank spaces in the walls, suggesting more doorways. He could make for those if his goal was to lose pursuit. But that wasn't his goal. Instead, Karl eyed the stelae. The rectangular, roughly headstone-shaped pieces appeared formed of stone harder and more durable than the ubiquitous limestone of the labyrinth. Karl's Mark-One Eyeball measurement put each one at about three feet tall and two feet wide.

Karl could hear steady, rapid footsteps approaching from the first hallway. It sounded like only a single hunter, and a confident one at that.

Karl sprinted down the passage, bypassing the first few stelae. He stopped at the third one on the right-hand side. He flicked off the light, crouched down behind the stone, and drew the pistol from the waistband holster. He rested the .45 atop the stela. Its four-inch width offered a comforting degree of protection from small-arms fire. The grip of the automatic felt familiar, a comforting talisman in an otherwise utterly alien environment. Karl had fought through many "there I was" moments, but none of them had offered any practical lessons for being stalked through the subterranean ruins of an ancient Mayan city.

The light of Karl's hunter washed over the passageway entry. It wavered, then swiveled away, illuminating a section of the left-hand passage that Karl had decided against entering. The flashlight offered a convenient method of keeping track of his pursuit. But the fucker was taking his sweet time about it. *Come on, you bastard. This way.* Karl had more of them to deal with and doubted he'd have all night to accomplish it.

The light narrowed as the gunman hunted down the wrong passage. Before it shrank to a point, the gunman apparently reached the conclusion that he'd guessed poorly. The beam expanded and grew, returning up the passage, across the initial hallway, then on into Karl's side of the passage.

Karl allowed his eyes to adjust, not looking directly into the beam, but allowing his peripheral vision to catch the darker, moving form behind it. He knew he didn't have perfect concealment behind the stela; it simply wasn't large enough. He couldn't wait forever. But neither could he risk a shot too early, a shot at a target that didn't yet present a good sight picture. A target that could shoot back if he missed.

The air smelled stale, with a graveyard whiff of dirt, decay, and old stone. The floor dug painfully into Karl's knees, the slightly damp mixture of who-knew-what soaking through his jeans. Karl hadn't gone through sniper school, so he hadn't been trained in enduring the torture of remaining motionless for hours in uncomfortable positions. But he'd waited through enough ambushes in a variety of unpleasant shitholes. He could ignore the creeping desire to shift, to fight the incipient itch or cramp.

He waited.

The beam shifted in a repetitive search pattern, left, then right, then back again. The tile murals on the walls flickered in and out of view in weird, disjointed scenes of ceremony, sacrifice, and war, all performed by squat, animal-visaged forms. The firm, slow footsteps of the gunman grew louder. Left, light. Right, light. The beam splashed over Karl's hiding place, continued on – hesitated…

Even with his eyes averted from the light, Karl could still make out the solid form behind the beam. Center mass must be immediately below the source of the light. Karl placed the green tritium dot of the front sight between the two dots of the rear sight and squeezed the trigger at the same moment the light swept back toward him. The white brilliance of the flashlight was joined by the orange flare of muzzle blast. The deep-throated bark of Karl's .45 mingled with the sharper, snapping bark of the hunter's carbine.

Karl's protective stela shoved against him, then broke apart into chunks. A hurtling fragment of stone gouged a line along the left side of his temple, right below the hairline. His forearms placed atop the stela had supported about half his weight. With the support abruptly removed, he fell forward, newly jagged edges of rock cutting into his arms.

He expected another shot, this one a nigh point-blank round into his back. But he refused to go meekly, raising the .45 for a defiant last shot.

The tac-light no longer threatened to dazzle Karl's vision. Instead it spotlighted a carven tile depicting some sort of bird-headed creature performing some action involving a snake and what might be a knife.

No shots.

Karl pushed himself to his knees, rising from the broken remnants of the stela. Keeping out of the light, he took three roundabout steps to the fallen gunman, .45 in a firm two-handed grip before him.

"Are you killed?" Karl asked.

No answer. Which was answer enough. But just to be sure, Karl reached out with the toe of his shoe and nudged. He felt a head loll and roll beneath his foot. "Yeah. Well, better you than me."

Karl holstered the .45, replacing gun with mini-light. His light showed him the blond, tattooed thug, lifeless before him. Karl's slug had taken the man in the sternum, at an upward angle that must have burst the heart, killing him almost instantly. Karl worked the tactical sling free from the limp body, securing the carbine for himself. A Bushmaster Patrolman. Close enough to the M4 to provide Karl a comfortable frisson of nostalgia. He hurriedly slung it over his shoulder. He bent again to rifle through the pockets of the tactical vest when a noise, like the whisper of two dry sheets of coarse paper rubbing against each other, stopped him.

Karl raised his head, bringing the carbine's flashlight up along with it. Into the circle of illumination shifted a form entirely new to Karl's experience. He couldn't categorize it. It fit into none of the Linnaean taxonomy he could recall. It presented an elongated shape, something akin to a monstrously expanded grasshopper. But no, that wasn't right. It didn't seem to have a single, defining shape at all. It unfolded itself as it stalked forward on a constantly shifting number of – feet wasn't right, limbs neither. Bent members of some ebony, chitinous material, temporarily positioned adjacent to the ground, served for locomotion. The entirety appeared a conglomeration of linear structural members, themselves composed of smaller lengths, in constant flux, like living origami, if origami consisted of folding oversized tongue depressors and toothpicks instead of paper. And if origami could fold in and out of more than three dimensions. The geometry of the thing was subtly, nauseatingly *wrong*. Compacted, it might mass no more than Karl himself. While moving, its accordion locomotion enlarged its width to nearly fill the hallway. A ring of eyes cast back a yellow-green reflection, the eyes semi-detached, free-floating, shifting from elbow end or point or whatever structural units momentarily faced front. A hint of something foul wrinkled Karl's nose, something crustacean, or perhaps something insectile with an added pinch of salt.

Karl looked into the abyss. This *thing* looked back. Neither blinked. Karl refused to allow horror to root him to the spot. And he was nearly incapable of panic. Whatever this alien menace was, it was a threat. A threat he must deal with prior to investing time wondering exactly what the fuck it was.

He put a shot into it. Or tried to. Karl stood, pulled the trigger, and stepped back, observing the result. The thing expanded to the extent the walls allowed, elongating into skeletal components, becoming as much empty space as mass. Whether the round had hit anything or not, Karl couldn't tell. But an icy blue gleam buzzed through the circle of eyes. The creature sprang forward. Karl spun on his heel and ran. He dodged and leapt stelae, hoping to lure the pursuit into stumbling over the stones. He heard only the papery rustle growing louder, nearer.

He felt a probing, tearing needle lance into the skin at his back, between his left shoulder blade and his spine. It ripped down, slicing through his shirt and about a tenth of an inch of flesh, a burning pain preceding a searing cold. The cut stopped at the bottom of his rib cage. Karl had been knifed before, but this felt like no stab wound or laceration he'd suffered. The pain stopped for a heartbeat, the wound gone numb. Then it throbbed to acidic life again, firing webs of agony through his back. Karl wanted to fall to his knees and tear at the skin of his back, to scream and curse at the anguish. He didn't; he kept running, running through the alternating numbness and pain, running for the dark opening drawing closer to his left.

And then the pulsating pain ceased, leaving nothing behind except the normal discomfort Karl associated with a scratch of that depth. He didn't pause to consider the positive change of fortune. Instead he reached out with his left hand, clamped it onto the edge of the doorway, and swung himself ninety degrees, remembering to duck beneath the lintel.

A short corridor opened before him, another with its tiles largely dislodged from the walls, leaving a mass of crumbled rubble paving the floor. At the end of the hall, a stairway descended into darkness. Karl sprinted to the head of the stairs, glancing over his shoulder as he ran.

The thing had cornered without any apparent loss of momentum. It was right on him; gleaming black pseudo-limbs, razoring to points and edges, reached for him. Karl danced a heel-toe turn as he reached the end of the corridor. He'd had a glimpse of steep stairway, plunging almost perpendicularly to disappear into a confused mass of toppled walls and fallen chunks of roof. His momentum carried him backwards, over the edge. He tried to shift forward, bending at the waist, giving up as a lost cause the idea of keeping his feet while falling backward downstairs, hoping to take the fall on his ass and thighs as long as possible before the inevitable tumble bounced his back and head off the unforgiving stones.

The thing flowed after him. Karl pulled the trigger as he fell through the air, pumping out rounds as fast as he could twitch his finger. Bullets sank into and passed through the flexing, polymorphous origami sculpture falling after him. Gleaming black spines reached closer, closer…

The back of Karl's ankles hit first, then his butt. After that, all became a whirl of light and dark and pain.

CHAPTER 17

Alejandra descended the shaft as the sun set. The delays and setbacks of the afternoon had planted a mounting irritation. This shit should have been settled. Hector had scouted a route through the tunnels and a subterranean river to where he'd seen lights and heard voices. Alejandra had men, ropes, boats, and guns. Moving them all into tunnels, moving through tunnels, rafting along a river, coming out the other side, and frightening off a bunch of students shouldn't be difficult. But it was one *chingada* thing after another. Staging the equipment required multiple trips. Someone forgot to bring the foot pumps for the rafts. These idiot boys couldn't coordinate trips to the toilet. Diego insisted on issuing lights to everyone. Then everyone insisted on carrying extra batteries, which required locating the box where those had been stored. But the earthquake had toppled the supply tent, and no one knew where the box had been relocated during the cleanup. Two of the rafts leaked, and the entire expedition had to wait while the holes were located and patched. And on and on.

These *idiotas* couldn't organize *un quinceaños* for a friendless orphan. So Alejandra followed Diego down a rope and into the bowels of the earth to instill some urgency and supply some sorely lacking leadership.

Her .380, freshly cleaned and oiled, rode at her hip. She wore a head-mounted LED flashlight, a maroon bandanna tied pirate style over the top straps for a touch of style. She'd tucked her jeans into the hiking boots she wore when inspecting expansions of her operation deeper into the jungle. She wore a bulletproof vest over a dark blue T-shirt. Not that she expected the college kids to start shooting, but it helped send the message to her crew that she wasn't fucking around.

Fifteen men waited for her below. She counted, aloud. "Good, no one's gotten lost already."

That garnered a few scattered chuckles.

"That wasn't a fucking joke," Alejandra said. The flat, hard edge to her voice stifled the laughter. "After the pathetic job you *maricas* did getting down here, I can't trust you to piss without dribbling on your legs. Now, here's what we're going to do. I know you've heard this already, but I figure at least half of you have already forgotten. You're going to follow Hector down these tunnels until we get to the water. Then – and only then – you're going to inflate the rafts. You're going to tie the rafts together so you don't get separated. Then you're going to paddle where Hector tells you. Then you're going up a wall. Don't worry, Hector or

Diego will go up first and drop a rope for you. Once you get up top, you're going to begin a sweep, up through some ruins, then out into a camp. Chase off all the good little university boys and girls. This place is ours. Our new distribution pipeline. These spoiled rich kids aren't welcome. Let them know it.

"Got it?" She traversed her headlight left to right, picking up nods of assent and the occasional "*Si, Jefa.*" Most of them were grinning, anticipating the fun to come. All of them carried rifles. Most had packed along more loaded magazines than the job should require, looking forward to the sheer pleasure of pumping dozens of rounds into trees, dirt, or the air while scaring the shit out of these soft, sheltered students. Alejandra didn't care. Let them have their fun so long as she secured her new route and got the shipment out to the *Grand Princess* in time.

"Have fun," Alejandra said. "But take your instructions from me or Diego. Okay, Diego, get them moving."

Alejandra took up the rear, watching for stragglers. She examined her surroundings as she trudged along. The tunnel showed signs of engineering, a geometrical regularity suggesting early architects taking advantage of existing natural passages, smoothing and widening the soft limestone. *Good, an easy section through which to move the merchandise.*

The breeze funneled down from the chimney soon dissipated. But the air did not grow stale. Alejandra could feel moisture in the air, a cool, pleasant humidity. A darker spot in the wall to her right caught her eye. A depression of some sort? She stepped closer. No, it went deeper than that. A cave or side tunnel perhaps. Once this business was sorted, she'd have to organize a proper mapping expedition. A few paces farther on, she saw another opening to her left, a low entry, partially concealed by a tumble of rubble.

She skirted around an obstruction in the passage. Some sort of worn, sculptural piece. It might have once been representational, but the years had weathered it to abstraction. She passed a few more, then a couple more organic obstructions – bodies.

Arturo was nudging one of them with the toe of his shoe. "Shivved him. Shit. Looks like El Rojo put up a fight, though."

"We'll avenge him," Hector said, placing a hand on Arturo's shoulder.

Like he thinks Diego would do, thought Alejandra.

Arturo shrugged off the hand and then just shrugged. "I don't think El Rojo gives a shit what we do at this point."

Diego approached close enough so only Alejandra could hear him. "Burial detail?" he asked.

"Maybe later," Alejandra said. "Priorities, Diego. Besides, this might be a fitting tomb. Imagine what archaeologists a thousand years from now would think, finding the bones of these two down here. Come on, we're wasting time."

She chivvied them into motion again. They passed another passage entry and maybe another – the fall of rocks, some of them perhaps from the recent temblor, made it hard to determine if it was merely a natural indentation or something man made. A growing rumble, rising to a stone-cracking thunder, accompanied by a vibration beneath her feet, made Alejandra fear she'd been caught in another earthquake. She'd be found by the same future archaeologists uncovering Miguelito and El Rojo. But the noise was localized, emanating from behind her. She spun, her head-lamp spotlighting the rubble-covered opening she'd passed a moment before. The jumble of limestone fragments shuddered, a rattling, grinding vibration growing in intensity. Then the quivering rock pile hurtled apart in a shotgun spread before two tumbling, entangled masses.

"*Que chingados?*" Alejandra spat. What emerged from the darkness triggered no recognition. Some demon from the pits of Hell rolled, flailing and twitching, into the tunnel. It spread, expanding. Like an unrolling centipede, or a beetle spreading its wings. But none of those analogies fit the reality. This thing possessed too many limbs – if those were indeed limbs. It seemed all rib cage, though the ribs were oriented wrongly and kept shifting. It sprawled, blackish members scrabbling for purchase.

Something else, man-shaped – perhaps even a man – rolled free from the cage of those pivoting, recursive ribs or limbs. Alejandra caught a glimpse of the man before he tumbled out of the cone of her headlamp: a shredded red shirt flapping about him, arms crisscrossed with bloody slashes, torn jeans damp with blood. He rolled past her, in among her crew, whom she could already hear swiveling about, profanities spicing the air about her.

Then she was on one knee, pearl-inlaid grip in hand, the

Sig Sauer popping off rounds at the demon already regaining its balance. The bullets disappeared within its spreading form, having no apparent impact. And it came toward her. Alejandra's pulse accelerated, her ears roared with the sound of her own heartbeat. Terror and anger flooded through her, each fighting for supremacy. She didn't know which won; all she knew was she would hold her ground. She wouldn't allow her boys to see her run.

And then a barrage of rifles opened up from behind her, a hail of lead cracking overhead. The riot of gunfire drowned out the sound of her heart. The very air above her fluctuated with the violence of the lead storm. The smell of gunpowder cut the faint smell of the sea that accompanied the creature. Many, perhaps most, of the rifle rounds passed through the gaps in the shifting, black skeletal demon. But not all of them. Some thudded home, and they had an effect. Heavy rounds, 55 to 70 grains of lead, slammed into the living, kinetic sculpture. Demon it might be, but the black substance that composed its structure chipped, cracked, or shattered beneath the close-range impact of supersonic projectiles.

The demon staggered. The right side gave out. It toppled, raising a billow of dust – a dust composed of lime-stone and other substances Alejandra preferred not to specu-late on as she breathed it in. The barrage dwindled to sporadic potshots. Alejandra's ears rang, but she could sense her crew forming up behind her, some of them probably reloading. She brought one foot beneath her, rested the elbow of her firing arm on it.

"How do you like that, *puta*?" she asked.

The demon lurched upright again, lunged forward. Alejandra jerked the trigger. A semicircle of startled gunmen behind her joined in, pumping in round after point-blank round. The creature neared, twitching beneath the punishment, but inching forward. Sharp, glittering points emerged from the nearer ebony lengths. Alejandra could nearly reach out and touch the closest. So she did, with the muzzle of her .380. She squeezed off the last round from the magazine. The pointed limb shattered, the substrate beneath too dark for even the brilliance of her headlamp to illuminate from mere feet away.

As if that shot had at last stilled whatever served it for a heart, the demon collapsed, that bullet-shattered extremity gouging a furrow in the filth of the tunnel floor up to Alejandra's toe.

She stood over it, shuddering and gasping for breath, the fear of death now entirely replaced by the fear of being seen as weak. She fought to slow her driving heartbeat and steady her hands.

She thumbed the magazine release of her Sig Sauer and let the spent magazine drop. Hoping her hands did not betray her, she removed one of the two spare magazines cased on her hip and – *bendito Dios* – slipped it into place without a tremor and then slapped it home with an authoritative click.

"Did anyone see him?" she asked, forcing the query to take the mildest of tones.

"What?" Diego asked, prodding the splayed carcass with the barrel of his rifle. "We all saw that, *Jefa*."

"No, not the demon. The man in the flowery red shirt," Alejandra said.

"One of those *Magnum, P.I.* shirts?" Arturo asked. "Shit, that's the *hijo de la chingada* who did for El Rojo and Miguelito."

"Oh?" asked Alejandra. "Well, he just slipped by you heroes while you were busy wasting bullets on my trophy here. Maybe you should go find this *hijo de la chingada* and kill him. What do you think?"

CHAPTER 18

The yellowed lens in Dexicos' hand cracked, emitting a sulfurous belch, like a bursting bubble of swamp gas. A shard calved off, the scalpel-thin edge razoring a red line along the outside of his palm. The web of jagged cracks multiplied exponentially, and the lens shattered into a cloud of glass powder.

"An unexpected eventuality, I will admit," Dexicos said. He lifted the injured hand to his lips and sucked the cut. Truly sharp edges seldom hurt badly. It could be hard to tell how severe an injury the sharpest weapon caused. But this one appeared no more than a scratch.

Dexicos looked up from the edge of his hand to the nine gunmen assembled in a semicircle about him in the treasure chamber. "If you want something done right...Or is it 'never send an eldritch nightmare from the farthest cosmos to do a man's job'? I always confuse those two."

His summoning had failed. Somehow, Karl had

destroyed it. How an unarmed, mundane man could have bested that particular entity remained a mystery. Dexicos set it aside as temporarily irrelevant. If Karl had handled the summoning, then presumably Snyder had offered little challenge. He could assume Snyder no longer numbered among his employees. As a corollary, he could also assume that Karl was now armed.

Good thing I have my own Praetorian Guard. Smith had led in the rest of the crew shortly before the lens disintegrated. All the rest, that is, except for one hapless slob tasked to watch an entire archaeological expedition, the lot of them ensconced in vehicles. In the growing dark. It would constitute a remarkable feat if he pulled it off. But he wouldn't. He would be the weakest of the hired gunmen, the outcast, instantly disliked by the rest and ostracized by unspoken consent. There was always one, the feckless, the less capable. And he was always stuck with the shit duty. No, Dexicos could rely on most of those vans and buses driving off at some point in the next few hours, some of them, perhaps, stitched with bullet holes and carting off bleeding or dying students. The luckless guard would be left to fruitlessly justify his fuckup to the rest of the men later.

Centuries passed; men did not change.

Dexicos again opened up his briefcase atop the altar. Sorcery, alas, did not consist of a wished-for result consummated by a snappy magic word. Crafting a supernatural result demanded time, energy, and a seemingly infinite variety of materials. Thus most sorcerers depended on prefabricated spells in the form of magical artifacts either painstakingly constructed over the course of weeks, found, or – most often – stolen.

The contents of Dexicos' case represented over a millennium of scrounging, artificing, research, plunder, and outright murder. He considered the options displayed within, selecting a verdigrised ring crudely hammered from impure silver. A hound or wolf was roughly depicted on the bezel, if one squinted at it the right way.

Dexicos closed the case and handed it to Potter, the man standing precisely where Dexicos expected him to be on turning.

"Right. We appear to have a manhunt on our hands," Dexicos said. "I fear Snyder was not up to the job."

Alexandros snorted.

"Yes, Alexandros," Dexicos said, "it seems doubtful Snyder was the elite Marine he purported himself to be, as you rightly suggested. Would you like a cookie? No? Well, my other tracking effort was equally fruitless. That leaves it to us to follow our quarry into the catacombs. Be aware that he is likely armed, and we have ample evidence that this man Karl is not to be underestimated."

Dexicos pondered the problem some more. "Smith, Alexandros, are your men all equipped with electric torches? Check the batteries." He waited while men shuffled equipment and clicked switches on and off. "I think two search teams would be ideal if we had reliable communications. But given that we'll have no signal down here below, I think it best to remain as a single unit – one that substantially outguns the pesky Mr. Karl."

Dexicos rolled the silver ring about his finger. It was at least a size too large. He'd need to ensure it didn't slip off. "We have neither ropes nor climbing equipment. We shall have to improvise. Now, I want Smith with me up front. Place our guests in the center. Alexandros, you command a rear guard, three men. I think even Karl would find it difficult to stealthily eliminate a trio."

The lessons of millennia instructed Dexicos not to put himself in harm's way. But with Smith and Potter at his side, he need little fear physical danger. Smith possessed decades of military experience, along with several years of what was apparently now euphemistically known as "wet work." Potter's skills included much more than those of butler and sommelier. The big man's past was a mystery even to Dexicos, but had decidedly involved a significant amount of hand-to-hand combat. Dexicos felt it worth the mild risk to place himself at the head of the search in the expectation that his distant memories of the catacomb would give them the advantage in the deadly game of hide-and-seek.

Dexicos' memories might be distant, but they remained sharp. The centuries had not dulled his recollections. His first memory was of the Valley of the Kings. The desert gave way abruptly to a swath of green stretching as far north and south as the eye could see and dipping down to meet the sluggish brown ribbon of the Nile. Whoever had brought him – his father, a slave master, or perhaps the man was one and the same – had sold him to the Priest-Magi of Thebes,

Dexicos' aptitude for the thaumaturgic arts apparently manifesting at an early age.

The monumental architecture of Thebes – its towering obelisks, massive tombs, and colossal statues – dominated his memories for much of the next thousand years. It was there that he learned the eldritch mysteries, growing in knowledge and power. It was from there that he had taken his first journeys into the wider world, assigned to join embassies to fellow practitioners dwelling in places that would come to bear the names of Timbuktu, Beijing, Tibet, Ayutthaya, and many others. One of the others was K'aay-Boox, roughly a century before dynastic intrigue led to Dexicos' unforeseen and abrupt departure from Thebes.

An eventful, circuitous, world-spanning century of travel had found him in the steppes of Central Asia, where he parlayed a series of coups into an evolving status of wizard, warlord, emperor, and god. He'd ruled with an unquestioned, near omnipotence for over fifty years before a loose network of shamans and the untimely arrival of a migrating tribe of horsemen had dethroned him. Frankly, Dexicos had felt relieved. The power had grown increasingly burdensome. And correspondingly dull.

Dexicos kept a lower profile after that, building wealth and power covertly. Enjoying himself. And why not? He felt little of the effects of time. As best Dexicos could tell, he'd stopped aging sometime in his mid-forties. Every decade or so he sensed a touch of weariness. But this, he'd discovered, he could alleviate with a certain ritual and a blood sacrifice. Eventually he learned the blood sacrifice did not require complete exsanguination, though by the time he'd figured it out, he'd probably become the source of more than one regional vampire legend. Lucky for the locals, Dexicos figured; it was better him than the real thing.

So Dexicos felt a warranted confidence leading the ensemble from the chamber onto the viewing platform.

The years had not been kind. What had been a clean, discreet back way from the Chamber of Mysteries – albeit one with cleverly hidden spy holes – appeared as much a natural geological feature as the work of man. But the bridge still stood.

"Light," Dexicos said, holding out his hand. Potter gently, yet securely, deposited a bludgeon-like flashlight into his palm. The thing must weigh two pounds, of metal construction, and – Dexicos guessed after switching it on – putting out over a thousand lumens. The beam cast the bridge in high relief. Dexicos played with the switch, discovering to his satisfaction that it possessed different settings. He dialed it back down to a more moderate output; no point in running through the battery too quickly. The centuries had taught prudence.

Smith took point, crossing the bridge a couple of strides ahead of Dexicos, Potter keeping pace right behind. The bridge had once boasted rope handrails. Now a slip of the foot to left or right would send a pedestrian plunging to the unfriendly bosom of the water below if one were lucky, smashing against a protruding rock if one were not. The footing felt dry and secure, though Dexicos found himself wishing he'd chosen his footwear with a mind to fieldwork rather than fashion.

Beyond the bridge commenced the Halls of the Gods, a subterranean complex exclusive to the priestly caste, with passages and chambers specific to clergy, magi, mathematicians, and senior adepts.

It seemed the Gods had abandoned it. The entry hall had once served as a showcase of religious art, known as the Hall of Spirits for its depiction of the passage of the dead into the underworld. Now it was a linear rubble field.

"Got sign, boss," Smith said. "I make two pairs of tracks."

"Well done, Cochise," Dexicos said. "We know Karl and Snyder went this way, considering it is the only option. You want to prove you're a true Indian chief, tell me which way they went at the intersection."

Smith grunted and moved on. Dexicos followed. The parade behind him sounded like a cavalry troop trotting along a gravel road. Feet ground once ornate tile reliefs into aquarium gravel. A pity.

Apparently he wasn't the only one feeling that sentiment. "Careful, you clods," the archaeologist said. "These fragments are priceless. Salvageable if you don't turn them to dust."

Dexicos looked behind him. The archaeologist was tiptoeing along the hall, walking stick held horizontally for balance – and to keep the tip from doing further damage. One of the gunmen placed the barrel of his rifle into the archaeologist's back and shoved him stumbling forward.

The woman reached out a hand to the archaeologist's shoulder, stabilizing him. "Watch it, asshole," she said to the gunman. "You bastards have worse field awareness than freshmen." She got the archaeologist moving forward again. "Are you okay, Jim?"

Jim nodded.

"Quiet in the rear," Dexicos said. "James Allison I know from my research. But you, madam…you are…?"

"Professor May Chen. That is who I am. And you are –"

Dexicos cut her off before she could reach the presumed insult. "Many things, my dear Professor, and I've been called all of them. Now, please bear with us patiently, and this will all end soon. Or do not bear with us patiently, and it will end for you much sooner. And you, my gentlemen adventurers, please treat our guests with a touch more courtesy until such time as they deserve harsher treatment. Agreed? Good."

"Boss? They went this way," Smith said, barrel of his rifle pointing to the rightward passage of the intersection. "Two sets of tracks to the right and one to the left, but that one's both coming and going. I figure one of them, Snyder probably, went a few yards down that way, then switched back." Smith had continued along while the rest had stopped at Professor Allison's interruption.

"Excellent work, Smith," Dexicos said. "An extra eagle feather for you."

The passage had not suffered the same degree of damage as the Hall of Spirits. It was still a mess, but at least the noise dropped. How could a hunting party capture any quarry while sounding like a family of elephants on holiday?

The Hall of Years boasted stelae depicting the important doings (either real or polite fictions) of the kings and notables of K'aay-Boox. Some of the stones still stood. Most had toppled, succumbing to the years. Unlike Dexicos, who remained standing and would continue to do so, no matter what the adversarial hand of Time threw at him.

"So much for Snyder," Smith said a few moments later. "Appears your man Karl was already armed. Nobody thought to frisk him?"

Dexicos frowned. "What's this?" he asked, approaching Smith, who was crouched over the corpse, playing the beam of his carbine's tac-light up and down it.

"Look here, boss. From the size of the hole, I'd guess a .45," Smith said, shining his light upon a bloody entry wound.

Presumably then, Karl now had two weapons. Dexicos cursed at himself. The wisdom of centuries had not, it seemed, taught him that removing one gun from a captive did not mean that captive was not concealing a second. That kind of slip could be viewed by his men as carelessness, carelessness as incompetence, and incompetence as weakness. That would never do.

"Alexandros," Dexicos snapped.

"Sir," Alexandros said, working his way up from the rear of the procession.

"You confiscated a pistol from Karl. A .38, I believe."

"Yes, sir," Alexandros said. Dexicos noted the man had

adopted a rigid posture, a perhaps unconscious return to parade-ground discipline while undergoing a dressing down.

"Did you frisk Karl?"

"No, sir."

"Did it not occur to you that a man concealing one weapon might well be concealing another?" Dexicos loaded the question with practiced scorn. And after all, he was paying Alexandros for security. An employer should be able to rely upon his employee to provide the services paid for. He shouldn't be expected to oversee every little aspect. This lapse was Alexandros' fault.

Alexandros said nothing.

"I expect rather more from you, Alexandros. The remainder of this little escapade should afford you a chance for redemption. Otherwise I fear I will need to reconsider our arrangement upon our return to New York." *There, sorted.* "Now, please return to your post. Please advise your compatriots that our quarry may now have both a pistol and the late Snyder's weapon."

Smith rose from his haunches and continued down the hall, his tac-light fanning ahead of him. "Gets kind of confusing down here, boss," he said. "Looks like Karl took to his heels. See, dirt kicked up all over. Killed Snyder, took his rifle, and hightailed it. So at least we don't have to worry about him popping up from cover and hosing down this hallway. But look here. All kinds of strange marks. Never seen shit like that."

Dexicos had. "Cast for blood sign. Karl will be wounded. Count on it." He hoped he was correct. He needed to reaffirm his hyper-competence, reinforce a sense of omniscience. He could feel events spinning more and more out of his control with each of Karl's slippery escapes.

"You called it, boss," Smith said. "Got a splash over here."

Dexicos looked over Smith's shoulder. Not a great deal of blood. His summoning did not appear to have inflicted a fatal wound – at least not here. But the splatters of red dampening the floor of the Hall of Years should be sufficient for his needs.

"Some room, if you please, Smith," Dexicos said. After Smith had moved a few steps aside, Dexicos used the heel of a shoe to scratch a circle in the dust and detritus around the line of blood drops. He squatted down, placing the head of the dog creature mounted on the silver ring directly in contact with a splash of blood. He closed his eyes and exerted his will, invoking the Spirit of the Hunt that dwelled in the ring. Summoning the Spirit of the Hunt required little ritual or ceremony. Tracing blood spoor was what it existed for. It fairly ached for invocation. The circle, the will – and above all – the blood, sufficed to draw it forth.

The ring on Dexicos' finger seemed to grow slowly heavier, as if some buoyant substance leaked from containment. Dexicos knew that if he placed the ring on a scale now, it would weigh the same as prior to the invocation, yet the illusion persisted.

A nebulous mist accreted within the circle. Over the course of half a minute, it took on a semblance of form: a low-slung canine of fluctuating feature and dimension that shifted erratically through phases from near invisibility to wispy ground fog to dense cloud and back again, though never congealing to anything truly substantial.

The Wraith Hound lowered its nose to the blood, appearing to draw in a deep draft of the scent. A pinkish hue suffused the mist form, then dissipated. The featureless head swiveled up and back, appearing to focus on Dexicos. The magus could almost hear an anxious whine emanate from the Wraith Hound.

"Seek," Dexicos said and scuffed the circle with the toe of his shoe. He'd have to replace the pair anyway once this debacle ended, so to hell with the creamy leather finish.

The Wraith Hound drifted away, nose to the floor. The flashlight beams crisscrossing through the shifting consistency of mist enhanced the dreamlike sense of unreality the Wraith Hound always carried with it. At times, it could be nothing more than a miasma arising from a damp section of limestone. At others, a nigh demonic apparition.

Dexicos loved summoning the Wraith Hound.

The hound led them down the Hall of Years without hesitation, locked on not to the scent of Karl's blood, but to its essence. It could follow Karl through water, even through solid stone.

It led only a short way before pivoting to the left at the head of a stairway leading down. The stairway, like so much of the rest of the catacomb, had seen better days. Rubble, fallen blocks of stone, collapsed fill earth, and chunks of limestone had congested the descent. But some more immediate event had forcibly cleared a pathway.

The Wraith Hound slipped onto the stairway and down, the severity of the remaining obstacles presenting no hindrance to its insubstantial form. It proceeded straight down, as if the stairway remained intact and unobstructed. It flowed through cracks and around boulders only to reform its shape at the next clear area in its path.

"Follow as fast as you can," Dexicos said. "The Wraith Hound will not slow to let us keep pace."

Following at speed, however, struck Dexicos as a daunting prospect. Dexicos supposed he could tuck into a ball and hurl himself down through the wreckage, following the path recently blazed. That looked…painful. Not to mention hard on the attire.

Smith showed no hesitation. He ducked beneath the lintel, stepped onto the first tread – that one cracked and canted at a near forty-five-degree angle – then turned sideways to fit through a passageway smashed through rubble. He braced himself with heavily muscled arms pressed against the stairway walls and lowered himself farther into the sloping, disordered chute, dislodging protruding bits of stone as he went.

Dexicos shrugged out of his jacket and handed it behind him to Potter, knowing the man would fold it neatly and find some way to preserve it. His trousers, however, he knew to be doomed.

No help for it. He followed Smith.

CHAPTER 19

Karl scrambled along on hands and knees. Or, rather, hand and knees. He didn't want to risk a light, so he kept one hand out in front of him, feeling his way forward through the dark – a darkness lessened unhelpfully by the flashes of gunfire behind him. All that these firefly bursts accomplished were intermittent reddish glimmers that illuminated nothing.

So Karl crawled in the dark, ignoring the discomfort of cold stone bruising his already damaged knees and shins. His legs still worked, that was the essential point, though it could easily have been otherwise. The memory of that *thing* closing about him remained fresh. Those ribs, or limbs, or whatever they were had folded around him, moving simultaneously with both the precision of one of those elaborate seventeenth-century clockwork mechanisms and the organic smoothness of an insect.

Karl disliked the imprecision of calling the creature a

thing. Even while he replayed the event, he worked on names, finally settling on Bandersnatch. The *thing* had been frumious enough to warrant the appellation.

The plunge through the collapsed stairway must have prevented the frumious Bandersnatch from simply folding itself further, crushing Karl to a bloody paste within. Instead, the Bandersnatch had to deal with a tumbling, crashing descent that taxed even its bodily control. Karl had been slammed and tossed within, like an agate in a rock polisher. The cage hadn't entirely surrounded him. In addition to being hurled repeatedly against the hard, chitinous structure of the being itself, he'd also bounced off bits of stone that protruded through the spaces between the "bars" of his cage while in an upward or freefall portion of his tumble and had been slammed against the remains of the stairs at the bottom of the fall, before repeating the cycle. Again and again.

Karl had tucked himself into a ball, hands over his head, hoping that he would not suffer any catastrophic blow to his head or spine. The fall had seemed interminable, and he'd felt every bruise, every gash torn into arms and legs. The sling of the carbine he'd taken from the man he'd shot parted on contact with something that sliced into Karl's shoulder. The weapon bounced along within the cage for a couple more revolutions, smacking once against his ankle before disappearing, probably slipping between the bars. The .45 tucked at his waist shoved and bruised his flesh, and every object in his pockets took little ball peen hammer shots at his inner thigh. He'd slipped the Jade Dagger through his belt after snagging it from the altar, and he could feel its point make occasional jabs into his outer thigh through his increasingly shredded jeans.

And then the pummeling stopped. The Bandersnatch rolled to a stop – into the stabbing beams of flashlights. The cage opened, and Karl crawled out, keeping low. This armed mob before him must be the narcos from near the dig site. Had to be. They'd kill him without hesitation, yet at the moment they appeared a welcome, friendly sight. Not friendly enough that he'd stand up and greet them though. His only thought was to stay low, get through them. Let that fucking Bandersnatch draw their full attention.

And that was what he did. None of the narcos appeared to pay him any heed as he crawled, bruised and bleeding, through their midst and out.

The gunfire behind him stopped. Karl did not. He didn't know where he was, had no idea where he was going. But – shaken, battered, rattled, and disoriented or not – he had to keep moving, find a place to hide or defend. Stay alive. And then? His job. May Chen and Jim Allison remained in the hands of Mago D. The rest of the camp were hostages. They were his responsibility, their release up to him. That was what he'd do.

Somehow.

His progress brought him brushing against a wall. With the gunfire ended, the distraction of the Bandersnatch might be ended as well. At least one of the narcos must have seen him. Keeping low and out of sight no longer seemed as important as speed.

Leaning against the wall for support, Karl got to his feet. He took a step. It hurt. Every part of the step hurt; his leg protested from ankle all the way up to his hip. But the leg worked. So he took another step.

Walk it off, soldier.

Karl pushed on, gaining speed, hoping he didn't stumble into anything. He did not yet wish to risk a light. His right hand brushed along the wall, helping him keep his bearings.

What had that *thing* been? Where had it come from? It wasn't of the earth no matter how many Charles Dodgson names Karl loaded it with. Alien? From some other dimension?

Nietzsche might not have been so keen on thinking cosmically rather than individually if he'd known the cosmos contained horrors such as that – demon. Karl didn't really like the term demon, with the hellish connotations of the word. But it seemed to fit. What had he stumbled upon? Was it connected to this place? Or was it somehow in league with Mago D?

Karl shook off the speculation. It wasn't pointless. It was untimely, a distraction from the need of the moment: survival.

His right hand lost contact with the wall. Karl stopped. He groped, delineating the outlines of a doorway by touch. The narcos would be in pursuit soon if they weren't already. Fleeing in a straight line violated all the basic tenets of evasion. So Karl went through the doorway, remembering to duck and probing ahead with an outstretched hand.

Nothing obstructed his passage. The floor felt level,

more level than the partially worked tunnel he'd been traversing. After a few steps Karl decided a light would be undetectable by any pursuit. To his relief, the mini-light had survived his spin cycle in the demonic washing machine. The narrow beam showed a cleanly cut hallway, about ten feet wide and six high. Karl put a hand atop his head, palm down, and could feel the ceiling brush against the hairs on the back of his fingers. *Tight fit.*

A series of evenly spaced alcoves had been cut, offset, into either side of the hall. The upper half of each alcove, starting about waist high, pushed three feet farther into the stone, creating some sort of workbench or desk. Dust, crumbled bits of pottery, and implements in various states of completeness littered the workspaces. Who had worked down here? Was it a school? Some sort of training area? Artisans' workshops? Had the stelae Karl had seen been chiseled and carved down here?

Again, Karl shoved the speculation aside, kept moving. He needed to stay a step ahead –

A chill dampness touched the back of his ankle, as if he'd backed up near an open freezer or into a high mountain fog bank. Karl spun. He grunted, took a step back.

"My day for weird," he said.

A wavering form, a sort of condensed, molded vapor, crouched before him in the shape of a dog. One paw, from which bits of mist drifted away to dissipate into nothing, was raised before it. The muzzle thrust forward. The mist dog quivered, but otherwise didn't move.

"Not straight out of Baskerville, then," Karl said. He

bent at the knees and leaned forward, holding his left hand out, palm down and knuckles curled. "Who's a good boy?" The clenching of his hand widened several of the cuts on his hand. Blood oozed, trickled between his knuckles, and dripped to the floor. The dog's muzzle snuffled closer, the body elongating. The nose proved predictably damp. Drops of blood splashed through it. The swirling vapor composing the nose took on a rosy hue that spread up the muzzle and throughout the head. The mist dog lifted its nose to the ceiling and opened its jaws from which issued a thin, spectral baying.

Some sort of bloodhound, then. A tracking dog, Karl figured. Had to have been sent by Mago D. Meaning he'd probably been responsible for the frumious Bandersnatch. Meaning also he was the real deal. *A fucking wizard.* The man holding Professors Allison and Chen and keeping the rest of the crew hostage, the man Karl would have to match wits with, was a wizard. Fine. More things in heaven and earth, Horatio. Karl would simply have to adjust his expectations. And whatever surprises Mago D had tucked away up his sleeves, he was just a man. Karl had yet to meet a man he couldn't tackle. He could devise a method of dealing with the hocus and the pocus. Or perhaps just could put a bullet in the wizard. Simpler.

There was also the matter of the platoon Mago D had brought with him. And the small army of narcos infesting the tunnels. Karl had his work cut out for him.

The ghostly howl faded. So did the ghostly dog. Coils of vapor rose and spread from the central mass, disrupting the shape and leaving an amorphous fog that continued to shred itself into nothing. With Karl found, it seemed the magical bloodhound's purpose had been fulfilled.

Back to the Downs.

Karl straightened. A tracking dog should have a handler. But this critter had been alone, which meant something had gone wrong for Mago D. The wizard showed fallibility. Good.

Still, fallible or not, presumably Mago D could follow his dog. Leading him here. Karl scanned his surroundings again. Should he set an ambush here? No. Too open. No cover. Perhaps he could backtrack into the main passage, continue on a bit and wait for Mago D to enter this hallway, then come up from the rear. Depending on the disposition of Mago D's troops and captives, Karl might have a chance to snatch May and Jim. Or shoot and scoot, whittle away the opposition. Whatever he was to do, he had to get moving.

Perhaps if Karl's eardrums hadn't endured such prolonged abuse, he'd have heard them coming earlier. Instead, the only warning he received was the light of mingling flashlight beams lighting one side of the hallway entry. Belatedly, the sound of scuffing footsteps followed.

Karl turned away and commenced a limping jog farther into the hallway. He scanned for a side passage or a collapsed wall or a stack of unworked stone blocks. Anything to provide cover or concealment. He saw nothing, nothing other than the workstations lining the walls, continuing as far as his light would show.

A rifle cracked, and a bullet sprayed stone chips from

the wall to Karl's right. Shouts followed. Karl considered flicking off the mini-light. He'd be less of a target that way, but he'd have to slow his pace. And he might miss seeing a way out or at the very least something to put between himself and the bullets.

He decided to risk the light. Another shot winged by him, that hypersonic, angry insect whine unmistakable. Karl neither flinched nor slowed. The thought of getting shot in the back irked him, but the probability of getting shot in the front while doing something stupid – say, spinning around and opening up with his pistol without the benefit of cover – troubled him more. It wasn't the thought of dying that concerned him – a streak of fatalism ran deep within him – it was the manner.

The shouting redoubled. Bullets ricocheted from the floor behind him; more zipped past. Karl kept on, his limp no longer acute, trying to ignore the lethal swarm but knowing one of the narcos would soon either get lucky or have ranged him properly.

A dark rectangle, foreshortened into a parallelogram, opened in the wall to Karl's left. He angled his approach and practically threw himself through the opening. His right shoulder absorbed the impact as he skittered into the wall of a narrow passage. He righted himself and got his legs moving again. The mini-light showed a cleared, unadorned passage, a merely utilitarian back way, lacking the artistry of the grander halls. Like an adit connecting the main lodes in mines. That simplicity suited Karl fine; nothing to obstruct his sprint.

His legs protested. Bruised and lacerated, his limbs wanted a rest. But that state of affairs had been rather common for the last decade or so. Karl had pushed his body beyond standard tolerance limits in war zones around the globe and over the course of various scrapes in civilian life. His legs could handle it.

Karl hoped he'd put some more space between himself and his pursuit. The narcos would interfere with each other if they tried to sprint down the hall, swinging elbows and rifles establishing an upper speed limit. If not, if one of the narco gunmen rounded the doorway from the hall within the next few moments, the narrow confines of the adit would help him channel his fire. A ricochet off the wall would do for Karl as easily as a cleanly aimed shot center mass.

The shot did not come. Instead the passage opened into a rectangular chamber, a sort of meeting of ways. Across it the narrow passage continued on. To the right, a broad hall – almost a boulevard in comparison – commenced, sloping up. Whatever had been to the left was no longer apparent, the ceiling having collapsed. A jumble of masonry and stone had fanned out into the chamber, blocking easy passage. Anyone crossing would have to pick his way through ankle-twisting rocks and around shoulder-high boulders.

That suited Karl.

He wended through the detritus until he found a pair of boulders that suited his purpose. He worked in behind them and turned to face his pursuit. The boulders leaned snugly against each other, providing excellent cover from incoming rounds. The juncture of the two rocks offered an ideal rest for Karl's outstretched arms and his .45. To his left he could sprint for the boulevard, though it would first require navigating more of the rubble field. Or he could turn around and run down the continuation of the utility corridor. Either way he had routes of egress, "stick and move" replacing "shoot, move, communicate."

Karl patted his pocket, feeling for the spare magazine. It had faithfully remained with him through his chaotic peregrinations. He thumbed off the mini-light and pocketed it. Then he braced the pistol on the boulders and waited.

The narcos didn't force him to wait long. Their wavering lights mingled and separated, a miniature klieg light display. Again Karl performed the exercise of averting his eyes, preserving his night vision against the threat of the oncoming dazzle. He let them come on. Their advantages were numbers and weapon range. His, cover. The balance of advantages tilted on a fulcrum of time and distance. Karl waited until the front rank grew near enough to enter the effective range of his pistol. That, he figured, tipped the balance to roughly equal: his cover offsetting their numerical superiority. At least, the balance was as equal as it was going to get. He couldn't call a timeout and negotiate new rules for the contest. Any illusions he'd ever had about fair play had long since been beaten from him by roadside bombs, ambushes, and drone-launched missiles.

The first narco entered the meeting of ways, the adit so narrow they'd proceeded in single file. From the movement of their lights, Karl had deduced a pairing: one narco following the first of the pairing so closely he could provide covering fire over the first man's shoulder.

The difficulty remained aiming. Looking directly at the targets meant looking directly into the cones of their flashlights, which would be tantamount to blindness. Karl would have to rely on instincts honed by years of experience. He let the first target pass into his peripheral vision, let out a half breath, and applied the last half pound of force with his trigger finger.

The muzzle flash splashed crazed shadows among the boulders. The crack interrupted the susurrus of rubber-soled footsteps and tense-nerved breathing.

"*Chinga!*" someone yelled. The lead flashlight fell to the ground. The utility hall lit up with a fusillade of muzzle flashes. Karl ducked. The barrage filled the chamber with the echoing percussion of rifle fire and the impact of bullets on stone. A scream punctuated the hammering cacophony as friendly fire claimed a casualty.

"*Alto!*" a female voice yelled above the din, then again as the firing continued, "*Alto, bola de pendejos.*"

A couple more shots smacked against Karl's redoubt, then stopped.

Karl popped up and fired again before the narcos could coordinate an assault. He didn't know if he hit anything. But he got a response: a second fusillade commenced. He grinned as another bellow of shocked pain joined the cracks and bangs.

Then the female voice called again. And the narcos moved in. It wasn't the most tactically elegant of entries, but with their numbers, it didn't have to be. Karl fired off double taps, hoping to stem the initial wave. An acrid pong suffused his nostrils. Hot brass bounced and clattered about him. A spent cartridge lodged in the collar of his shirt, scorching the back of his neck. The slide of the Taurus locked back, the magazine empty. A couple more flashlights had fallen beneath Karl's assault, the beams now shining, unmoving, at ground level. But more gunmen came on, spreading out into the meeting of ways. The narcos fanned out, taking cover and trying to outflank him.

Shit.

Karl thumbed the release, dropping the spent magazine. With his left hand he retrieved the spare mag and slammed it home. During those two seconds, he considered his options. He discarded the notion of running for the continuation of the adit. He'd be too exposed. They'd probably nail him in the back before he reached it, and certainly would once he entered the featureless, extended linear kill box. He'd have to make for the boulevard. At least he had more cover along the way.

Karl stood. He fired two quick shots to his left, hoping to at least suppress the narcos whose field of fire intersected his route to the boulevard. He moved in a bent-over shuffle and dove to the next covering boulder. Unsteady flashlight cones caught and lost him as he went. Bullets sang and sparked in his wake.

The boulder he sheltered behind did not possess the same degree of protection as the paired boulders of his first redoubt. Karl got to one knee and faced back the way he'd come. He scooted in closer to the rock, feeling exposed as the narcos worked around to his flank. More shots came his way, some obviously intended only to keep his head down, others with more lethal intent. A couple skipped and sparked near his right leg. The narcos were closing more efficiently than he'd hoped, moving unhesitatingly through the rubble field, ignoring the risks of turned ankles and return fire. Karl sent a round their way, just to keep them honest. The incoming slowed them momentarily, at least those in the rear.

To his three o'clock came a sustained burst, three or four rifleman firing as fast as they could squeeze the triggers. That suggested covering fire. One or more narcos would be scrambling toward him beneath that horizontal hail. Karl crept around his boulder, leaned from cover and looked. Two were coming in a crouching trot, sans light, perhaps hoping that turning their flashlights off would allow them to approach unnoticed and relying on the flashlights behind them to illuminate the path. But those same guiding flashlights also lit them up well enough for Karl to target.

He put a round in each, going for center mass but settling for one kill shot and one disabling hit. Then he moved again, darting for the next, even smaller boulder. The narcos could see him go. A near miss punched a hole through the flapping fabric of the remains of his shirt, right below his hip. Another grazed his boot heel as he lifted his foot for another lunging stride. The force almost overbalanced him. Karl caught himself on his left palm against the top of his target rock. He threw himself over the top. He failed to entirely clear the boulder, his upper thighs grazing against the rough surface as he passed over and turning what he'd hoped to be a tuck and roll into a flop and wriggle. Rising ground, noticeably less rubble strewn, met him on the far side.

Karl scrambled once again to his feet and turned about-face, leaning forward against the boulder for support and to get as low as possible. The rock barely reached higher than his lower ribs. The narcos came on, inexorably, spreading out into an arc. The boulder only offered protection from a narrow section of the arc.

The woman's voice came again, from somewhere behind the gleaming band of light. The shooting stopped. "*Mas cerca*," she said, the words clear in the sudden silence.

Not getting out of this one. See how many I can take with me.

Karl selected a target. No one was requesting his surrender. They were simply getting closer, intending to finish the job more efficiently, stop wasting bullets now that he was a lone fish in a small barrel. No point prolonging it.

He squeezed the trigger. The pistol bucked against his palm. The target emitted a grunt and sat down. Karl moved his point of aim to the next man and squeezed again.

Nothing. Empty.

"It's been a laugh," he said. He dropped the pistol and tugged loose his big jungle knife. That elicited a wave of cruel guffaws from the firing squad.

Karl's last choice was left, right, or back over the top. He'd just decided on right when gunfire erupted once more.

The shock Karl felt was the shock of feeling no pain. He hadn't been hit. He hadn't even been shot at. The firing wasn't coming from the narcos. It emerged from the utility tunnel he and the narcos had recently exited.

Mago D, you wizard, you pulled a rabbit out of a hat.

Karl turned around and ran up the boulevard.

CHAPTER 20

Dexicos Megistos watched his men roll up the drug gang's firing line. Even without having trained together, most of his hirelings worked with a coordinated precision that bespoke years of ingrained military training. Smith and Alexandros had performed a tolerable job of recruiting, especially considering the time constraints. He'd never tell them that – a fat pay envelope was praise enough – but he recognized it.

Two-man fire teams continued to exit the narrow tunnel ahead of him, entering the chamber beyond and engaging the retreating narcos. There was something familiar about the place. It appeared to Dexicos rather worse for wear, though he could not yet get a good look at it from where he stood near the rear, next to Potter, Festo, the prisoners, and one gunman whose name he hadn't bothered to learn.

"Move in," Dexicos called out. He slipped back into the

jacket Potter handed him, the garment still pristine as expected. "Faster. Get some people after Karl immediately." Dexicos rather doubted anyone involved in the firefight could hear him, let alone would pay any attention. But the need to assert his will underpinned many of his actions. He knew himself with a degree of precision that would give a psychiatrist a clinical case of envy.

The arctic cold that engulfed his finger had announced the return of the Wraith Hound to its silver prison. Or kennel. Dexicos had not been overly disappointed. Once they'd lost contact with the hound as it bounded weightlessly through the ruined stair, Dexicos had despaired of catching up to it before it had tracked down Karl. In fact, he kept the homecoming to himself.

Discovering the remains of his initial summoning had been a greater blow. At first. Once he'd realized that Karl could not have been responsible for its defeat, that in fact another group shared the catacombs with him, and that this group was likely in pursuit of Karl as well, Dexicos felt cheered. He offered some oblique suggestions that it was all his doing. The plan then became to follow this other group – presumably the narcotraffickers he'd overheard Miss Chen mention in the tent the moment before he'd introduced himself. Let these cartel soldiers hunt down Karl; then his boys would take them down in turn. Preferably before they killed Karl; Dexicos did not wish to risk harm to the Jade Dagger. A stray bullet could shatter the artifact. And where would that leave his scheme?

So now he encouraged his troops.

The narcos, caught entirely off guard, put up little resistance. Those who lived ran for the continuation of the adit, some sprinting all out, others, more disciplined perhaps, turning to offer a semblance of a fighting withdrawal. Dexicos' troops moved forward in teams from cover to cover, driving the narcos on while taking minimal risks. Why should they? Killing drug dealers wasn't the contract. Still, the contract might require adjustment. Dexicos considered.

His moment of contemplation was the one May Chen chose for her escape attempt. She turned on Potter, snapping up a kick Dexicos guessed she'd learned in the gymnasium at some sort of aerobic kickboxing class. She possessed both speed and flexibility. But unfortunately for Miss Chen, the exercise class had not imbued her with any true martial art skills. Even more unfortunate for Miss Chen was that Potter was well versed in multiple martial arts disciplines, as well as built along the general lines of a forklift: a solid mass with a low center of gravity.

With quiet efficiency, Potter interposed an arm, grasping May Chen's ankle and hoisting her off the ground.

Professor Allison deemed it the part of a gentleman to add his efforts. He hefted his walking stick directly into the crotch of the unknown gunman. The gunman folded in upon himself and fell to his knees, his rifle swinging free on its sling while both hands clutched at his wounded pride. Then Professor Allison laid into Potter, driving the folded seat of the stick into Potter's midsection with an impressive thump.

At least it impressed Dexicos. It seemed to create little impression on Potter, who registered the merest grunt. The butler neither budged nor released his grip on Miss Chen.

Festo entered the fracas. When Professor Allison lifted the walking stick back up over his head for a second blow at Potter, Festo reached out and plucked it from his hands. Allison, unbalanced, staggered back, tripping over the still doubled over gunman. They both went down in a heap.

Potter, still holding Miss Chen dangling a foot above the ground, took two steps, leaned over, and with his free hand snatched up Professor Allison by the fabric of his vest and shirt collar. The professor, substantially heavier than Miss Chen, only rose up on his toes rather than swinging freely.

"Neatly done, Potter," Dexicos said. A good butler was, in his estimation, a rare commodity. More rare than competent killers like Alexandros or Smith, and thus worth the expenditure of the occasional attaboy.

The gunman rose to his feet, the extended wince beginning to release its hold on his face. He reacquired his grip on the carbine and menaced Professor Allison, fury replacing pain.

"You there," Dexicos said, "let us not kill our hostages just yet."

The gunman shifted his gaze from Professor Allison to Dexicos. "Burgher," he said, the tone indicating he was nearly as aggrieved at being referred to as "you there" as at Professor Allison's attack. He blinked, looked back to Professor Allison, then his weapon. He lowered it, seeming to realize he'd been caught in an impropriety, like a schoolboy discovered yanking the pigtail of the girl in the desk before him. Burgher was another of the heavily tattooed contingent of the hired mercenaries, a hair over six feet tall and approaching Smith and Alexandros levels of muscularity. He had tousled red hair and about a week's worth of ginger scruff on his cheeks. Couldn't be a day over thirty years old. "Skip Burgher, sir. My friends call me Scratch."

"I'm sure they do, Mr. Burgher," Dexicos said. He dismissed Burgher from consideration as he would a boxed chardonnay. "Now then. Miss Chen, Professor Allison, let us have no more of that sort of behavior."

"*Professor* Chen," said Miss Chen. "Say it with me: *Professor.*" The indignation with which she delivered the remarks was somewhat lessened by her inversion, her hair sweeping back and forth across the detritus of the floor.

Dexicos offered a smile and slight bow. "If you good professors would give me your parole, I'll ask Potter to set you down."

"No," Miss Chen said.

"Very well. Mr. Burgher, kindly put a bullet through Professor Allison's heart."

The mercenary shrugged, then raised his weapon.

"Wait!" said Miss Chen. Professor Allison remained speechless, struggling uselessly in Potter's grasp. "You have my parole."

"Thank you, Professor Chen. Stand down, Scratch." Dexicos addressed Potter. "Please set Professor Chen down.

And, should Professor Allison be so good as to give me his parole, let go of him as well."

Professor Allison nodded weakly. "I won't try to escape."

There, sorted. Now, Dexicos considered, he had a choice to make.

He moved on into the Processional Antechamber. He'd gotten his bearings now, recognizing the place despite the wreckage. In the swirling lights he could make out three dead narcos as well as one of his own.

The gunfire came now in only sporadic bursts. Dexicos' men had driven the narcos from the Processional Antechamber and occupied positions before the continuation of the utility hall, content with having driven off the enemy and securing the room.

"Smith," Dexicos said, "Alexandros, please attend me." He gazed about while he waited for his captains to arrive. The cluttered, cavernous room failed to bring on clear memories, the damage from the collapsed corridor having exceeded some recognizability threshold that allowed a place to trigger memory. Too bad. He recalled, though without clarity, that the Meeting of Ways had once been a grand foyer or antechamber.

Alexandros and Smith stood at ease before him. He could feel the heat rising from the barrels of their rifles. Neither man displayed any overt emotion, though Dexicos thought he detected the faintest of smiles on each, the merest trace of upcurled lips.

Men never change. Being on the sunny side of an

uneven fight brings out a certain good-natured predation, like that of a well-fed cat given a wounded mouse.

"We're going to split our forces," Dexicos said.

"Sir?" Smith asked. "The fuck?"

Alexandros said nothing, no doubt still smarting from the last ass chewing he'd received from Dexicos and eager to retain enough buttock to sit down on.

"Commendable brevity, Smith," Dexicos said. "To answer your query, I've determined that the remaining narcotics traffickers constitute a clear and present danger to our mission. Either during the search for or the capture of Karl, they might interfere. Or afterwards, they might inhibit our exfiltration. Or a stray bullet might *damage my fucking Jade Dagger!*"

Dexicos enjoyed seeing Smith rock back a few millimeters on his heels. "So, if I've explained myself well enough to my employees?"

"No questions from me, boss," Alexandros said.

Smith merely nodded.

"Then send the troops after the narcos. Put Scratch in charge; he seems psychotic enough. I want you two with me."

"Scratch?" Alexandros asked.

"Mr. Burgher. The ginger with the playing cards tattooed across his arms."

"Yes, sir," Smith said. "Might be some…pushback from the boys. They didn't hire on for combat."

Dexicos *tsked*. "Offer them double. Any who decline such generosity are free to leave my employ. Immediately.

I'm sure they can find a way out. And a ride back to the airport. I understand Über is ubiquitous in the jungle." He turned off the sarcasm and leveled a cold, flat stare at Smith and Alexandros. "Move. Now, if you please. Karl is gaining a lead."

CHAPTER 21

Karl ran up the boulevard, the slope imperceptibly growing steeper, providing a workout for the glutes and hamstrings that he might have appreciated on any less taxing day. His mini-light suggested the boulevard had once been some sort of elaborate, formal passage. The sheer size of it indicated it had been an important route intended for important people on important occasions, the steep inclination suggesting a metaphorical as well as actual ascent. The footing was dry and even, consisting of closely set paving stones that might once have been incised with images. The ceiling was high and vaulted.

Vaulting ambition, which o'er leaps itself and falls on the other side, Karl thought. Then again, he remembered, Shakespeare had also written "Ambition, the soldier's virtue." The man had known how to come down on every side of an issue. He shook off the digression. His mother ensuring that his childhood was steeped in the classics offered certain benefits. Helping him navigate through an ancient Mayan catacomb while pursued by monsters, wizards, and gunmen probably wasn't one of them.

The gunfire diminished in both frequency and volume as he neared the summit of the boulevard. He stopped when he reached the top. There didn't appear to be anywhere farther to go. The boulevard ended in a sort of short plaza or rectangular cul-de-sac. The walls on either side displayed age-weathered images, some of which Karl recognized as various and sundry gods of the Mayan pantheon. Ahead rose only a dead end, the wall unadorned, seemingly untouched by tools, only bare, rough stone meandering in a sort of vertical wave pattern.

Shit. No cover up here. Terrible spot for a last stand. Not that he would make much of a stand with only his jungle knife.

Then he noted a break in the wave pattern near the left side of the plaza. He hustled over for a closer examination. The wall, he discovered, was thin, surprisingly thin: a granular, pockmarked stone varying in width from maybe a foot to the thickness of his palm. And it only partially blocked the rear of the plaza, covering about three-quarters of it starting from the right side. Another wall of the same type of rugose carbonate rock commenced from the left side of the plaza, but about four feet deeper in, and ran back to the right, passing behind the other wall, suggesting the entry to some sort of labyrinth.

And me without my ball of twine.

Karl didn't hesitate. Running away galled him. He had a

job to do and people relying on him to do it. People back there, not somewhere ahead of him in this maze. But taking on the assorted thugs below with only a knife was suicidal. Let the narcos and Mago D's boys whittle each other down. The survivors would come in pursuit later. Meanwhile, he'd take advantage of the respite to find an edge, locate a good spot for an ambush. Something. He'd find something. Or he'd make something.

No victor believes in chance.

"Damn straight, Nietzsche," he muttered.

It did prove to be a sort of labyrinth, formed of wavy curtains of delicate, frangible rock. At the second turning Karl nearly stumbled over a scattering of stone fragments from a hole in the rock that might have allowed a dog or small child to crawl through, further evidence of the relatively delicate nature of the walls. The surroundings induced a close, almost pelagic sense of claustrophobia. Karl wouldn't have been surprised to find fossils of extinct marine species embedded in the walls. He didn't stop for an inspection.

The third turning offered options to the right or left of a diagonal wall. Karl chose right.

The silence contributed to the feeling of deep, aquatic immersion. The overlapping walls formed ideal sound-proofing baffles. If the gun battle had renewed itself down below, Karl doubted he would have heard it. Though with his hearing, the bar was set rather low.

A short length of wall – made even shorter by the collapse of its last yard or so into a heap of shards – opened into a tall, narrow chamber with additional limbs of the labyrinth opening to the left and right. A ledge or stone platform abutted the far wall, at about chest height. Scintillant flickers and gleams cast back the beam of Karl's mini-light. He moved closer for a better look.

A dazzling ossuary met Karl's eyes. Skulls and bones lay across the surface of the ledge, as if on exhibit. The orbits of the skulls bore glittering crystals, brilliant fire opals, vibrant amethysts, and other gems beyond Karl's limited store of mineralogical lore, while incised golden ideographs covered the remaining surface of the skulls. Malachite filled elaborate, flowing incisions in femurs. Jade dots traced the edges of yellowed pelvises. Gilded arm bones crossed others intaglioed with silver. Gleaming heaps of gemstones lay amidst the remnants of smaller bones gradually disintegrating into dust, perhaps one day to become a constituent part of the limestone beneath.

It was like a scene from *The Thousand and One Nights*, one of the adventures of Sinbad the Sailor. The thought *I'm rich* mingled with *Professor Allison would prefer to see the site untouched. So would May.* And that cut short any chance Karl would waste time in a state of amazed awe and greed. Neither archaeologist would get a chance to see this if he didn't get off his ass and rescue them.

A glance down the other two exits from the room told Karl that this chamber wasn't the only burial site. From either side the sparkle of jewels reflected the beam from his mini-light. If he had time to reconnoiter a section of the labyrinth, perhaps he could set a surprise or two for the pursuit. But first…

A scattering of thumbnail-size fire opals rested in a mound of powdered bone. A pocketful of those might go some way to recompensing him for the injuries of the day. Professor Allison paid him well, but the contract included no contingency for combat pay. The casual interest in archaeology that his proximity to the dig had engendered failed to curtail his inclination to snatch a handful of loose loot.

Hand extended to scoop up the gemstones, Karl stepped to the ledge. And right into the pit trap that pivoted open beneath his feet. He dropped, the shock of the sudden fall freezing his lungs in mid breath and shooting panic signals through his nervous system. Then the drop halted, Karl's body wedged into the trap at his hips. The hinges of the mechanism had not, it appeared, endured the centuries in pristine condition.

Karl swore, then chuckled. *Should have seen that coming.* Apparently it wasn't only pride that preceded a fall. Greed also got its shots in. At least greed not accompanied by sufficient caution.

He placed his hands on either side of the pit and pushed. Something caught on the underside of the pit. He could feel his jeans slipping down a fraction of an inch. Something on his belt, then, was the culprit. Karl let himself slip back down. By tightening his abdomen and shifting his hips slightly, he was able to fit a hand into the pit and feel around his waist. He got hold of the hilt of his jungle knife.

Gingerly, he drew it free of the sheath. Taking pains not to slice himself on the razor edge, he lifted it free and set it beside him on the edge of the pit. He started to lift himself again, then hesitated, remembering he had another knife stuck through his belt. He repeated the ab tightening and hip shifting, this time to the opposite side, then retrieved the Jade Dagger, depositing it next to the heavy steel number.

Hoping that had done the trick, Karl tried again, palms flat on either side of the pit, triceps tenting the sleeves of his shirt. He hoisted himself out of the trap, grating off a few more swathes of denim and leaving behind a couple of patches of skin. He stooped to retrieve the knives and replaced them at his belt. Then he headed for the left-hand exit – though not before snatching up the fire opals and slipping them into his pocket. He figured he'd left more than sufficient on the shelf for Professors Allison and Chen to catalog.

The next burial chamber boasted an equally opulent abundance of richly adorned bones. A diagonal passage offered exit to the right of the ledge, while immediately to the left another curved into the darkness. Karl followed the latter passage, following the curve past the fallen remains of one of the curtain walls to a reverse curve that terminated a few paces farther on at a four-way intersection.

Karl tapped his chin, thinking. Then he continued his recon, assembling the pieces of an idea.

CHAPTER 22

Dexicos halted his reduced band at the foyer of the Halls of Glittering Repose. The Grand Processional sloped away behind them. The murals depicting the underworld, which the kings, priests, and higher functionaries believed they were to enjoy, no longer possessed that depth, color, and clarity that had impressed him upon his first visit as an ambassador observing the internment of a young prince, dead of some tropical disease.

Distant, sporadic gunfire informed him that the narco hunt continued down in the Processional Antechamber and points beyond. Behind stood his remaining attendants – and guests. Smith and Alexandros flanked him, with Festo a step back. The professors followed, with Potter's silent bulk urging them on.

"Right, then," Dexicos said, putting a spritely effervescence into his words. "Smith, Alexandros, off you go. Karl is somewhere in the labyrinth of the Halls of Glittering

Repose. Find him, kill him, retrieve my dagger. You can alter the order of events if you like."

"The Halls of Glittering Repose?" Smith asked.

"I didn't name it, Smith. Anyway, you can decide for yourself if the name was warranted."

"And you, sir?" Alexandros asked.

Dexicos raised an eyebrow, considering if the question was insubordination or proper gathering of mission intel. He split the difference, letting Alexandros wither beneath that raised eyebrow for a long moment, unanswered. Then he said, "I will be preparing contingencies. Reserve force, rescue, reinforcement. That sort of thing. With any luck, you will be back with the prize before I complete my preparations. Without luck, perhaps you'll be glad I remained here with my case of wonders."

"Yes, sir," Alexandros said. "Ready, Smith?"

"Bottle of Jack says I get him first," Smith said.

"Make it tequila, something high end," Alexandros said. "We're in Mexico, *amigo*."

"I'll take the Jack," Smith said. "Tequila tastes like skunk piss."

"Peasant."

"Grease ball."

"Are you gentlemen quite finished?" Dexicos asked.

There followed the clack and clatter of weapons checks. Dexicos tapped his wristwatch. "Ticktock," he said. His captains exchanged glances, then disappeared into the labyrinth.

"Potter," Dexicos said, "my briefcase, if you please."

Potter appeared, proffering the case. Dexicos took it. "Festo, we appear short of furniture. If you would please extend your arms, you will oblige me in remedying that lack."

Festo frowned. "*Que?*"

Dexicos sighed. "Hold out both arms, please. Palms up."

Festo's frown remained, but he complied. Dexicos placed the case on the outstretched arms and opened it. As he did so, a greenish light appeared in the foyer. Dexicos nodded his approval as Potter paced about, activating and dropping chemlights. *A prince among gentlemen's gentlemen.*

Dexicos returned his attention to the case. He perused the familiar objects within, considering the options. Time factored into his planning. He doubted he had the hours – or days – to complete any of the Greater Conjurations or Puissant Evocations in his arsenal. On the other hand, he wasn't limited to spur-of-the-moment, slapdash wizardry. He could put together a competent bit of combat magery.

Dexicos nodded to himself. He selected a number of items from their custom recesses in the case and got to work.

A crude chain of rusted iron links bore a medallion in the form of a full-visored basinet helm. Dexicos donned it, grimacing as the chain left ochre stains on his jacket and shirt. The medallion brushed against the button just above his navel. Dexicos gripped the medallion, closed his eyes, and found his center, a frigid pool of rigorously enforced calm. Eyes still closed, he felt for the magic imbuing the chain, connecting with it, memorizing its pattern and flow.

He opened his eyes. "It occurs to me that, in a confrontation with this man Karl, a degree of imperviousness to metals – whether ferrous or leaden – would accrue to my advantage. The Armor of Ficino fits this requirement admirably. Or it will, once I complete the ritual. But that is merely defense. Karl possesses a certain edge in youth and strength. He can likely deliver a powerful blow. It behooves me to punch back. Or, preferably, punch first."

The other two items he'd selected still rested in the case, though free of their cutout slots. Dexicos reached for the first, a twist of copper wire about which wound the cracked and frayed remains of an ancient leather thong. The briefcase shifted as Dexicos picked up the wire, disrupting his grip. Bits of leather flaked off beneath fingers that exerted more strength than Dexicos had intended in order to compensate for the movement.

"Damn you," Dexicos said. "Hold still, Festo." He closed his eyes again, regaining his icy focus.

"*Perdón*," Festo muttered. Dexicos opened his eyes again. Festo looked to be a man unraveling.

Dexicos offered a reassuring smile. "All will be well, Festo. Don't worry. You see this? Milo's Fist, it is called. Said to be the remains of the hand wraps of Milo of Croton. I have my doubts. Yet what is beyond doubt is its ability to amplify the power of a blow." Again Dexicos let himself attune to the power imbuing the artifact, awakening it though not bringing it to its full puissance.

"Milo of Croton?" May Chen asked. "Wouldn't that make your artifact there twenty-five hundred years old? Give or take a few decades."

"Yes, my dear," Dexicos said. "I did say I had my doubts. Magical preservation or no, a couple of millennia are tough on leather."

"I don't suppose I could…" Professor Allison began, then dwindled off as he recollected his situation and to whom he was speaking.

"No, my good Professor, you may not examine Milo's Fist, nor any of the other items in this case. Few of them possess any real value for the antiquarian. Their value lies in other properties." Dexicos finished adjusting the wrap, easing a painful constriction about the knuckles. "Now then, one more, I think. This? Yes. Oh, yes."

Dexicos held up what appeared to be a gentleman's pocket watch from the late eighteenth or early nineteenth century. Gold links composed the watch chain, a chain devoid of charms or fobs. On closer inspection, what made up the body of the watch itself was a sort of clamshell cage of small, tightly spaced bars of some black, or age-blackened, metal.

Dexicos raised the watch to eye level. He let a dry tongue snake out to touch his lips, hardly aware that he did so. With the edge of a thumbnail, he cracked open the clamshell a merest hair's width. Once more, tentatively this time, Dexicos allowed himself to reach out to contact the power within the object. This time, almost subvocally, he spoke a Name.

A flicker of blood-red light rimmed the hairline crack and filled the lacunae between the little bars. Incongruously, given the hellish gleam, Dexicos felt a suggestion of immense cold, a probing, bitterly gelid touch responding to his own probe. He nearly uttered an Abjuration, a heartbeat away from thrusting the pocket watch back inside the case and terminating the disquieting connection. But he mastered himself, as he always had and always would.

"You wait," he snarled. "I command. You obey. There are fates worse than confinement, and I can introduce you to them all if you challenge me."

"What the hell is that?" May Chen's words came out in a choked hush. She'd no doubt felt something too.

"That is a question I'm afraid no man can answer with any specificity," Dexicos said. He offered the confident, self-possessed grin of a man unconcerned. Appearance counted. "From what I have ascertained from my own studies, as well as research into the esoteric sources, this containment vessel holds a physical specimen. Not the entirety, but a fragment of an entity, a paring from the *corpus* of an alien intelligence."

"A little green man?" Professor Allison asked.

"Hardly little. Hardly a man. Though I suppose some portion of it might be green. No man living has seen It *in toto*. Man had barely risen from ape when It arrived from some unfathomably distant corner of the cosmos. They worshipped It, and It consumed them. When at last It departed – returned to Its home, voyaged on to other worlds, or withdrawn into hibernation in some bathic trench – It left behind minuscule portions of its bulk. And these fragments – or at least this one – retain some semblance of Its power, and some semblance of intellect and will."

Allison grunted, raised a skeptical eyebrow. "What's it look like?"

"I could open the shell for you, allow you a peek. If you'd like to go utterly mad just before you die. Just before we all die, horribly. But I don't think I shall indulge you."

"Let's keep it a mystery, why don't we?" May Chen said. "Put that thing away, Mago D. Whatever it is. Why send it after Karl if it's going to kill you as well?"

"Astute, my dear. You are a quick study. It would indeed slay me if I released it. Therefore, I will keep it caged. I intend merely to allow a fraction of it to calve off. That I will direct to burrow into a wound, drawn by the blood. The result shall be sufficiently lethal. And unpleasant. But limited to Karl."

Festo shuddered again. "*Señor*, my arms. They grow tired."

"Courage, Festo. The ritual will soon be over and with it, your weariness."

Dexicos slipped the pocket watch into the front right pocket of his jacket. He took a crystal salt cellar from the case, filled with ground hematite rather than salt. With a practiced ease, he laid a circle of dark reddish powder around him and Festo. He replaced the shaker.

Dexicos examined the circle. It appeared unbroken, evenly drawn. "My good Potter, I imagine you have a bottle of something robust and flavorful on your person." From one of his pockets the big man produced a bottle, a thick white towel wrapped protectively about it. From another he retrieved folding silver traveling goblets, a set of four nested together.

"As ever, you provide satisfactory service, Potter. Now, my good Professors, I'll be gone for a short time, ensuring that Alexandros and Smith's errand does not go uncompleted. While you wait, you might enjoy whatever fine vintage Potter has brought along. I'd be surprised if you did not discover a block of cheese and perhaps a flaky loaf to accompany the wine."

Dexicos picked a sommelier's corkscrew from the case. He opened the foil-cutting blade; then with his right hand he drove the blade into Festo's throat and jerked it viciously across through carotid and jugular. With his left hand he grabbed Festo's collar, holding the man upright while he jerked and gurgled, surprise and pain written across his features. Blood arced and jetted, splattering Dexicos and placing his outfit beyond the best efforts of any dry cleaner to salvage.

Festo clutched uselessly at his severed throat. The briefcase fell, its support withdrawn. It hit the stone floor, bounced once – the relics remaining secure in their cushioned recesses – then slammed shut.

Spatters of blood met the circle. An exsanguinating blood sacrifice delivered considerable energy, and human provided the greatest. The power of Festo's dying life force ignited the circle like a wheel of fire. To Dexicos' attuned senses, the ring of magic burned hotter, like a magnesium flare. Energy flooded into the Armor of Ficino, the chain radiating heat that grew uncomfortably warm even through the insulating layers of jacket and shirt. Milo's Fist writhed and twisted, actinic blue worms arcing about the copper, sending light galvanic pulses up Dexicos' arm. The pocket watch reacted not at all, the remnant within too utterly alien to interact with human nigromancy.

Dexicos let Festo fall. The corpse collapsed across the ring of powdered hematite, breaking the circle. The eldritch fire winked out. No matter, the circle of power had served its purpose. "There," said Dexicos, "dressed and accessorized."

May Chen and Jim Allison stared back at him. Allison's open jaw and wide eyes betrayed shock and horror. Chen appeared to have stopped herself in mid-scream. The narrowing of her eyes suggested more anger than shock.

"You murdering pig," she said.

"May?" Professor Allison said, the word coming out in a sort of querulous uncertainty. He closed his mouth, swallowed. "May, perhaps this is not the time to level accusations."

Dexicos laughed. He felt – full. Swollen, but not unpleasantly so. He nearly vibrated with his desire to *go*, to move, like a child suffused with suppressed excitement.

"My dear Professor, the man is dead. I killed him. Murdered him, if you like. Should I do the same to you, it won't be due to the lovely Professor Chen's imprecations. If I slay you, I will do so for reasons entirely of my own. And my sweet May, do not fret. If I kill Professor Allison, I shall show no exclusionary sexual discrimination: I'll kill you as well."

May Chen extended both middle fingers.

Dexicos laughed again, a long, deeply mirthful expression of sheer joy. "Potter, look after our guests. And, Professors, save me a glass of wine. Killing Karl will earn me a celebratory drink."

He produced a flashlight and strode into the Halls of Glittering Repose.

CHAPTER 23

Alejandra ejected the spent magazine. She retrieved another – her last – from the inner pocket in the custom lining of her jacket. She should have carried more. But this was supposed to have been a simple sweep and clear mission, not a fucking battle. Alejandra inserted the fresh mag into the well of the pistol grip. The Sig felt uncomfortably warm and exuded the odd combined smells of hot oil and fireworks.

She'd fled with the remnants of her crew down the narrow hall until they'd emerged in a dark, cavernous space. Sweeping light suggested it had been a quarry. Chisel marks etched irregular linear patterns in the high walls. Talus, rubble, and broken stones lay piled up near the base of the walls and formed little cairns here and there.

"Get behind cover," she'd heard Diego yell. At least he remained alive. Those should have been her commands, but since he was her head of security, she figured she'd simply preemptively delegated. That counted as foresighted leader-ship, didn't it?

Alejandra had found a jumble of cracked and jagged edged blocks of some soft, greasy-feeling stone that reached up to her knees. Someone had preceded her. Arturo, she thought it was. Yes, she recognized the street fashion and the blinged-out piece-of-shit rifle. Alejandra dropped beside him as incoming rounds announced the attackers were right on her heels.

"Who are these *jotos*?" Arturo had asked. His voice sounded shrill, terrified, louder than required even given the need to be heard over the racket of gunfire.

Good question. One Alejandra had been asking herself ever since the first rush of shock eased from the surprise onslaught. Out of habit, she replied with assurance. "The archaeologists hired security. *Gringos*. Ex-soldiers. *Pinche* mercenaries." It might even be true. It didn't really matter. Killing them or escaping them mattered, whoever they were.

And she'd tried. The mercenaries had come at them, following bursts of gunfire that encouraged Alejandra to keep her head down. They were good, disciplined, these mercs. Her own crew fought back enthusiastically, filling the cavern with the chattering of fully automatic and rapid, poorly aimed semiautomatic fire.

But enthusiasm failed to compensate for the lack of skill and experience. Arturo bought it during the initial merc advance, the kid leaving cover, standing up and firing from the hip while screaming obscenities. He'd taken a round in the chest and another in the forehead for that mistake, a lesson he'd never get the chance to learn from. His rifle had tumbled from his nerveless fingers to cartwheel off into the darkness.

Alejandra had kept low, behind her protective bulwark of stone, firing only when a target presented himself. But the dark cavern, illuminated only by the chaotically bobbing and wavering beams of flashlights, was not conducive to marksmanship. She had no idea if she'd hit anything. From the shouts and screams, she gleaned that others had connected, but that those hit were more often her men rather than the mercenaries.

And now she'd been reduced to a single mag.

"Diego," she called. "Diego? Is there an exit?"

The reply came. "Diego's dead." She thought it was Hector's voice. "No way out." The kid tried to sound macho about it, ready to make a manly last stand, but Alejandra could hear the panic beneath the words.

Little blossoms of red and orange answered Hector, the mercs targeting his voice.

She heard Hector yell, a shocked, pained sound. He'd been hit, she guessed. But return fire came from that direction. Hit, but not killed. Yet.

The blossoms of red and orange moved. Fire and maneuver. Alejandra wished she could have afforded soldiers like this. Fire teams working together, closing on Hector's position, one team moving while another kept up steady, controlled bursts. Alejandra doubted Hector had much longer.

But the flashes and bangs were moving away from her. Leaving a way open back into the narrow hallway.

Alejandra rose to her feet, bending at the waist to lower her profile. She took a sighting on the hallway, then flicked off her light. She ran, the contorted position making for an awkward, ungainly stride through the dark. But no one stopped her. No shots followed. She heard screams behind her, rising above the gunshots.

Her foot connected with something soft but unyielding as she neared the hall, sending her sprawling. She clambered back to her feet, feeling pain bloom in her right knee where it had collided with the stone floor and feeling a rising heat from scrapes on her left palm. She fumbled for her light, flicked it back on to get her bearings. The corpse Alejandra had tripped over appeared in the beam. Not one of hers. *Good, got at least one of the fuckers.*

Scrambling up from the fall had gotten her turned around. She found the hallway again, only a few steps away, and started off again in a limping jog. But she'd drawn the mercenaries' attention. Shots followed, striking the walls and floor about her as she gained the hallway.

Alejandra moved, gaining speed as her banged-up knee loosened. Bodies created obstacles in her path. She leaped over the first, stumbled, then righted herself. As she cleared it, she thought she recognized who it had once been, though she couldn't remember the name. Once she'd reorganized, recruited more security, she'd have to make an effort at learning names.

The next corpse wore the polo shirt and khaki pants with

cargo pockets that she associated with the American mercenaries. The next two were hers. Given the firefight she'd just escaped, Alejandra doubted she had any soldiers left to her. Dead. All of them. This escapade had depleted her personnel. And for any drug-transport purposes, this route was compromised. How was she supposed to get the shipment to the *Grand Princess* now? She could, she supposed, abandon her guiding principle. She could eschew the carefully developed layers of secrecy she'd built her business on. Get a van, load it up, and drive to the port herself. Other organizations did it all the time, relying on luck and bribery to see the shipment through. But those other organizations were willing to accept occasional losses of goods and couriers, whether to law enforcement or competition. Alejandra's model possessed no margin for error, not yet. With the earthquake and the near one hundred percent losses suffered by her security force, the survival of her business depended on this single shipment getting through. She would have to risk it.

Risk it or run? Maybe cousin Maria could wrangle her a job folding laundry aboard one of the cruise liners. Give up the money and the promise of vaster sums to come. Give up the clothes, the fine food and wines, the cars. Live little better than an animal, like that stupid *puta* of a cook who'd given her lip yesterday.

No. The hell with that. One single risk, then rebuild. Rebuild smarter, contrive even more redundant layers of stealth. Evaluate what had failed and compensate for it in the next go-round. If, that is, she could get out of here alive.

The hallway emptied into the large chamber, picking up again on the opposite side. Alejandra thought, running through scenarios at furious speed as she took those last few long, limping strides. The mercenaries, she guessed, would most likely expect her to continue on. After all, that was the way she'd come. The only way she knew to get out. *So don't go the way they expect. Hide, let them pass. Wait. Then get out. Simple.*

Alejandra turned to her left, weaving through the boulder field. She cleared it, then felt the ground rise, noting with a flick of her flashlight the tile paving beneath her feet. The climb steepened, and she slowed, her exertions catching up with her.

From ahead of her came the sounds of a commotion. An eerie green glow appeared over the brow of the rise. She reconsidered her plan. Perhaps returning to the hallway and making a run for it was the best bet after all.

Behind her came distant conversation, the words unclear, but Alejandra could guess at the speakers and the context: the mercenaries sharing the tactical situation, discussing which way she'd gone. So stick to the plan, risk the unknown ahead rather than the certain lethality behind.

Alejandra dropped to her hands and knees and eased her head up. Even with the mercenaries gunning for her below, she could still exercise caution. She had no wish to rush into an even worse situation.

Over the rise, the tile road ended in a sort of plaza. The green glow came from a ragged ring of chemlights. A body lay in the ring, within the confines of an even smaller circle of some reddish dust. Three living people staggered about the plaza, in the midst of an earnest, deadly struggle.

A woman held the neck and jagged-edged shoulders of a wine bottle. She waved it menacingly. A man wielded some sort of umbrella or walking stick with which he belabored another man, a massive, broad figure like a circus strongman dressed as a butler. A dark stain dampened the hair on the back of his head and soaked the back of his jacket. Alejandra corrected her initial assumption that the stain was blood when she noticed the shards of a bottle crunching beneath the feet of the combatants and recalled the broken bottleneck in the woman's hand. Wine, then. Or blood and wine.

The big man staggered around the circle. He threw punches, looping lefts and rights, at his antagonists, but his blows were as errant as his movement was unsteady. The crack in the skull delivered by the bottle must have scrambled his gray matter.

The man with the umbrella ducked beneath a slow haymaker. He thrust the umbrella between the big man's legs and dove forward. The umbrella acted like a stick through the spokes of a bicycle. The big man sprawled on his face, the circle of chemlights jostling as the ground transmitted the force of his fall. Before he could recover, the woman was on him, driving the sharp edges of the broken bottle into the back of his thick neck.

Alejandra had no idea what sort of drama she'd just witnessed culminate. But she did have a gun. These two obviously did not. She'd be better off up here, in charge at gunpoint, rather than down below facing the mercs. Maybe these two knew where she could hide. Maybe they'd serve as hostages; could be they'd employed the mercenaries in the first place. Either way, she needed to move.

A shout and gunshots reinforced the point. Looking behind her, Alejandra saw four of the mercenaries ascending the slope toward her, firing as they came. They advanced in pairs, keeping to the sides of the wide hall. Bullets smacked into the tiles below her, coming closer as they dialed in the range.

Alejandra tensed, ready to scramble to her feet and over the lip of the rise. Before she could, more figures entered her field of view. They came in a rush, at least a dozen black-clad men decked out in body armor and tactical vests and carrying the sorts of battle rifles Alejandra associated with European armies.

Zetas. They'd caught up with her at last. She wasn't going to deliver the shipment to the *Grand Princess*. She wasn't going to rebuild her organization. In fact, her organization was probably destroyed, her camp demolished, finished product, precursor chemicals, and raw leaves stolen. Her workers dead, every chemist, mixer, cook, and general-purpose laborer. All dead, slaughtered by the Zetas after torture and interrogation. They'd trace her relatives, kill them too. It was over. She wasn't going to retire early and fabulously wealthy. She'd been so careful, refusing to commit the same error her father had. She'd been smart, innovative. But it had all availed her naught.

The four *Americano* mercenaries faced about, their

flashlight beams playing across the oncoming Zetas. Alejandra wasn't sure which side opened fire first. She didn't care. She no longer cared about anything. She pushed herself to her feet.

Grasping her Sig tightly, she began walking back downhill. Strolling, really. *Un paseo.* She picked a target and pulled the trigger. Casually plinking, like shooting Coke cans with Diego when he could talk her into target practice.

Something metallic bounced and clattered against the tiles near her feet. It started to roll back downhill just about the same time it registered for Alejandra as a grenade.

Chinga, she thought, more in resignation than despair, as a flash birthed an enveloping cloud.

Darkness followed.

CHAPTER 24

Without his rag of a shirt, Karl began to feel chilled. Absurd, he knew. The temperature remained even, cool but comfortable. One layer of clothing made no practical difference. No breeze disturbed the still air. Though up above the jungle might be enjoying the lower temperatures prevailing between midnight and dawn, down here the catacombs maintained an unvarying atmosphere.

Still, Karl felt the absence of his shirt. Removing it suggested bedtime, and that reminded him of the hour and of how tired he was. But he figured more exertion lay ahead of him before he could rest. Meanwhile, he could enjoy the respite provided by the temporary lack of activity, let it stand in for actual rest, while he watched his shirt from his hiding place.

His concealment consisted of a hollow at the base of one of the maze walls, this one flaring to greater thickness where it met the floor. He'd lined the edge of the hollow with fragments from one of the holes that riddled the maze walls like a termite-infested house. Another of the bone display platforms flaunted its macabre and gaudy burden across from his hiding spot. Though this one now housed a few bones less.

The wall hosting Karl's hollow ended at a T-intersection. At the junction where one wall crossed the T of the other, the red of Karl's Hawaiian shirt signaled. Or would have had there been any light to see it. Karl waited in darkness, but his memory showed him the shirt, its shoulders stretched across a scrounged scapula to provide structure, fragments of arm bones dangling from ancient, desiccated ligaments slipped through the sleeves. He'd wedged a protruding spur of the scapula into the porous rock of the wall. A skull added to the illusion, pegged onto a chunk of bone thrust into a depression in the wall immediately above the shirt.

Hardly convincing, Karl knew. He wouldn't place this staging on his résumé if he applied for a job arranging display mannequins in a department store. But in the nighted recesses of an underground labyrinth, it should serve. He hoped it would serve.

The longer he waited, the more Karl began to wonder if ambush hunting hadn't been a mistake, if he'd be better served actively stalking his pursuit instead of lying in wait. What if no one came this way? What if they'd given up pursuit, decided to leave him down here? Perhaps at this very moment Mago D's goons were dragging Chen and

Allison topside, figuring they could simply wait until Karl emerged, driven by hunger.

He began to itch. The local insect ecosystem had discovered him. Subterranean creepy-crawlies began to explore. None were so impolite yet as to bite, for which Karl was grateful, though the sensation of their tiny feet moving across his skin was unpleasant enough. Still, he'd sat through worse while dug in, waiting for insurgents to enter the kill sack.

Light warned Karl of company before the sound of rubber soles making a cautious but steady advance reached his ears. No surprise; the ears just weren't that reliable anymore. The tight beam of a tac-light worked along the floor and walls of this section of the maze. One beam. One set of footsteps. *Good.* Karl had worried about facing an entire squad. He'd guessed he might be able to take two if he could put down the first immediately. But it appeared he'd only need to deal with one man first. One trained, experienced, ex-military soldier for hire. Like Karl.

Karl performed the mental equivalent of a shrug. Karl Thorson was more than a match for any man walking the planet. *Übermensch*, he thought as the steps neared, *but not in any creepy Nazi way*. The thought almost made him laugh out loud. That he'd heard the thought in May Chen's voice did make him smile.

The light allowed him a glimpse of his stalker as he paced closer and closer. A big man. A big man who slowed a trifle as he passed the treasure shelf. Karl had counted on that when he'd selected his hiding spot. It would be a rare man indeed who would glance down and away from a glittering, exotic argosy such as these gilded, bejeweled bones presented. The reflected light showed darker skin tones. *One of Mago D's goons I haven't seen yet.*

The man continued on, passing Karl by, not even glancing at his side of the passage, entranced by the shine of gems on bones. He paused momentarily, though he must have seen a few such displays already during his hunt. He moved on, tac-light showing the way, showing…

The man stopped, swinging the rifle up to his shoulder, drawing a bead on Karl's decoy.

Karl stabbed the button of his carefully positioned mini-light. He had no intention of fighting in the dark if he could help it. At the same instant he burst from the hollow, taking the man after four driving steps in a kidney-high, blindside tackle. He'd considered simply shoving his jungle knife through the back of the man's spine. But the hostages remained uppermost in his planning. Keeping the man alive might allow him to glean some intel, or perhaps provide him some leverage, a hostage of his own. Dead, the gunman would be so much meat.

The man staggered beneath the impact of the tackle and went hard to his knees. The rifle flew from his grasp, the sling catching it to dangle beneath him. Karl scrambled atop the mercenary's back. He reached down, grasped the rifle by stock and barrel, and yanked up, hoping to pull it tight into the gunman's throat. But the man was fast. He got a hand in the way, grabbing the rifle by the forestock. He was also strong. Even with Karl on his back and only one hand for leverage, he rose to his feet, grunting an exhalation of effort.

Karl adjusted his grip, shifting his hands to the attachment points of the sling. With one smooth motion he slipped the sling free and dropped from the mercenary's back, bringing the rifle with him, his weight tearing it free from the mercenary's one-handed grasp.

Surprised, attacked from behind, and disarmed, the mercenary might be. But the mercenary remained cobra fast. Even as Karl rose from the crouch he'd dropped to and started to bring the rifle to bear, the mercenary spun, his sidearm appearing in his hand with a speed to rival a legendary Old West quick-draw gunslinger.

Karl didn't have the rifle positioned for a shot yet, his right hand still near the neck of the buttstock, not close enough to the trigger guard to slip a finger inside. So he snapped the rifle around, slamming the buttstock into the wrist and hand holding the pistol. The pistol spiraled off into the darkness, bouncing off a wall and clattering down the passage.

Karl's opponent's other hand shot forward and seized the rifle. He yanked, tearing the rifle free, but losing his own grip in the process. The rifle sailed off in the opposite direction from the pistol.

"Well, shit," the mercenary said. "Looks like Mr. Smith is going to have to earn his Jack Daniel's the hard way."

Karl considered going for his knife then. But Smith closed the gap so quickly that he couldn't spare a hand. Smith was a good six inches taller and probably twenty-five pounds heavier. Karl didn't doubt his ability to take him, but he figured it would require both hands.

Smith used both of his, reaching out for Karl's throat in a throttling grasp. Karl dug his chin into his chest, tightened the muscles of his throat, and lifted his own shoulders as he reciprocated, getting both hands around Smith's neck.

Karl didn't know what Smith thought was going to happen here. Did he believe he could snap Karl's neck? Smith was a big guy, no question, but Karl doubted he was any stronger than Karl, and he looked to be at least a decade older. Pound for pound the advantage might lie with Smith. But those ten years would be an equalizer. Squeezing each other's throats like this, the best either could hope for was to deprive the other man of oxygen before he ran out himself. The odds were just as good they'd pass out simultaneously, leaving it a contest as to who would revive first.

Karl hadn't broken the neck of a wild Idaho bull as a teen; he'd no precocious, prodigious feats of strength to draw upon as inspirational memory. He wished he did. Karl knew from experience that snapping a man's neck wasn't as easy as the movies would suggest. He watched Smith's eyes bulge with strain and pain, and imagined his own looked something similar. Then, certain Smith was committed to this absurdity, Karl took a half step forward and rammed his knee into Smith's groin. Smith tried to move his thigh into a blocking position, but he'd noticed Karl's intent too late.

The pain of the blow drove the breath from Smith's lungs, and his grip momentarily loosened. Karl's grip did not. He took advantage of the lessened constriction to draw in another lungful and twist his neck free of Smith's grasp.

Smith reached again, hands slipping from Karl's throat as Karl shifted from side to side. Then he regained his grip, tried to dig his thumbs in. But by this time, lack of oxygen began to tell. He abandoned his throttling hold and gripped Karl's wrists instead, trying to tear Karl's hands free from his throat. That failing, he went for his knife.

"Shit," Karl said as he caught the gleam of the Ka-Bar. He twisted, driving power through his legs and hips into a throw that heaved Smith into and *through* the frangible labyrinth wall.

Smith's skull proved no more durable. Blood and brains mixed with fragments of rock and bits of fossilized, crypto-zoic sea-life.

"Mr. Smith goes to Hell," muttered Karl. *So much for a hostage*. Or any information Smith might have been able to provide.

Karl returned to his hollow. He retrieved the mini-light and searched the passage for the fallen rifle. He found it, an HK416 with a tac-light affixed beneath on the mounting rail. He slung the rifle, getting a feel for it. Karl flicked on the light, checking to see if the fall had damaged it. It worked, so Karl turned off his own mini-light and pocketed it.

He returned to Smith's body held mostly upright by the head and neck's insertion into the wall. Karl intended to rifle Smith's pockets for spare magazines and whatever other useful items he might find, then retrieve his shirt from the bone hanger making up the decoy. He figured a hundred rounds or so of 5.56 should offer him some powerful arguments in any negotiations with Mago D and his boys. And if he could find the dropped pistol, so much the better.

Karl dropped to a crouch, patting a cargo pocket on Smith's still twitching leg.

"Fuck," Alexandros said from behind. "Who is going to buy my bottle of tequila?"

Karl was up and sprinting for the T-intersection as the first rounds gouged splinters of stone from the wall at his heels.

A sharp slash of fire burned along Karl's lowest rib on his left side. A bullet graze or flying debris from a miss. He didn't know or care. It didn't matter either way; a surface wound, painful but not debilitating. He could still run, try to get some distance from Mago D's gunman Alexandros. Karl remembered him: older, keen-eyed, with the impassive, watchful face of an experienced killer.

Karl feinted left at the T-intersection, then darted right. For a fraction of a second he was tempted to make a snatch at his shirt, try to tear it free of the scapula anchoring it to the wall. But only for that fragment of time. It might not come free; tugging on it might hang him up long enough for Alexandros to get a clean shot at him. Wasn't worth the risk. Getting killed over a shirt would get him laughed away from the gates of Valhalla.

He needed space now. Cover would be nice as well. Maneuver failed as a tactical concept if there was nowhere to move. If Karl were pinned, without anything solid to duck behind, with a rifle trained at his back, then *these violent delights have violent ends*. He could spin about, try to get off a shot in reply at the very least. There were worse ways to go. Everyone dies at some point. It wasn't the thought of dying that irked him, it was the idea that he'd fail at his job, that May and Professor Allison and Judy and all the other college kids remained at risk. They were his responsibility. If he let Alexandros shoot him, then he'd failed his responsibility.

So don't fucking fail, then. "Screw your courage to the sticking place." Karl's mother had always liked that one, and even liked Lady Macbeth herself, always inventing excuses for the murderess, imputing benign motives to her beyond any reasonable interpretation of the play.

The passage he'd entered looked no different than any other stretch of the labyrinth. About ten long strides ahead, it veered at an obtuse angle to the right. *Shit*. No options and not a sharp enough angle to provide cover. He kept running, making the bend as another round buzzed by him, missing wide, a rushed wingshot, but indicating Alexandros was still too close on Karl's heels for him to risk spinning about in an attempt to return fire.

Another fifteen strides ahead, the lurching, bouncing beam of the HK's tac-light showed the passage terminating in a sort of gallery filled with the end points of walls, wall segments, pillars, and stubs of pillars. Karl felt a savage grin stretch his lips. Cover, concealment, room to move, hide, and stage ambushes.

"The game is afoot, motherfucker," Karl called over his shoulder. His mother largely sniffed at Conan Doyle, but his father was an avid Sherlockian, with only his fondness for Kipling vying for place of honor.

A low wall reaching about mid-thigh on Karl capped the passage before it entered the gallery, leaving a gap about a foot wide on either side. A stump of a shattered pillar jutted up behind it to the left, a couple of intact pillars or wall segments rose centered behind it, and a wall beginning a passage beckoned to the right. More obstacles presented a stony tangle farther back. Karl dove over the low wall as Alexandros triggered a three-round burst.

Grit and stone scraped more shreds of skin from Karl's palms and forearms. The HK stock banged into an elbow, and the barrel rebounded from his chin. He pushed himself up to his hands and knees and scrambled behind the cover of a stretch of wall that had never developed as had the others composing the labyrinth.

He stood up and turned around to train the HK on Alexandros, exposing only a fraction of his right side, the left concealed behind the wall segment. Alexandros had noted the changed tactical scenario. Instead of leaping the low wall, continuing his pursuit, he'd gone to a knee behind it, unwilling to follow Karl into this hide-and-seek paintball arena, this maze within a maze. Karl could see his head and shoulders, the beam of Alexandros' tac-light threatening to dazzle his vision.

The lessons of the midnight warrior were deeply ingrained in Karl. He figured he could teach a course on the subject. He'd nutshell the class with notes from this little escapade, assuming he survived it. *Fighting in the dark presents a variety of unique problems. Night-vision goggles can go a way to alleviating some of these. But they can play hell with depth perception. And as they function by enhancing ambient light, they aren't of any use in the total subterranean darkness of – for example – catacombs beneath a forgotten Mayan ruin. A laser sight can be a useful close quarters targeting adjunct, but you need to be able to see the target in the first place, as the laser itself provides no effective illumination. That's where a flashlight mounted on the weapon comes in handy. It lights up a target nicely. That benefit does, however, come with some drawbacks. For one, shining a light on the target pinpoints the shooter's position with precision, making the shooter a bright, shiny target as well. Another problem is that while the shooter can now see the target, aiming in the traditional sense is impracticable. The illumination comes from the front of the rifle. Without any light source from the rear providing a glimpse of the front and rear sights, getting a proper sight picture is tough. The bright beam fucks up electronic red-dot sights as well. So it comes down to instinctual point shooting.*

Karl squinted into the beam of Alexandros' light, settled the rifle into the hollow of his shoulder, and squeezed the trigger. The recoil offered a solid, reassuring familiarity. The report, like a sledgehammer striking rock right beside his ear, was less pleasant. So was Alexandros' return fire, slamming rounds into the stone beside Karl's head. One round punched through a particularly narrow section, showering Karl's shoulder and back with splinters.

Shoot, move, communicate.

"That the best you've got?" Karl called. "Think I'll be drinking that tequila myself."

He turned, put his back to the wall, and scanned the terrain, trying to memorize the features and distances at a glance. Then he flicked off the tac-light.

Karl wouldn't recommend navigating blindly through a maze of unforgiving stone to anyone. But staying put and shooting it out with Alexandros would mean failure to take advantage of the terrain. It would mean accepting a more or less fair fight when he could stack the deck in his favor. Hell, with only the single mag in his confiscated rifle and Alexandros carrying who knew how many rounds, the odds probably favored Alexandros.

So Karl jogged toward his first goal. With Alexandros scanning the cavern with his tac-light, Karl wasn't moving through stygian night. That helped. On the other hand, Karl did not want to get caught in the beam as he crossed open ground. A great way to take a bullet in the back.

He kept low and moved fast toward a half-pillar joined by a thread of stone to a wall angling farther back into the gallery. He almost made it unnoticed. A hummock of rock or stray boulder he hadn't noted in his visual sweep of the ground caught his foot and threw him forward. He lost more skin, this time from chest and chin in addition to his palms. Alexandros must have heard the sound of impact and Karl's involuntary exhalation of surprise. The tac-light floated by as Karl heaved himself back to his feet, then swept back. The light centered unwaveringly on his back showed Karl his goal, the cover of the half-pillar mere steps away. He took those steps as Alexandros fired.

The difficulties involved with aiming apparently bedeviled Alexandros as much as Karl, because the two shots Alexandros managed to snap off both missed. As the second shot kicked up dirt at his heels, Karl hooked his left arm around the narrow half-pillar and hurled himself sideways behind cover.

The half-pillar provided scant protection, leaving bits of arm and leg exposed unless Karl intended to cower behind it sideways. He didn't. He darted across the largely open stretch to the wall. He felt the air behind him disrupted as Alexandros' next shot winged within inches of his spine, the merc dialing in his reflexive point shooting.

Karl wanted to stop there, send a shot back to put the fear of Karl in Alexandros, but he might need to husband his ammo. Besides, a part of him was beginning to enjoy this game of cat and mouse. A Nietzschean conception, one which he'd considered as amusingly overblown as many of the great philosopher's other exhortations, now felt relatable. He felt the "eternal joy of becoming, beyond all terror and pity – that joy which includes even joy in destroying." A savage grin stretched his features into an almost bestial snarl.

Karl scooted along the wall. The angle of the wall soon occulted the light Alexandros provided, leaving Karl shuffling as fast as he dared in the dark. Karl trailed his left hand along the rough surface to help give him some bearings. The wall ended after only a dozen paces. Karl leaned around it, but saw not even a glimmer. Perhaps Alexandros had switched off his own light, intending to join the lethal game. Or perhaps Karl had misremembered the terrain, and this short wall actually led to a section of the gallery he hadn't noticed, one sheltered from Alexandros' light.

Karl wasn't buying the latter. He seldom second-guessed himself. Alexandros had snuffed his tac-light. That meant Karl could no longer be certain where the man was. But he couldn't have moved far. Not yet.

Karl stepped catfooted from his cover, back toward what his mental map told him was the low wall behind which Alexandros had crouched. Presumably he was no longer there, but perhaps Karl could catch him in transit, the man blundering along in this troglodyte's sphincter of total darkness.

Karl's outstretched hand found cold, hard stone. Right about where he'd anticipated, though that was no guarantee that his dead reckoning was accurate – this could well be a different terrain feature. He stopped, listened. He thought he heard the scuff of a shoe. He well knew that the imagination got up to all sorts of shenanigans in the absence of stimuli, especially when an edge of excitement or fear was added to the psychic stew. And, frankly, his hearing was for shit.

Bending down, Karl felt around until his fingers encountered a fragment of rock, too irregular and rough to be considered a pebble. Staying crouched, he flung the rock in the opposite direction from which he guessed the shoe-scuffing sound had come. Before the rock landed, he'd brought the HK to his shoulder.

The bit of gravel struck, a tinny stone-on-stone tinkle in the distance. He heard – distinctly now, not an auditory mental figment – the sound of a body shifting, presumably Alexandros swiveling about in response to the noise.

But Alexandros was canny, too experienced to flick on his light and reveal himself. Perhaps he'd already considered that gambit himself and thus was armed against Karl's use of the ploy. Nonetheless, he'd given away his general location – the two men having, broadly speaking, switched positions. Karl flicked on the tac-light, the HK pointed in the direction the sound had originated. Alexandros was already in motion. Karl caught the man's calves and heels in the circle of light and shifted to track him. He squeezed the trigger. He watched the puff of grit and dust erupt from the wall behind which Alexandros ran.

Karl allowed himself another whisk of the tac-light, absorbing as much as he could at a glimpse. Then he switched off the light again before Alexandros could reorient himself and return fire.

Keeping low, Karl moved toward the nearest cover in Alexandros' direction. He was safely hidden by the time Alexandros flicked his own light on, then almost instantly off again.

That feral grin crossed Karl's face again, the joy of the contest suffusing him. *The man's good. I'm better.*

Karl moved toward that last flicker of light, trusting largely to his memory of immediate obstacles, though keeping the rifle in his right hand thrust forward and his left hand outstretched as well. There was, after all, such a thing as overconfidence. He kept his eyes open; afterimages showed blue and yellow when he closed his eyes, disrupting his mental map.

A rock clattered somewhere nearby, Alexandros trying Karl's trick. Karl froze, refusing to emit a sound. A reasonable move from Alexandros, though not particularly imaginative. So, Karl faced an experienced, canny opponent, but one unlikely to pull off the unexpected. He'd respond by the book. Alexandros' was a long book, containing years of tactical situations, true enough, but he was still limited to it. Karl would be a fool to underestimate that degree of experience; the man had lived this long undertaking dangerous jobs, after all. But perhaps the years might to some degree favor Karl. Considering Alexandros' age, for example, his hearing was likely even worse than Karl's.

Karl crept on. Somewhere out there in the dark Alexandros did the same. They could conceivably stalk each other through the darkness until they died of hunger. But each man wanted to end this quickly. Almost inevitably, one of them would make a mistake.

A shaded glimmer appeared ahead and to the right, then vanished. Alexandros needed a peek for some reason. *Someone just made a mistake.* The light might have helped Alexandros. But it also served Karl, granting him a view of the path toward the light source. He sprinted in the dark, trusting his memory. *Five paces, veer right, three paces, stop.*

He'd nearly mistimed his stop. His nose grazed the surface of the pillar, the barrel of the HK halting millimeters away from a telltale scrape of metal on stone. Karl preferred to consider it precision performance. He leaned around the left side of the pillar. *Time to make a mistake.*

He clipped the side of the pillar with the buttstock and emitted a surprised grunt. Then he shifted to the right side and sprinted for the wall a few steps away, left hand held before him, partially relying on his memory of the relative position of the wall to avoid running headlong into it or missing it completely.

It was there. His palm encountered the rough stone, with its whorls and patterns reminding Karl of weathered reefs. He turned and knelt, placing his shoulder against the wall and bringing the rifle up to firing position.

He thought he heard the scuff of Alexandros' feet. Then light bloomed a conical beam illuminating the pillar Karl had vacated moments before. Alexandros was a dim, barely perceptible form behind the originating point of the cone. Alexandros swore, then disappeared as he flicked off the light.

Alexandros reappeared as Karl switched on his own tac-light, the beam snaring him completely, not ten yards away.

"That's game," Karl said and squeezed the trigger.

Alexandros tried to move, but managed only to pivot a quarter turn toward Karl before the first bullet struck him, low on the right side, just above his belt. Karl adjusted his aim point, and the next round punched completely through Alexandros' upper torso, tearing through his heart en route.

Karl stood. The fierce grin was gone. Now that he'd won, killed his man, the joy of combat and the anticipation of victory vanished, leaving a cold dispassion. He preferred not to contemplate the ruined husks of the dead, especially not when he'd caused that death. That kind of thinking could lead down dark rabbit holes he'd rather avoid. Better to ponder practicalities.

For example: "I appear to be lost," Karl muttered, looking about him. He recognized none of the maze about him, could not see the entry to the gallery. In fact, he was pretty sure he'd left the gallery and reentered the narrow passages that comprised the bulk of the labyrinth.

"Allow me to show you the way," Mago D said.

CHAPTER 26

Karl froze. Mago D's voice had reached him clearly enough, but he didn't think it had come from nearby.

"Projecting your voice?" Karl asked. "Get much use for that in your act?"

He received no immediate answer, so he padded over to Alexandros' body. Karl had nearly depleted the ammo in Smith's HK. Alexandros had been, Karl recalled, a Heckler and Koch man himself, though he preferred a different model. Presumably he carried extra mags.

"I do not see much profit in your attempting to goad me, Karl." Mago D sounded closer. "Perhaps Smith and Alexandros were insufficient to the task of putting you down. I assure you, I've slain many of your sort over the long centuries."

Karl finished swapping rifles while Mago D spoke. He patted down Alexandros for magazines.

"What, not going to offer me a job as their replacement?" Karl asked, speaking over his shoulder in hopes that the sound-baffling properties of the subterranean labyrinth would lead Mago D astray.

"I suppose that would be traditional. I suspect, however, that you would not accept."

Karl shoved a spare magazine into each of his back pockets. Then he found Alexandros' sidearm: a .357 Python with a six-inch barrel. He raised an eyebrow. He hadn't figured Alexandros for the revolver type. And a vintage Python smacked of sentiment. People could always surprise you. Even dead ones.

Karl started to strip off the leg holster, but the initial *skrtich* of Velcro made him pause. Too noisy, the sonic equivalent of a flare gun. *Here I am!* Besides, if he couldn't take down one man with a 5.56-caliber rifle, then he doubted the pistol would help much. Let Alexandros take his pistol with him across the Styx.

Time to move. He'd given Mago D too long to track him as it was. He'd rather do the finding than be found. But he'd had enough of playing hide-and-seek in the dark. He kept the tac-light on as he stalked through the maze.

"You're probably right, Mago D," Karl said. "I don't think your company's core values align with mine."

"Please, Karl. You can dispense with the 'Mago D' sobriquet. You may refer to me as Dexicos Megistos. Or simply Dexicos, as you have not yet offered me your surname. We may as well treat each other with decorum."

Karl turned left at an intersection. The sorcerer's voice

seemed to have come from that direction. "Sure thing, D," he said. "When a man's trying to kill you, it's only right to observe the proper etiquette."

"Karl, is the effort of forced levity how you wish to expend the last moments of your mayfly existence?"

Dexicos' voice had faded somewhat. Karl took the next turning back in the general direction he'd come.

"We all have to go sometime," Karl said. "Might as well go with a smile."

"*You* may die," Dexicos said, sounding somewhat nearer. "In fact, I intend you to do so shortly." Dexicos laughed. "You know what the builders called this labyrinth here beyond the Halls of Glittering Repose? Of course you don't. How could you? They called it Beh Xibalba, roughly meaning the Paths of the Dead, or the Road to Hell. How appropriate that I kill you here. You will die, but I will continue. I will continue to defy the darkness as I have for thousands of years."

"Why?" Karl asked. "Didn't you start getting a bit tired after the first three or four centuries?"

"Why? Because life is all there is. When the mind is extinguished, that is the end. I do not wish to end. I wish to endure. I admit to a certain weariness. That is why I indulge myself in such activities as this, my little game with the Jade Dagger. Watching you all scramble around like ants whose hill has been kicked over is tremendously entertaining. It helps pass the years." Dexicos' voice shifted in volume as he spoke on, Karl guessing the sorcerer was navigating through a twisting section of the maze. "Admit it,

Karl, mine is the only rational response to the absurdly ephemeral nature of existence."

"What, try to live forever and stave off boredom by fucking with everyone? I don't admit that at all."

"The only alternative is despair, Karl. That is all you have. You may mask it, ignore it, or attempt to delude yourself. But in the end you have only despair. Do you know what is at the end of this labyrinth, this Beh Xibalba? Only the far wall of the cavern. A dead end. Nothing. A fitting metaphor, don't you think? I'll give it a name: The Wall of Despair."

Dexicos sounded much closer now. Karl checked that the safety was off and stalked toward the sound.

"Some may despair. But that's no way to live. What you should have learned in all your centuries, D, is that what keeps us going is hope." Karl saw a gleam of light and moved that way, skirting a half-pillar and toppled wall. "Hope is irreplaceable. It underpins all religion, all belief systems." The light grew, shining through a hole near the foot of a wall about a dozen yards farther along the passage he was using. He kept talking, keeping his voice even, not showing his growing eagerness. "Even atheists, knowing the end is final, knowing the end is inevitable, hope to see the next day. Hope to see the next moment, and the moment after that, staving off the inevitable with an imaginary pole of stacked moments, hoping each moment isn't the final one."

"Until it is," Dexicos said.

Even though he knew Dexicos couldn't see him, Karl

shrugged. "Until then, we continue to hope." Then he dropped to one knee and stuck the barrel of the rifle through the hole.

Karl caught Dexicos in mid-stride, passing by the hole with purposeful steps. Karl did not hesitate; he squeezed the trigger. Then again, and again.

The first round hit Dexicos at upper thigh. A dull orange pulse of light intercepted the bullet, the light spreading in concentric circles, then dissipating. A flattened bullet dropped straight down. The second round drew forth the mystical orange light at the abdomen. By this time Dexicos was beginning to swivel toward the aperture in the wall. The third round hit directly in the center of Dexicos' chest.

Dexicos laughed. "My body armor is an older model, Karl. But effective, don't you think?"

Karl shot him again, in the face. It was worth a try. And besides, the man talked too much. The orange light stopped this one as well. But at least Dexicos stopped laughing.

"All right, Karl. My turn," Dexicos said. From a jacket pocket he produced a Taser.

The best way to handle the debilitating jolt of electricity from a Taser is to not be hit in the first place. The length of wire, which varies from model to model, limits the effective range, but Karl was well within the reach of even the most limited Taser, practically point-blank. As soon as he saw the Taser, Karl was moving; the powerful muscles built through endless series of squats and deadlifts uncoiled like a spring, pushing him up from his crouching position and off to his right.

In any other situation, even Karl's speed and strength would probably have been insufficient. Dexicos was simply too close to miss. The hole in the wall saved him. Karl's reflexive leap moved him just enough that Dexicos could not track and fire fast enough. One of the darts passed through the hole, its trailing wire grazing Karl's pant leg. The other, which would have embedded itself in Karl's calf, instead caromed off the inner edge of the hole, missing entirely.

Karl landed on all fours, pushed himself to his feet. He heard Dexicos spitting curses. Then the shattering impact of metal and plastic on stone.

"Fine, Karl. It will be more satisfying to take you apart personally." Dexicos sounded calm again, his frustration passing like a flicker of summer lightning.

"What, are we going to duke it out?" Karl asked.

"Why not? Let us come to grips like men. Continue along this wall. Beyond the bend is a way meet. It should provide us an ample arena for our combat."

Why not? Karl had the advantage of size, strength, and youth. Doubtless Dexicos hid a card or two up his sleeve. But Karl was confident he could overcome whatever trick the sorcerer pulled. Besides, people were counting on him. Better to settle this issue now.

"You're on, D," Karl said.

He unslung the rifle and left it there after switching off the tac-light. Mago D might be bulletproof. Karl wasn't. Why allow Dexicos a chance at snatching up the rifle? Karl fished out his mini-light, turned it on, then strode down the hall.

Dexicos proved as good as his word. The wall curved, then ended. Several other passages ended at roughly the same point, creating an oval-shaped clearing about ten feet across its long axis and six or seven on the short axis. Dexicos waited in the center of the arena. He'd already wedged a flashlight into a fissure of one of the walls.

Karl stopped at the entry to the arena, flashing his light around, looking into the darkness of the other passageways. Perhaps Dexicos had allies hidden away. Or had stashed a weapon. Or had May gagged and tied up. Or…

Dexicos waited patiently, an amused smirk on his face.

Karl gave up his search. He stepped into the arena. Keeping a healthy distance from Dexicos, he found a hole in the porous surface of the arena wall nearly opposite to that in which Dexicos had lodged his own flashlight. Karl thrust the butt of his mini-light into the hole, ensured it was secure, then turned to face the mage.

Dexicos Megistos faced him in turn, his expression unworried. In fact, he appeared confident, even expectant. He looked fit enough, trim and in condition. But age and sheer mass would ultimately tell. Dexicos must know that. Meaning he had more surprises than the rusty lightshow armor plating.

No point in prolonging this. Karl would simply have to keep his eyes open.

Dexicos began, "I believe we can dispense with –"

Karl rushed him, intending to hoist him off his feet and

body-slam him. Driving the breath from a man's body and dazing him ends a fight damn quick. But that wasn't what happened. Dexicos shifted with the practiced ease of an aikido master, adding an assist with one hand to propel Karl into one of the wall ends defining the arena.

Karl got his hands up in time to prevent a collision between stone and chin that stone would inevitably win. Right. Millennia of life would allow the leisure time to absorb any number of martial arts techniques. Meaning…

Karl spun, ducking away. A kick blurred above his head.

"Oh, this will be fun," Dexicos said. "And I must remember to thank my tailor. These trousers are every bit as unrestricting as advertised."

Karl straightened. He raised his hands before him and took a boxer's stance. He moved to the center of the oval ring, giving himself some room and preventing Dexicos from using the surrounding stone to further batter him.

"Lay on, MacDuff," Karl said. "And damned be him that first cries 'Hold, enough.'"

"Oh, that will be you, Karl."

Dexicos leapt into a flying side kick from farther away than Karl deemed possible. Karl moved aside and raised a bent arm, brushing aside the attack. Even avoiding the brunt of it, Karl still staggered back a step. His arm would bloom into a bruise where the sole of Dexicos' shoe had grazed it.

Dexicos landed gracefully on the balls of his feet, beside Karl. He struck with blistering speed, driving an elbow at Karl's head. But Karl was moving himself with equal alacrity. He had a hand up, interposing between elbow and face. He caught the elbow in his palm. The strength of the blow still pushed the back of his hand into his own nose hard enough to make Karl blink, but he'd sapped it of the knockout power it otherwise would have delivered.

At the same time Karl threw his other hand in a short arc, driving into Dexicos' ribs. He feared that mystic rusty light would flare up, stopping the blow, but it did not. Perhaps that magical defense was limited to bullets. Or to metal objects in general. If that was the case, Karl felt gladdened he didn't wear a ring.

Dexicos grunted and took two staggering steps away. The condescending smirk disappeared from his face, replaced by a snarl.

"Fine," Dexicos said. "Playtime is over."

Dexicos clenched his fists, and Karl noticed the wrapping of leather and wire around his right hand.

The next rabbit out of the hat.

Karl feinted a left jab as Dexicos moved in. Dexicos swayed back slightly. When he did, Karl dropped all pretense of fisticuffs. Instead he bulled in, going for a clinch, hoping to take Dexicos to the ground, where Karl's greater mass and strength could tell.

Again, Dexicos was faster and more skilled than Karl could credit. The mage slipped the hold and shifted laterally. Coming in close beneath Karl's arm, he slammed the metal-wrapped fist into Karl's side, approximately at the same point in the short ribs where Karl had hit him.

The power of the blow lifted Karl from his feet and propelled him a yard away. He landed on one knee, pressing a hand to his side. Pain sparked in rapid, percussive sequence. Karl glanced down. He figured that punch had cracked a rib. He was surprised to see a deep laceration, blood already welling up between the lips of the gash.

"Ahhh," Dexicos said, his satisfaction emerging in a feline purr. "Does that hurt, Karl? Enjoy it. In a few moments you will look back in longing for the relative bliss of such minor pain."

Karl got to his feet, pushing down the pain, telling himself he'd had worse.

"What, you got more rabbits in the hat, Doc?"

"Indeed. My hat is a veritable warren, Karl. For example, observe this."

Dexicos eased what looked to be a pocket watch from his jacket. With thumb and forefinger he levered the case open a crack. A glint of red light filled the hairline space. And with the light came a lance of frigid air and an accompanying unease that threatened to grow into outright terror. Whatever that pocket watch contained generated an unreasoning fear in Karl. He wanted no part of it.

"The contents of this yearn for blood. Once I release it, it will burrow into your open wound. And there it will feed, delving inside you in the most unspeakably painful manner, eating you from the inside out. At the same time it will send a psychic tendril drilling into your brain, describing what it is doing to you. And as it does so, it will whisper to you secrets. Secrets of the entity of which it was once a constituent part. Vile secrets of dark, alien stretches of the cosmos. Secrets that will drive you mad. What will happen first? I wonder. Will you die screaming from pain before you are driven mad? Let us make the experiment."

A portion of Karl's mind clamored for him to run, to run screaming away from this thing. But he was Karl. So he charged.

With the pocket watch in both hands, Dexicos was unable to nimbly step aside. Karl got an arm wrapped around the mage's waist. His other hand dropped for the hilt of his jungle knife. But would the magical protection that stopped bullets also stop the steel blade of the knife? Did he have another choice? If he failed to put Dexicos down before he released whatever was contained in the pocket watch, then the Book of Karl ended right here.

Karl's hand brushed against something else as he reached for the jungle knife. It was the hilt of the Jade Dagger. *Not metal.*

Karl tugged it free, feeling the tip of it draw a line of blood from his leg as he did so.

"Yes, Karl," Dexicos was saying, "let me get a close-up view of your death."

Karl could hear the creak of hinges. The red light increased, bathing the arena in a blood-red glow. The arctic cold intensified.

Karl hugged Dexicos to him. "Not today," Karl said. He punched the Jade Dagger into Dexicos' abdomen, between the second and third buttons of his shirt, twisted the serpentine blade, and tore it free. Then he stepped back, pushing the mage away.

Dexicos gasped, an exhalation carrying both startlement

and pain. The pocket watch fell from his hands, the clamshell bouncing, clattering in a lazy spin that came to a stop facing Dexicos.

The pocket watch sprang open.

A crimson light bathed Dexicos, the burgeoning terror displayed on his face appearing in stark detail. A sheen of ice crystals manifested on the floor, fanning out from the pocket watch. They crunched beneath Dexicos' feet as he backed away, but he was able to move only a few paces before reaching the arena wall. He clamped one hand against the blood-pumping wound in his gut. The other felt behind him, feeling out the extent of the wall at his back. His mouth moved as he struggled to speak. His eyes widened. What he was seeing, Karl did not want to know.

Then *something* emerged from the clamshell. Karl saw only a squamous appendage scaled alternatingly in acid green and dull scarlet. It was too small for him to make out details. What little he saw disturbed him, knotting his stomach in a spasm of nausea and sending horripilation rising along every inch of skin. The appendage stretched forth, dragged itself nimbly from the pocket watch, revealing a larger mass behind it, a mass that shouldn't be able to fit within the clamshell. Karl turned away, refusing to see any more of it, feeling his mind on the verge of shutting down at the glimpse he'd already suffered.

He heard a scraping noise, then a wet, bubbling squelch, like a serving spoon thrust into a tray of Jell-O.

And then Dexicos began to scream. It commenced as a sort of whimpering disbelief, but instantly elevated to panicked denial. Then it intensified, proliferating into pain that ratcheted up the rungs of agony. And accompanying those purely physical screams were shrieks of utter madness.

Karl ran, stumbling, from the arena.

CHAPTER 27

Karl remembered to grab the HK. He'd left his mini-light in the arena, and without the tac-light, he'd have been left in total darkness. Total except for the dimming, blood-red glow of the arena. Dexicos' screams trailed Karl as he tried to escape the labyrinth.

That proved less difficult than he'd feared. Dexicos might well have possessed an astonishing memory, but he hadn't been an idiot. Karl found an illuminated chem-stick a few turnings away. It had been placed carefully in the center of an intersection. Karl noted the direction it pointed to – assuming he hadn't been completely turned around, and it was actually pointing the opposite way. He followed the suggested line of travel and, sure enough, found another chem-stick beacon.

Ten minutes later Karl emerged from the labyrinth. He found May Chen and Jim Allison waiting for him. He felt a degree of pleasure when he saw May's expression shift from worry to relief. Professor Allison's might have gone through a similar transition, but Karl didn't pay any attention.

The two archaeologists waited a discreet distance away from their primary light source, a circle of dimming chemsticks. Karl wondered why they avoided the relative cheer of light in the darkness until he saw the two bodies.

"Karl," May said, her voice breathy and catching, "you made it. I knew you'd make it."

"She did, too," Professor Allison said. "I wanted to hike out of here as soon – well, as soon as events allowed. But May insisted we wait for you."

"Events?" Karl said. "Is that what you call taking down Potter? Nice work, you two. I'll admit I wasn't looking forward to tangling with him." He strolled over, taking a look at the big man's corpse. Some people appeared to shrink after death. Potter still looked larger than life. Festo did appear smaller, somehow deflated. His blood-soaked shirt, a putrid shade of chartreuse in the light of the chemsticks, seemed oversized.

May smiled proudly. "The butler didn't seem to think a woman was any threat. So I brained him with the wine bottle when his back was turned. And then Jim went to town with his walking stick." She stopped smiling. "It took longer than I thought. Wasn't much fun. That guy was tough."

"Are you all right?" Karl asked. Killing a man wasn't paintball. Some people were not equipped to deal with the notion of taking another's life.

"Now? I'm holding it together. A day from now, maybe

a week, who knows? I might lose my shit. But it had to be done, so I did it. We did it."

"And *it* coincided with all the shooting down below," Professor Allison said.

"The narcos and Mago D's boys?" Karl asked.

"At first," May said.

"We think a third group joined the fun, jumped the narcos," Professor Allison said. "We kept our heads down up here until the shooting stopped. That's when I suggested we skedaddle."

"Did you get a look at the third group?" Karl asked. He stooped over a cloth upon which it seemed Potter had begun to set out a picnic. A heel of bread and a wedge of cheese appeared to have avoided any blood spatter. Karl picked up the bread and began munching.

"I did," May said. "Dressed all in black, with those military weapons harnesses on. They looked like some sort of special operations force, y'know? Like in the movies."

"Do you think it was the army?" Professor Allison asked.

Karl shook his head. He swallowed a mouthful of bread. It was good. Say what you would about Dexicos Megistos, the man had known how to live.

"I don't think it was the army. My guess is Zetas. A lot of ex-military in that cartel. But let's go see. Time to get out of this hole, don't you think?"

"Please," May said.

"Hole?" Professor Allison sounded indignant. "This is a priceless archaeological site. But yes, let's call it a day."

"What happened to the other one?" Karl asked. He gestured at Festo before he bent down to retrieve the cheese, a crumbly, fragrant wedge, possessing a green cast in the light of the chem-sticks. *Moon cheese.*

"Mago D stabbed him," May said. "Part of some ritual. Creepy, Karl. The man has power. Real magical power." She began to lead the way down onto the boulevard.

"Had," Karl said. "He had power."

"You killed him?" Professor Allison asked.

"Let's say I helped. May I suggest that if you start exploring the labyrinth, you bring security? Heavily armed security. Maybe flamethrowers."

"That thing in the pocket watch?" May asked.

"Yes," Karl said. He shivered. "You mind if I don't talk about it right now?"

May patted him reassuringly on his arm, the left; the right held the HK and its tac-light, with which Karl was examining the battlefield.

"Looks like the men in black cleared up their own dead," Karl said. "That is, if they suffered any casualties at all."

"What do you think happened?" Professor Allison asked.

"Turf war," Karl said. "Zetas eliminating some competition. Our little local group of narcos were relying on stealth, sneaking product through the tunnels. But I guess they weren't stealthy enough. Zetas caught wind of them, tracked them down. And —" Karl waved the light over a pile of bodies. They'd been stripped of weapons and dumped in a heap. Commingled in the pile were Dexicos Megistos' mercenaries and the local narcos, at least one of whom appeared to have been killed by an explosive device, probably a grenade. Karl saw no sign of black military fatigues or other equipment suggestive of Zeta soldiers.

"Do you think the Zetas will use the tunnels now?" Professor Allison asked.

Karl shrugged. "I don't know. My guess is no. They were eliminating competition, not attempting to take over a smuggling route. They've already established their pipeline; don't need another. Probably trashed the production facility, burnt it to the ground. They're distributors, not producers. Still…"

"Yes, why take chances," Professor Allison said. They continued walking, back along the narrow hallway. Professor Allison spoke as he walked, letting entire minutes pass between sentences. "I think it is time to push this one up the ladder. This site is too important for me to let my ego obstruct the discovery. Let the Mexican government take over. They can bring in the army, place a cordon around the entire site. And I imagine they will keep me on in at least a consulting capacity. This place is bigger than one man. The secrets it holds!"

"Are you sure you want all of these secrets revealed?" Karl asked.

"What do you mean?"

"We've seen some crazy shit. Crazy shit you might not want to mention to the *federales* if you want to be taken seriously."

They'd emerged at length onto the broader gallery leading to the rubble-congested stairway through which Karl had tumbled. The origami-like skeletal structure still sprawled where it had fallen. The girders comprising its body no longer possessed the high-gloss, chitinous sheen. But even unmoving and presumably dead, Karl still approached it with caution.

"You mean crazy shit like that?" May asked.

"Yeah," Karl said. He prodded the nearest member with the barrel of the HK. Commencing with the spot where the barrel touched it, the body of the creature began to crumble. When the process stopped, there remained only an elongated mass of coarse, ashy dust.

"I guess some problems solve themselves," May said.

The ascent up the stair was arduous. Karl's side ached; fresh blood leaked from the scabbing wound on his side where Dexicos Megistos had punched him. Professor Allison was breathing heavily, and May looked little better. But no one wanted to sit and rest yet, the subterranean environment too oppressive. So they pushed on, through the halls, out over the bridge and at last back into the treasure chamber.

There at last they halted for a breather. Professor Allison unfolded the seat of his walking stick and sat. Karl and May sat next to each other on a wooden pallet.

It was Professor Allison who rose first. He glanced at the disordered collection of artifacts on the altar shelf. "They no longer seem quite so impressive, do they?" He looked at Karl and May. "I'll see you two back at the dig.

But don't dally, Karl. I need to drive into town as soon as possible, make some phone calls. But before I do that, I might need your help if one of Mago D's men still has our people held at gunpoint."

Karl doubted it. Either the mercenary had gotten tired of waiting for instructions and bailed, or he'd been overpowered by the archaeologists and workers. But he nodded. "Sure, Jim. I'll be right behind you. I just need another minute."

Professor Allison nodded in turn, but not before shooting a significant glance at Karl and May. He offered a tired smile before he trudged out of the treasure chamber.

His blessing?

"So what now?" May asked.

"Now? I was thinking I might magic up some jade," Karl said.

"What? How?"

Karl stood and produced the Jade Dagger, still tacky with Dexicos Megistos' blood. He went to the altar and picked up a necklace, thumbing along the beads until he found one of jade. "I've got the Jade Dagger. I remember the incantation. If it doesn't work, I'm out nothing. If it does, then I've got jade beads. Nice, portable wealth."

"Weren't you the one talking about devaluing the market?"

"I'll magic up *some* jade. Not a mountain of it. Just enough to fund maybe a month at a five-star hotel in, oh, let's say Paris. Know anyone who might want to come with me?"

May stood up, facing him. A half smile raised one side of her mouth. "What about the Jade Dagger? What about Jim and the dig?"

"I'll leave the dagger here once I've finished my production quota. And it sounds like Professor Allison is making other security arrangements, the kind involving uniforms and armored personnel carriers. I was thinking of moving on anyway. So, want to spend some of my ill-gotten gains with me?"

May took a couple of steps closer. "I'm a modern woman, Karl. Modern women are not susceptible to this sort of bribery. We don't fling ourselves at the nearest man with a wad of cash and bulging pecs." She took another step closer, looking up at him. "In fact, as a modern woman, I feel it is my duty to go to Paris with you and explain this to you in greater detail. Teach you the error of your ways – in cafés, wine bars, Michelin-starred restaurants. Between twelve-hundred-thread-count Egyptian-cotton sheets."

Karl put his arms around her waist and pulled her to him. She draped her arms around his neck.

"Do you think there's a chance of my reforming you?" May asked.

Karl kissed her. Thoroughly. Her eyes shone and her smile now encompassed both halves of her mouth.

"We continue to hope," Karl said.

R.J. SIERRA
GAIA FILES
DEAD TO THE WORLD

Jane's young. She's broke. Oh, and she just discovered she has supernatural powers so bizarre they may end up killing her.

GET INDIE SAINT TODAY!

For all our books, visit our website.